Anya Bast

Blood of the Damned

Ellora's Cave
Romantica Publishing

What the critics are saying...

✎

"From the beginning to the end, this book satisfies everything you want!" ~ *Erotic Escapades*

"This story may be very short, but it definitely packs a punch." ~ *A Romance Review*

"A superb mix of romance and suspense that is just too hard to put down." ~ *Ecataromance*

"This is an incredibly erotic story." ~ *Love Romances*

"BLOOD OF THE DAMNED is a dark, sensual read with many layers." ~ *Romance Reviews Today*

"An exceptional vampire romance." ~ *Coffee Time Romance*

5 Angels "This was a fabulous read." ~ *Fallen Angel Reviews*

"This is a well-rounded keeper that will add heat and excitement to any day." ~ *Just Erotic Romance Reviews*

An Ellora's Cave Romantica Publication

www.ellorascave.com

Blood of the Damned

ISBN 9781419955839
ALL RIGHTS RESERVED.
Blood of the Damned Copyright © 2006 Anya Bast
Edited by Briana St. James.
Cover art by Syneca.

This book printed in the U.S.A. by Jasmine-Jade Enterprises, LLC.

Electronic book Publication January 2006
Trade paperback Publication June 2007

With the exception of quotes used in reviews, this book may not be reproduced or used in whole or in part by any means existing without written permission from the publisher, Ellora's Cave Publishing, Inc.® 1056 Home Avenue, Akron OH 44310-3502.

This book is a work of fiction and any resemblance to persons, living or dead, or places, events or locales is purely coincidental. The characters are productions of the authors' imagination and used fictitiously.

Content Advisory:

S – ENSUOUS
E – ROTIC
X – TREME

Ellora's Cave Publishing offers three levels of Romantica™ reading entertainment: S (S-ensuous), E (E-rotic), and X (X-treme).

The following material contains graphic sexual content meant for mature readers. This story has been rated E-rotic.

S-*ensuous* love scenes are explicit and leave nothing to the imagination.

E-*rotic* love scenes are explicit, leave nothing to the imagination, and are high in volume per the overall word count. E-rated titles might contain material that some readers find objectionable—in other words, almost anything goes, sexually. E-rated titles are the most graphic titles we carry in terms of both sexual language and descriptiveness in these works of literature.

X-*treme* titles differ from E-rated titles only in plot premise and storyline execution. Stories designated with the letter X tend to contain difficult or controversial subject matter not for the faint of heart.

Also by Anya Bast

And Lady Makes Three *(anthology)*
Edge of Sweetness
Ellora's Cavemen: Dreams of the Oasis IV *(anthology)*
Ellora's Cavemen: Tales from the Temple III *(anthology)*
Ordinary Charm
Seasons of Pleasure 1: Winter Pleasures: The Training
Seasons of Pleasure 2: Spring Pleasures: The Transformation
Seasons of Pleasure 3: Summer Pleasures: The Capture
Seasons of Pleasure 4: Autumn Pleasures: The Union
Seasons of Pleasure 5: A Change of Season
Seduced in Twilight
Tempted by Two
The Embraced 1: Blood of the Rose
The Embraced 2: Blood of the Raven
The Embraced 3: Blood of an Angel
Torrid Tarot: Whisper of the Blade
Water Crystal

About the Author

Anya Bast is a multipublished erotic fantasy & paranormal romance author. Primarily, she writes happily-ever-afters with lots of steamy sex. After all, happily-ever-afters with lots of sex are the very best kind.

She enjoys the study of Celtic myth, dreaming, and shamanism and incorporates what she learns into her paranormal stories.

Anya got her start writing fantasy romance. Since writing a little hotter seemed to come naturally to her, she had no trouble making the move to erotic romance. She loves writing books that are heavy on plot, emotion and character development, and also have spicy, no-holds-barred sex scenes. Exploring the elements of dark sexual fantasy in her writing is what Anya does best.

She lives in the country with her husband. They share their lives with eight cats and one perplexed dog.

Anya welcomes comments from readers. You can find her website and email address on her author bio page at www.ellorascave.com.

Tell Us What You Think

We appreciate hearing reader opinions about our books. You can email us at Comments@EllorasCave.com.

BLOOD OF THE DAMNED
☙

Chapter One
Harcourt Maximum Security Penitentiary
Zhejiang Province, China–Sometime tomorrow
∞

Jade's heavy boots clanged on the metal walkway as she trekked across the heart of Harcourt Prison. All around her men stood at the bars of their cells catcalling and shouting obscenities. Thirteen levels could be seen in the cellblock she walked through, each floor lined with at least three hundred rusted iron cells, and every single prisoner in them seemed riled up by her presence.

But she was only interested in one man here.

She ignored the rest of it. Ignored the sound of their voices, and the noise of the clanging iron bars and the metal walkway beneath her boots. She closed her senses to the stench of the place—unwashed human body, rotten food, old semen and blood. Jade closed her extrasensory perception to their emotions as well, their rage, their desperation at being out of control. She cut herself off from all of it. Fifty years of training as a Priestess of the Morrigan gave her that ability.

She approached the end of the walkway and the armed guard who waited for her. The red-haired prison guard had bad teeth and a profane grin. His gaze trailed from her heavy combat boots, up her leather-clad body to her face. Apparently the prisoners weren't the only ones who hadn't seen a woman in a while. She flipped her long black leather coat open so he could see the two weapons—two high-caliber pistols—holstered on her waist. His grin faltered.

To further dampen his spirits, she reached into her back pocket, pulled out her ID and release order, and flashed them at him. "Jade Xiang, officially empowered by the International

Federation. I've got a remand order for Niccolo Romano. Take me to him."

The guard snorted, expelling a bit of spittle that Jade moved to the side to avoid. "That crazy fuck? You can have him." He peered behind her. "But I don't see any Federation agents with you. You sure you can handle this guy on your own?"

She stared at him as she slid her documents back into her pocket. "Let me worry about that."

He looked at her doubtfully and shook his head. Then he turned and led her down a row of cells. Jade made sure she walked close to the railing on her left to avoid the inmates' grasping hands. If only she could avoid their spit and their words as well. A lot of them growled out things they were thinking about her, things she didn't want to hear. Her close proximity seemed to whip them into an even greater frenzy. She couldn't wait to be out of here.

The guard led her down a hallway, away from the inmates' housing. They took an elevator down several floors, and then walked down a corridor lined with heavy steel doors. Her gaze flicked to the small viewing slits set in each one as she walked past. This was solitary confinement, Jade guessed.

It was quiet here. All Jade could hear were their footsteps and the guard's breathing. The quiet was a blessed thing to her ears and senses. Even so, she could still feel the tormented souls who clung to this place, the ones who lurked in the shadows of the living and screamed soundlessly. They were imprisoned here for eternity in anguish.

The guard stopped in front of one of the doors, punched in some numbers on the lock by the knob and the door swung open. "There he is," the guard said.

Jade stepped into the nearly pitch-black room. It took a second for her eyes to adjust to the darkness. The floor and walls were concrete. The ceiling appeared to be constructed of that same ancient steel that comprised the rest of the prison. No furniture decorated the cell. There was nothing at all.

Except him.

The man she sought knelt on the floor, his arms strung out on either side of him and bound at the wrists by thick chains attached to the walls. They'd left his chest bare and his dark head was bowed. Long, straggling dark hair and a beard shadowed his face. They'd put him in an uncomfortable position, obviously designed to punish. Though Jade figured this vamp hardly felt the pain.

"Why is he restrained this way?" she asked sharply of the guard.

"Killed an inmate last week. Some asshole stupid enough to mess with an Embraced." The guard spat on the floor. "Saved us the cost of executin' him."

Niccolo Romano raised his head and let his gaze slowly rove her in the same way the guard's had earlier. He parted his lips a little and she saw his fangs—white and sharp—in his mouth. She stifled the urge to kick him in the face. Had they been feeding him synth-blood to keep him sated? Or maybe blood hunger had been how he'd killed the inmate. Maybe Romano had drained him.

"Leave me alone with him," she said without looking at the guard.

"You sure—"

Keeping her eyes on Romano's face, she ground out, "I said leave me alone with him."

She heard the guard turn and leave.

Romano just stared at her. His long black hair hung around his well-chiseled face. The darkness of his hair seemed to swallow up all the light around his head, giving her the impression he thirsted for it...or maybe she was just projecting. She'd done her reading on this guy, knew what a hard history he'd had.

She knew a lot about him, but they hadn't told her what the Embraced would look like. She hadn't been expecting this. Even dirty and unkempt this man radiated power, strength and overall physical perfection. She let her gaze trace over his muscled legs, torso and arms. The man had to be unstoppable in a fight. She was preternaturally strong, but she doubted she'd be able to take this man in combat. She certainly didn't want to try.

"Niccolo Romano," she said, her voice loud in the small cell. "You've been remanded into my custody."

"Have I been loaned out again?" His voice was a deep baritone and smooth, silky dark chocolate. There was just the faintest trace of an unplacable accent. Jade knew his original tongue had been Latin, but he'd sailed through several civilizations since then.

She took a couple steps toward him, her boot heels clicking on the concrete floor. "You've been passed around a lot in the last two hundred years, I've heard. In and out of different agencies, bartered around for special initiatives." She shrugged. "But every time they're finished with you, they throw you back in here like a well-used whore."

His dark eyes flashed with anger and his huge hands fisted loosely.

So, he wasn't broken and he still had pride. That was good.

She paced in front of him. "Yeah, you're being loaned out again, but this time when you're finished you get your freedom."

His body went very still and power sizzled through the air, a flare of his glamour brushing against her magick. The powerful force raised the fine hairs on her arms and at the back of her neck. She stopped pacing.

"My freedom." His voice sounded flat, expressionless. She could get no emotional read on him because he was an Embraced. The man was stoic as a rock, anyway.

Jade crossed her arms over her chest, hearing the creak of the leather she wore. "Don't you want it? I mean, everyone knows how you allowed yourself to be arrested so long ago. Still, don't you think two hundred years is punishment enough?"

"What's the job?"

"You won't object to it, Romano. Anyway, we wouldn't be able to keep you if you did."

Niccolo Romano—that wasn't the name he'd been born with, of course—had a knack for death, a talent for it. It was what he did best; bring death to those who deserved it. She'd heard all the stories. When this man had walked down the street, everyone had gotten the hell out of his way. On some level, most of them could probably sense that death walked beside this man, that it was an old friend and constant companion of his. Everyone had a little psi ability, a little intuition. This man sent out a danger signal louder than a storm siren. Someone would have to be near brain-dead not to perceive it.

This was a man who'd murdered his way through the centuries. Innumerable men had lost their lives to him. Still, she'd done enough research on him to know that he wouldn't kill innocents. The vamp wouldn't aid in senseless destruction. He couldn't be used as force against the greater good...well, not most of the time. If someone had the right leverage on him, he could be forced into it. That was his biggest weakness. But the bottom line was that, even two thousand years since he'd been Embraced, the man was still a protector.

That's why they needed him.

He said nothing. He only lowered his gaze to her boots.

She raised an eyebrow. He didn't want to talk anymore? Fine. It was past time they got out there, anyway. She turned. "I'll get the guard and the keys for those chains."

"How do you know I won't just kill you and take off?"

She stopped, but didn't turn toward him. Jade smiled a little. "I know a lot about you, Romano, more than even your closest friends. I know you won't."

She tracked down the guard who cast a nervous glance at her before he plied the security code to the release mechanism on the outside of the cell. The hydraulic cuffs released and fell with a ringing clank and chink of the chain. She noticed the vamp's wrists bled from the rasp of iron against skin. Dried blood marked him from fingers to elbow.

He pushed to his feet with muscles that didn't seem the least fatigued from the awkward position he'd been sustaining. Romano stood before her dressed in a pair of gray prison pants, a pair of black prison-issue boots and nothing else.

He was tall and he was ripped. She'd seen that when he'd been kneeling. He made her respond like a woman did to a man. Her reaction was instant, primal and wholly unwelcome. This man made her whole body sit up and take notice. He made her heart rate and breathing speed up. He made her cunt cream just a little. She couldn't remember the last time someone had made that happen. She thought it had all but dried up.

He walked toward her with menace set into his shoulders and his swagger. She had the urge to back away from him, but stood her ground. He stopped right in front of her, so close his breath—the sweet, calm-inducing breath of the Embraced—stirred the fine hairs around her face. The heat of him rolled off and warmed her. Despite the threat in his eyes, her body started a slow burn. Her sex began to throb and nipples became sensitive.

Man, oh man.

Romano's eyes were hard and cold, the lines of his face set in a cruel expression. He had a face that could be either beautiful or brutal depending on the light, his expression...or his mood, she'd make a guess.

"Who said I'd agree to help you?" he snarled in a low voice. "Who said I was ready leave this place? Who sent you for me?"

A flicker of apprehension raced through her stomach, but she held his gaze steadily. *Goddess, please, sweet Morrigan, I hope we haven't misjudged this man.* "The Council of the Embraced," she said in a steady voice. "The Federation, the Order of the Morrigan...and Gabriel Letourneau."

Niccolo's eyes blinked and unfocused for a moment as she uttered the last name on the list.

She took advantage of his surprise, and turned and walked out the door and past the guard. Her heart pounded in her chest. Romano would follow if he wanted out of here.

"You don't want him cuffed?" the guard asked as she passed.

Yeah, she kind of did, but she waved him off without a glance and continued down the corridor.

She'd been expected to arrive here, and if they could plan on her being somewhere for any length of time, bad things tended to happen. Very bad things. They needed to get out as quickly as possible.

"You have a lot to explain," Romano called from the cell.

"Somewhere other than here," she yelled over her shoulder.

Niccolo caught up to her. "You've been reinstated," she said without looking at him. "You're a Council Executioner again."

"No. I will never hunt and kill others for money again."

"It's part of your current deal."

She found herself slammed up against the wall in less than half a blink of an eye. His hand fisted in the leather of her jacket at the shoulders. She stared at him, her heart pounding and her breath coming fast. For the speed and strength it had taken him to get her into this position, he hadn't hurt her.

Instantly, she took stock of how she could defend herself. Eyes, throat, balls. That's what she'd go for to free herself.

His face was close to hers. His chocolate-brown eyes narrowed. "I will never be an Executioner again," he growled.

She shrugged, trying to appear as though he hadn't just scared the shit out of her. "You do this work, we all get through it alive, and you can quit being one. After this, you can go become a goat herder in Inner Mongolia for all I care. As they used to say so long ago, scout's honor."

A muscle worked in his jaw. He stared into her eyes. Finally, after several tense heartbeats, he relaxed and backed away. Jade took several shaky, shallow breaths. "I will go with you," he said in a low voice. "I will see what this *job*—" he snarled the word at her "—is. If I don't like it, I'm not doing it."

Jade passed him, walking down the corridor once more. Once he found out what it was, he'd agree. "Fine," she shot back at him. "Can we please get the fuck out of here now? It's like you want to stay or something."

They continued on in silence and when they hit the metal walkway, that silence became a necessity. The prisoners were whipped into an even greater frenzy now than when she'd come in. The noise was deafening. The emotions ran high. She could feel their rage, their lust, their despair. The combined sensation felt cloying to her. It caught in her throat and made her gag. It was like having a sweaty sock stuffed in her mouth.

Finally they reached the tall, wide chain barrier that separated the exit corridor from the cellblock—the main gate. The guards there let them through and they turned the corner to proceed down the long hallway that led to the first checkpoint.

The prison was a huge square building, the bulk of which was comprised by the open cellblock. It was an old prison, built right after World War III. The Chinese government and the I.F. didn't have a lot of money to keep it up, even though this was an international prison—the largest in the world.

Jade understood that the prisoners were controlled in groups of fifty cells apiece. Corridors led off the main cellblock to other parts of the prison. Around the perimeter lay a large secure outdoor exercise area. When the temperature rose above freezing, the prisoners were allowed out there. Four towers armed with guards stood at each corner of the prison yard. Two security checkpoints stood between themselves and freedom—one inside and one outside.

She led Romano to the first of the two checkpoints. Even here the echo of the prisoners back in the cellblock filled her ears and their emotions scraped her acute senses. Guards stood on both sides of metal doors tall enough to allow a bus filled with convicts to pass through.

One of the guards, a black-haired Caucasian, rose from his desk where he was munching a sandwich. Jade flashed her papers at him while he wiped some mayo from the corner of his mouth with the back of his hand. They'd done all the hard stuff on the way in, so Jade was hoping this would go fast.

One of the guards took Romano aside to a small cage-covered window and gave him a black duffel bag, likely filled with his possessions.

The Caucasian guard nodded and she slid her papers and ID back into her pocket.

"No cuffs?" he inquired.

She shook her head.

He stared at her. "Don't you know who you just took into custody, Xiang?" He dropped his gaze, taking in her tall, slender body. It wasn't a sexual assessment, but a practical one. She knew she looked like a helpless female, but she wasn't. "I know you think you're pretty tough and all, but—"

Her temper flared. "I'm a Priestess of the Morrigan," she ground out.

He blinked and his eyes filled with understanding and respect. "Okay."

Romano came back to stand beside her, and the guard pressed the buzzer that opened the heavy gates. They slid apart slowly, revealing the blinding white environment beyond, and she and the vamp stepped through. A blast of frigid air froze her lungs, but the man beside her didn't even flinch. In the swirling snow a distance away was the second checkpoint.

That's when all hell broke loose.

Behind them, the lights shut off, plunging the prison into complete and utter darkness. Tension flared through Jade's body as she turned. Romano stood beside her. She could feel his body heat radiate out and hit her, warring with the cold air. The auditory chaos within the prison had quieted, though the sound of the hydraulic security doors still sliding open sounded loud in her ears. Emergency lights turned on, bathing the corridor walls in red light. Somewhere deep in the prison, an alarm sounded.

The erratic yelling of the prisoners swelled. Their emotions swelled, as well. A sharp, poignant flare of hope emanated from them and then a desire for pure, unadulterated violence.

It wasn't the violence that bothered her, it was the hope. Her brow furrowed. Hope? That had to be a bad thing. It just had to be. Then everything started happening all at once, and far too quickly for her tastes.

"Shit! Something's overridden the cellblock door control and the main gate! Close these doors! Close these doors!" one the guards yelled.

He meant the gate separating the cellblock from the exit corridor, Jade guessed. Not good. The guards started punching buttons on the control panel, trying to get the ancient doors to stop their slow slide open and begin to close. They made a grinding, groaning noise that didn't sound promising.

At the far end of the corridor, Jade could see men rounding the corner. They appeared to be running straight for freedom. Unfortunately, that path led directly through where she and the vamp stood.

"Fuck," Jade breathed.

She'd actually thought for a minute she'd be able to get Romano out without incident. She turned and ran for the second set of gates with Romano beside her. Resisting the urge to move as fast she was able, she forced herself to keep pace with him. If she didn't get out with Romano, she might as well not get out at all.

Her boots crunched over the ice on the concrete walkway and the cold wind whipped her hair into her eyes. That combined with the swirling snow made it hard for her to make out their goal, the final checkpoint.

A loud scrape and groan sounded behind them. She chanced a glance back and saw the escapees had wedged a desk between the closing doors. The heavy piece of furniture was partially crushed, but it had served its purpose. Prisoners scrambled over the desk into the exercise yard in a trickle that was fast becoming a flood.

From the towers above them, the guards fired at the prisoners breaching the gate. The *pop, pop, pop* of the tower guns sounded not at all comforting…especially when bullets hit the snow-covered ground beside them. She tuned in with all she had on her environment, not an easy thing to do under the circumstances. She heard a stray bullet whizzing through the air near her and dodged to the left to avoid it.

She felt two others flying toward Romano, one going for his head, the other his leg. She shoved him to the side but it was like trying to topple a tree. One of the bullets missed him, but the other hit him high in the chest. Blood sprayed out onto the snow and Romano went down beside her.

She stopped and knelt, helping him up. It took more than a simple bullet to kill an Embraced, and they had to keep moving. At least his leg hadn't been wounded. He could still run.

He pressed a hand to his chest and lunged to his feet. She wrapped an arm around his waist and propelled him forward. They left his duffel bag behind on the ground.

"You just dodged a bullet," he rasped at her. "What the hell are you?"

"Uninjured. Come on, move!"

He shrugged her off and started to run. Behind them, the prisoners gained on them.

The heavy solid iron gates ahead of them were closed. Jade pulled both her guns and ran to the small door to the right of the gates. She had no wish to shoot unarmed men, but she knew what they'd do to her if they made it to this gate before she got through it. Romano, he might survive...maybe. She wouldn't, and she had no desire to die by being raped and beaten to death.

She pounded on the metal door. "Open up! I've been empowered by the International Federation to take a prisoner out of here!"

The small round viewing hole in the door opened. "No way. If I open this door more than one prisoner is walking out."

Behind them, a couple of the fastest prisoners had reached them. One went for Romano and Romano gave him a quick, clean death in half a blink of an eye. No hesitation. No mercy.

The other ran for her. She whirled, drawing her weapon, but Niccolo was there first. He grabbed the man by the throat and cracked his neck. The prisoner slumped to the ground and Niccolo turned with a ruthless look on his face.

The noise of prisoners behind her was becoming louder by the heartbeat. Their pounding feet filled her senses. She turned and stuck the muzzle of one of her guns against the guard's forehead. "Open this door right now," she gritted out in a low voice.

The man blanched. He fumbled for the door's release while staring straight into her eyes. It opened a crack. She pushed it, forcing the guard back, and she and Romano surged through it. She whirled and slammed it shut with her foot. The guard bolted it about a half a second before a force of men hit it on the other side. The gates groaned ominously under the weight and Jade staggered back and fell, ending up on her ass in the snow with both barrels pointed at the door.

"Holy shit," she said in a shaky voice. Their collective emotions bathed her now. It was almost more than she could bear.

Rage, deep, horrifying rage. It rasped against her mind like sandpaper on a baby's bottom.

Pounding fists beat on the metal gates and on the thick metal walls that surrounded the prison's exercise yard. Jade was glad she couldn't see their faces. For several moments she just sat there, feeling the cold seep through her clothing and watching the five guards at the outside gate run around like they didn't know what to do. The other guards inside were probably already dead. Mayonnaise man was probably dead. Beyond the gate came the *pop, pop, pop* of the tower guns...and more men died.

It was possible there had been some internal error in the Harcourt security system that had thrown the cell doors and the main gate...but she suspected it had been no accident.

The gate groaned again and she forced herself to push to her feet. They needed to get out of there in case that thing gave. She looked up and her breath caught in her throat as she registered Romano.

He stood staring at the gates and seemed to be absorbing and radiating back all that thick, cloying anger. His body, even though the temperature was well below zero, looked hot to the touch. It was as if he identified and reflected that rage. The lines of his body, which seemed powerful and strong before, now appeared brutal to her.

She holstered her weapons and touched him on the arm.

He jerked and looked at her. His eyes were clouded, distant and a muscle worked in his jaw. He blinked and they cleared, leaving behind pools of deep brown. His body relaxed.

The spell was broken. Jade took a deep breath.

"Come on," she said. "We have a bullet to get out of you." She turned and walked toward where she'd parked her snow glider.

"Hey," the guard she'd threatened yelled at her. "You're I.F. Aren't you going to stay and help?"

She wasn't I.F. She'd only been empowered by them. Her allegiance lay elsewhere. "Not my problem," she called over her shoulder. She'd been there to get Romano out and she'd done that…barely.

Chapter Two

She led him across the snow-swept expanse in front of the prison and past the vehicles parked there. The thought of what had occurred still had her shaking. Someone had overridden Harcourt's main computer, opened all the cell doors and the main gate. She'd expected something nasty, perhaps an attempt on their lives by one of the guards, but she'd never expected that. Someone had wanted them both dead and had wanted to remain blameless for it. They'd gone to a lot of trouble to achieve that end and they'd almost succeeded.

Jade was almost inclined to feel flattered.

"What the fuck is going on?" the vamp asked in a low, rasping voice. He held a hand to his wound.

"We're almost to the glider, Romano," she answered.

"My name is Niccolo."

She glanced at him. Touchy. "Does your wound hurt?"

He grimaced at her. "What do you think?"

She raised her hands in surrender. "Hey, sorry. I don't know much pain an Embraced can handle."

He just grunted at her in response.

They reached the self-propelled glider and she opened the hatch. She climbed in after Niccolo. The warm air of the temperature-controlled cabin enveloped her and she rubbed her hands together, trying to get the feeling back into them so she could get the craft in the air.

Spotting the bottle of twenty-six-year-old single malt scotch that Charlie had left behind, she grabbed it and drank deep. The alcohol burned its way down her throat and into her stomach, lending her body a welcome heat. Charlie would have been horrified she wasn't sipping it.

Niccolo settled himself into one of the copilot's chairs at the front of the craft. He still had a bloody hand pressed to his wound. They wouldn't be able to treat him until they were in the air and far from here, however. She capped the bottle, handed it to him and sank into the captain's chair.

Jade fastened her seat belt and flipped the engine switch. The control panel lit up and a gentle hum filled the air of the cabin. She loved the slight sound of the glider's engine. It was so comforting, and was doubly so now since it meant they were *leaving*. "Seat belt," she said to Niccolo.

He ignored her and took a drink of the scotch.

She took the wheel, unlocking it and pulling it toward her. His big hand came to a rest over hers, stilling her movement. She looked at him.

"What is your name and where are we going?" His voice held a thread of violence.

"My name is Jade Xiang and we're going to Tibet."

He grimaced in pain and removed his hand, leaving a smear of blood behind. "Tibet? Why the hell are we going there?"

"It's its own country again. Did you know that? The Dalai Lama is back and everything."

"Very interesting, but that didn't answer my question. What's in Tibet?"

"All your friends, Niccolo. Your cat. A full explanation that will come from someone other than me. I'm just the delivery woman. Now…seat belt."

He grunted and grumbled, but he still belted himself in.

She put the craft in the air and charted a course for the Akaya Monastery. She only hoped nothing interfered with them between here and home. They not only had the Dominion manifestation to worry about, but the weather.

Global warming had made meteorology dicey at best. It was supposed to be clear from here to there, according to the onboard navigation system, but you never really knew. If it stayed clear, the craft would zip over the snow-covered ground at a great speed. It wouldn't take them long to get to their destination, barring complications.

About twenty minutes into the flight, once they were straight, level and on course, she flipped the craft's autopilot on and unbuckled her seat belt. "Let's go ahead and..." she trailed off as she got a glimpse of Niccolo.

He sat in the chair beside her with his head tipped back and his eyes closed. The blood had clotted around the wounds on his chest and wrists. She traced the lines of his face and body with her gaze. There was something about him that made her very aware that he was a man and she was a woman. She hadn't felt that way in a long time. Just looking at him made every hormone in her body fire to life.

She looked up from his stomach and into his open eyes. The look in them was smoldering. She'd never known brown eyes could look that hot. It made her whole body tighten with sexual awareness. Worse, his gaze probably mirrored her own.

Well, shit.

She cleared her throat and stood. "Let's get you cleaned up and bandaged."

He stood and followed her to the back of the craft. This was a state-of-the-art piece of machinery. The Council of the Embraced had a hell of a lot of money at its disposal and they didn't skimp on their equipment.

The craft fit six, though it wasn't meant as a long-distance vehicle as there were no sleeping quarters, but there was a full medical kit, a bathroom with a small amount of heated water and a galley. She fished out a preheated bottle of synth-plasma as Niccolo took a chair in the back of the craft. The smooth silver walls behind him leached the color from his olive complexion and made him seem pale and in pain.

She handed the bottle to him. "It's French," she said. "Just like Fontaine bottled water...sort of."

He took it and just stared at it.

"Go on," she waved her hand. "Drink it. It'll help you heal."

"It will sustain me," he said. He looked up at her, his eyes darkening. "But only real blood from a real vein will help me heal." He set the bottle on the floor near his chair.

"Well, don't look at me." With a shake of her head, she turned and gathered what she would need to draw the bullet from him and dress his wound from the medical cabinet to the left of the galley.

She set the items down on the table by his chair, then doffed her coat and holster and laid them on the galley counter. "Do you prefer to lie down or sit up?" she said as she picked up a pair of long needle-nosed tongs.

"Which will hurt less?"

She shrugged. "Doesn't matter."

He grimaced. "I'll sit up."

"Lights on max," she said and the area brightened enough for her to see. After she turned his chair a little so there wouldn't be shadows in her work area, she gritted her teeth and knelt. "Goddess," she muttered. "I hate doing this."

"You're not the only one," he answered. "Talk to me. It will help if you talk to me while you dig around in there for the bullet."

She winced. "Do you have to say it like that? What do you want me to talk about?"

"You."

She blew out a slow, careful breath. "Okay."

He gripped the chair arms, straightened his shoulders, and looked straight ahead.

"You probably already guessed I'm not human," she said as she set the instrument into the small wound and pushed in.

She bit the inside of her lip as Niccolo grunted and stiffened. "I'm an OtherKin Sidhe...well, half, but that half is enough to make me immortal and give me some OtherKin abilities." As she spoke she centered her awareness on his wound, sensing for the location of the bullet.

"I thought so," Niccolo said through gritted teeth. "You're half Chinese, half..."

"Welsh. Odd combination, I know. Hold still." The OtherKin Sidhe were all descended from the Tuatha Dé Danaan, who had once resided in the British Isles, Ireland specifically. She had a schizophrenic heritage.

She slid the instrument in a little farther and to the left. "I was raised OtherKin Sidhe, by my Welsh mother. Almost fifty years ago, I became a Priestess of the Morrigan."

Figuring it was better to rip the bandage off instead of pull it slowly, she found the bullet, clamped down on it and yanked it out fast.

Niccolo's back arched and he roared. The sound went straight through her, poured ice into her blood. She fell back on her ass for the second time that day, holding the bloody tongs with the bullet in one hand and staring up at him.

Niccolo closed his eyes and breathed heavily in and out through his nose. Blood streamed from the fresh wound and a nearly inaudible growl trickled from between his lips.

Jade's heart pounded in her chest. She still wasn't sure of this man, what he was capable of. She wasn't sure how much prison had changed him.

The growl stopped. He opened his eyes and the look of pain slowly bled away. His big body relaxed. Since she still had all her limbs attached, she started to breathe again.

Jade pushed up from the floor, disposed of the bullet and tongs, and then carefully shot the wound up with MedicFix. He reached up to touch the soft white paste that covered the bullet hole as though he'd never seen it before.

"No," she said sharply. "Don't touch it. Give it a minute to dry. It disinfects the wound. Not that you need that, but it will keep it from bleeding and hurting. The paste will be absorbed into your body as the wound heals and closes up. You can do everything you'd normally do now without worry that you'll reopen it."

His gaze darkened as he looked her. "Everything?"

She blinked. Was she the only one who'd heard meaning inflected into that one single word? Shaking her head, she turned away to clean the tongs and replace the materials into the cabinet.

He pulled her down into his lap, facing him in a straddling position. She'd barely seen him move, let alone had time to react. She tried to jab him in the eyes and throat, but he grabbed her wrists.

Her fear spiked. She didn't like being grabbed or restrained in any way. Bad memories rose up, along with the bile in her throat. She thought about slamming him in his fresh wound...but a barely coherent voice of reason within her knew he probably didn't mean her harm. Her reaction came from her memories and her fears.

Still, all she'd have to do was twist her wrists down to be free of his grasp. She swallowed her fear and fisted both her hands to restrain herself until she felt her nails dig into her palms. On the heels of her panic rose a much different reaction to being so close to him.

"Let me go," she said carefully. She took measured breaths in and out, calming herself.

He ignored her request. "You're a Death Priestess."

She gritted her teeth and counted to five. That was the derogatory title for her kind. The Morrigan was a triple aspect goddess and *death* was only one of them. That slight was enough to make her ignore the fact she was straddling this man and that her body was becoming very aware of the close proximity of his cock to her pussy. The fact that she was having that reaction at all, while he held her this way, was beyond surprising.

"Yes, I'm a *Priestess of the Morrigan*," she said pointedly. "So what?"

"You are much as I was…before."

"These days we work alongside the Council Executioners, yes. Is there some reason we have to have this conversation while I'm on your lap?"

He let one of her wrists free and snaked his hand to her nape before she could even draw a breath. Then he compelled her mouth to his.

The breath of the Embraced had a calming component to it. It lulled their human victim into a relaxed state and allowed the vamp to feed much easier. In most cases, the breath of the Embraced wouldn't work on the Sidhe, but it worked quite well on her human half. Her body relaxed as his sweet-scented breath bathed her mouth and nostrils.

His lips brushed against hers with a gentleness she never would've guessed this man possessed. She fought through the fog in her mind, trying to grasp some thread of sanity. It kept slipping away like the memory of a dream in the morning.

His huge hands moved to her waist and slipped under her leather vest. She relaxed into him, feeling his thumbs brush back and forth against her sides. The sensation of his skin on hers felt mesmerizing. She put her hands on his shoulders just to get more of it. Back and forth he stroked, until her breath caught in her throat and she shuddered in pleasure.

Niccolo moved his hands down her hips, almost cupping her ass, and pulled her forward a little against his body. She clearly felt the outline of his aroused cock through his pants. Her pussy responded by growing hot, damp and sensitive. He increased the pressure of his mouth on hers and she felt the tickle of his beard.

She sighed against his mouth, and he nipped her lower lip, demanding that she open to him. Her cunt seemed to catch fire when his tongue slid in to leisurely stroke against hers. She felt every caress of it between her thighs.

The man had had a long time to learn how to kiss well…and he could. His tongue played with hers and then slipped out as he alternated nipping at her lips and then slanting his mouth across hers to penetrate once again. The kiss was soft, then demanding, then a tease and then the promise of something more. It confused her, stole her breath and made her needy as hell. It made her want that *more* with everything she was.

She hadn't wanted sex for nearly fifty years.

That realization caused her to grab on to a thread of sanity and yank on it hard. She brought a hand down, punched him in his wound, got up and spun back away from him in one smooth move.

Niccolo grunted and bent over. He swore loudly in about five different languages.

Jade put a hand on the counter and closed her eyes briefly, trying to get her head together. She stared at the side of the heating unit as she spoke. "You trying to lull me in donating, Niccolo?" she asked in deceptively soft voice. She looked at him.

"It's not your blood I want," he said.

Well, he'd made his meaning clear enough. She turned, leaned up against the counter and crossed her arms over her chest. "Gee, and you didn't even buy me dinner first. Where are your manners?"

He straightened. "You didn't seem to mind."

"*Your. Breath.*" She snarled the words at him.

"I didn't think you'd respond to it."

Hell, everything about him made her…*respond*. Damn it.

"Well, I do." She turned away from him and pointed at a small door to the left of the medicine closet. "The MedicFix is dry by now. There's the bathroom. Shower. Razors. Towels." Then she walked past him, back to the cockpit.

Niccolo watched her walk away from him. The taste of her still lingered on his lips and tongue. She tasted good and he wanted more. It had been about five years since he'd had sex, the last time he'd been borrowed out from Harcourt, but that wasn't the only reason he wanted her. He'd met only a few Sidhe in his life, and all of them had been powerful, but strength seemed to leak from this woman's pores. It wasn't just physical, but mental and spiritual.

It drew him.

The Priests and Priestesses of the Morrigan were the OtherKin version of the Council Executioners. They policed the OtherKin population around the world, a thing the humans had trouble doing.

While the Executioners simply stalked and punished the Embraced who transgressed, the Order of the Morrigan were just as their name implied, a religious organization. They lived cloistered together and devoted their lives to the service of the Morrigan. They trained both their minds and their bodies with a dedication that made them walking lethal weapons. That explained how Jade had been able to dodge a bullet. It was something no ordinary OtherKin Sidhe would've been able to do. Niccolo suspected not many priestesses had that kind of speed, either.

In addition to her undoubted deadliness, she was beautiful. There was no doubt about that. She was tall and slender, lithe. Her breasts weren't that large. Just about enough to cup in his hands. He'd like to find out for sure, instead of just imagine. Her skin was the pale coffee color that came from a mix of Asian and Caucasian. Long, straight corn-silk fine black hair that probably fell to her ass unbound. She had it confined in tight French braid, but he wanted to see it loose. He wanted to feel it brushing over his skin.

Her eyes were the most compelling thing about her. They were light blue, almond- shaped and twinkled from a delicately boned face. Dark hair and blue eyes had always been his favorite combination.

Maybe he'd moved a little too fast, been a little too aggressive. That was his way. Seduction wasn't something he'd ever done subtly. He didn't do anything subtly. She wanted him in spite of herself, though. He could scent the changes in her body that signaled her attraction to him. He could hear the beat of her heart and the increased pace of her breath when he touched her. Niccolo wanted to make that happen again.

He stood up, grimacing at the ache of his chest, and headed to the shower. He'd have to make it a cold one. He didn't much about his future at the moment. In the last two hundred years he'd grown used to that, but he knew one thing… He wanted Jade.

* * * * *

Driving music poured from the powerful speakers of his living room. Drayden hummed along and whirled on the smooth marble floor, dragging the heel of one expensive polished shoe to meet the other. He turned, stopped and took big drag on his thousand-dollar cigar.

Life was good.

He closed his eyes and let his fangs extend as he contemplated his impending dinner. No bottled synth-plasma for him, only the finest blood directly from the finest, most expensive veins around the world. These days he didn't have to feed from the Demi since he had beautiful human women with sweet blood clamoring to serve him. He had everything he wanted…almost. Soon he'd have it all.

Even if he'd had to sell his soul to get it.

Something flickered in his awareness, a human approaching the door of his house with one of his minions. He just loved to refer to his loyal vamps and OtherKin wolves as *minions*. It amused the absolute fuck out of him. He opened his eyes and blew out a puff of smooth smoke from his lungs. "Music, decrease volume," he commanded the house computer.

The thump of the bass lessened as Eric entered with a lovely dark-haired Italian woman on his arm. Drayden had enjoyed this very expensive blood whore before. They were both dressed head to toe in thick winter coats and heavy hats against the cold.

Drayden heaved a sigh as he walked over to snuff out his cigar in a carved ivory ashtray. "Italian again?" he mock-whined.

The woman dropped her black fur coat to her feet, revealing a body that would make any man slobber. She bent a knee, allowing the hem of her long red silk dress to come up and reveal a sexy red shoe. "You want someone else? I'll go," she said, looking confidently into his eyes.

He licked his lips. His fangs were already extended. "No. I don't want another. I want you to take off that dress."

She smiled slyly. These blood prostitutes got more brazen by the day. She stripped her gown off, revealing a black lace teddy and thigh-high stockings. She had very pretty ankles and very pretty breasts. Drayden wanted to see everything else on her that was pretty. He never got sick of women. Tall, short, skinny, round. He loved them all.

He tore his gaze away from the woman to Eric. "And why are you still here?"

"I have news, boss."

Drayden pointed at the woman and then at his bedroom door. "You go in there. Make yourself ready for me."

He watched her walk away in appreciation of the sway of her ass, and then turned back to Eric. "Good news or bad news?"

"Boss?"

"Just make it fast."

"Harcourt Prison...failed."

Drayden blinked. He turned and paced away from him. "Well, that's *bad* news, isn't it?"

"Niccolo and the Sidhe woman almost didn't make it out."

Drayden clenched a fist and turned. "Almost," he said in a deceptively soft voice. "Almost?"

"I've had a report that Niccolo Romano was wounded, shot in the chest."

Drayden clapped his hands. "Oh, goody. That probably caused him about five whole minutes of pain," he spat.

"Maybe if the computers had released the inmates just a little sooner." Eric's voice shook, probably sensing how close he was to being a very *killed* messenger.

"Maybe if?" Drayden roared. He launched himself into the air and caught Eric by the throat, slamming him back onto the smooth Oriental tile floor behind them. Eric's dark eyes bugged and he made a pleasing gurgling noise.

"*Maybe* now I have to tell Mr. Jones that his plan failed. Can you comprehend, Eric, just how much Mr. Jones hates the words *almost* and *maybe if*?" His rage tainted his words with the Hungarian accent that was his birthright. He shook him up and down, slamming the back of his head down on the tile over and over. "Well, do you?"

Eric grasped Drayden's wrists and choked out, "No."

Drayden gave him one last squeeze and released him. He rolled away and sat up as Eric gasped and wheezed beside him.

Mr. Jones. The man creeped him out. Just thinking about meeting those dead-fish eyes gave him the willies. Mostly, Drayden tried to keep as far from the man—if that was what you could call him—as possible.

Now he'd have to deliver bad news to him.

"Get out," Drayden snarled.

Eric scrambled to his feet and hastily left the house.

Drayden took a moment to compose himself before standing. The addition of the old, powerful Vampir Niccolo Romano to this equation was not to their benefit. They needed more time and Niccolo and his merry band of do-gooders would fuck with them royally while they took that time.

Drayden swore low in Hungarian, then smoothed the lapels of his blue silk shirt and ran his fingers through his hair. He headed into the bedroom, needing blood and sex to clear his head and ground him. Then he'd go play messenger boy and hopefully not be killed in the process.

Drayden opened the door to find the woman reclining in a position she probably thought was alluring. He wouldn't think she was alluring until she was restrained. He walked to the bed silently and picked up the ties already bound to the headboard and snaked them around her wrists one by one. Drayden tightened them until she lost her coy little smile and whimpered.

He needed to be in control. Always and in everything.

Once she was properly splayed and at his mercy, only then did his cock harden. Drayden ripped his shirt off, revealing the mottled and scarred skin of his back, chest and stomach. The vicious marks momentarily wiped the sly, sexy look right off the woman's face, just as the sight of the scars always did.

Yeah, he was a monster inside *and* out.

* * * * *

Jade stretched in the cockpit of the glider, watching the winter-white ground zip past below them. She turned at the sound of Niccolo approaching behind her.

He came into the cockpit barefoot and wearing only the pair of loose drawstring pants she'd left for him in the bathroom. His skin was free of blood and his wrists were already healing. The circle of MedicFix marking his gunshot wound had adjusted to his olive skin pigment. He'd shaved, revealing his strong chin and better displaying his full, sensual lips. The memory of those lips on hers tightened every muscle in her body, and her fingers itched to feel his newly smooth skin.

His hair hung long and damp around his shoulders and he held a pair of scissors in his hand. "Can you cut hair?"

She glanced at the scissors. "You sure you want to trust me with those after what you just pulled?"

His full mouth ticked up in a smile that made her heart skip a beat. Great goddess, she was acting like a schoolgirl with a crush! This was ridiculous. "I think I'll be able to defend myself."

"You're a little overconfident there, I think." She stalked forward and plucked the scissors from his hand before he responded. "Go, sit down in the back."

She followed him into the back and picked up a comb from the bathroom. "I'm surprised to see you have no tattoos," she commented as she started to comb out his long hair. "I mean, considering your past. Didn't they mark you guys?"

Niccolo groaned at her fingers on his scalp, a deep sexy sound that shot straight to her pussy. She fumbled a length of his hair, then regained control and dragged the comb down through it.

"I did have tattoos once, but when I was Embraced all my scars healed. That happens once in a while," he murmured with closed eyes.

Man, she wished she'd had that luxury, something to heal up all her scars. Not even extensive reconstructive surgery had been able to fix them all. "A tattoo is a scar, I guess. And I remember Scythchilde telling me his face was deformed before he was Embraced and that it healed."

"Charlie. I haven't seen in him centuries."

"You're about to see him now, Niccolo. We're almost at our destination. How do you want your hair? Long? Short?"

"Short. It's easier to fight with short hair."

"How do you know we'll be fighting?"

"Come on, no one ever wants me for anything else."

"Roman style, then." She fell into a zen-like rhythm of comb and snip. She knew a lot about him, and so she knew that he didn't like to talk of his past. It fascinated her, however. She'd spent a long time researching him for the alliance that had been formed between the Council of the Embraced and the Order of the Morrigan.

He'd started out in life as a Roman soldier. Proving himself early and often as a beyond average fighter, he was promoted quickly into the elite ranks of the Praetorian Guard, the Caesar's personal bodyguards. But the Caesar had been a corrupt man who most everyone had wanted off the throne— wanted *offed* in general. So, Niccolo had plotted with a group of senators and praetorian and had killed him.

Niccolo had committed what amounted to regicide. Worse, perhaps, since he'd killed an emperor.

This was a secret that he had kept from his Embraced brethren. Jade knew it only because of the extensive historical records kept by the Priestesses of the Morrigan. She'd vowed never to reveal the information because she suspected Niccolo held a measure of shame within him regarding the act, even though most back then had agreed the Caesar needed to be taken from power by any means.

Even though the praetorian's act had been fully sanctioned by the incoming Ccaesar, politics demanded the plotters pay for what they'd done. So, Niccolo and the other praetorian had been forced into slavery as punishment. Back then the strongest slaves had been forced into the gladiatorial ring.

Niccolo fought for years and had gained a fame reached by only the best of them. Even though gladiators of the status he'd reached had been treated in a fashion equivalent to a star professional athlete, he'd been denied any luxury or benefit from it. He'd been kept poor and isolated. Niccolo had simply fought and killed to stay alive. Until one day his *mere de sang*, blood mother, found him and Embraced him. After that, his reality had changed drastically.

His had been a very violent life, filled with bloodshed and killing. From the time he'd been fifteen and had become a soldier, his world had been infused with the sounds and sights of death.

Was it any wonder he'd allowed himself to be arrested back in Minnesota all those years ago? Was it any wonder he'd allowed them to lock him away for a crime he hadn't even committed? Jade didn't think so. All he'd wanted was a little peace. Prison was the only place he could get it. He'd have to be sociopath to not have all that death affect him, and Niccolo was no sociopath in her estimation.

She understood all too well the need to seek solitude and a cloister, of sorts. She understood the need to escape a traumatic fate.

The last lock of his hair fell to the floor of the glider and Jade wiped a towel over the back of his neck to clear it of the stray clippings. His thick dark hair just brushed his nape now. She went around the front of the chair.

Nice. The shorter hair made him even better looking, if that was possible. She cocked her head to the side for a moment, considering him. What drew her to this man? She couldn't put her finger on exactly what made him different from all the other gorgeous men that surrounded her on an almost daily basis. Many had tried to seduce her, but Niccolo had gotten much further than most of them...and she'd only known this man for a very short time.

"Done," she said. She turned to replace the scissors and Niccolo grabbed her wrist. A shock of apprehension and arousal shot through her body at the contact.

"You mentioned at the prison that you knew more about me than even my friends. How much do you know?" he asked.

A flutter of regret moved through her stomach. She hoped she hadn't inadvertently broadcast her thoughts. She was skilled at keeping up shields, but sometimes when she was relaxed she let them slip a little, and Niccolo was a very old and powerful vamp with a great telepathic ability.

"I know...a lot," she answered carefully. "I know everything about you that was made available to me through the records of the Priestesses of the Morrigan. I know your origins, the particulars of your Embrace. I know about your *mere de sang* and what happened to her and how you became an Executioner for the Council."

He stood and plucked the scissors and towel from her and replaced them. "You know everything about me. I know nothing of you except that you're a half-Chinese, half-Welsh Priestess of the Morrigan."

Like Niccolo, talking about her past wasn't her favorite thing to do. He'd touched a nerve. She turned and walked to the cockpit. "You don't need to know anything more about me," she muttered as she walked away from him.

He caught her arm and whirled her around. "So you uncover my deepest secret, yet decide to keep all yours?"

Yes, she'd broadcast her thoughts. She must've. "Look, I don't think badly of you for what you did. Hell, it's *literally* ancient history. I know what I know about you because it's part of my job, not because I want to. Regardless, your secret is safe with me. I consider it sacred information."

They stood staring at each other as if in challenge. His eyes snapped with anger. Obviously, he was unhappy she'd been poking around his past, but he was just going to have to fucking live with it.

The navigation system in the cockpit sounded. The beeping filled the cabin, signaling she needed to take the controls over because they were approaching the monastery. She shook off Niccolo's grasp, turned and attended to it.

The Akaya Monastery sat on the side of a snow-covered mountain. In the foothills below the monastery nestled the small town of Akaya. Before the war, it had been rife with tourists coming to visit the monastery, especially after Tibet's annexation. The tourists were gone now...with most of their money, but the town still seemed to flourish in the shadow of the holy place.

In the summer the moss-covered boulders that surrounded the building and the town could be seen. Streams gurgled gently down through them, lending instant peace to those who heard them. Tall aspens and trees of unidentifiable origin to Jade sprouted in warm weather and dressed the mountainside in shades of a silver, cinnamon and gold.

She felt Niccolo come up next to her and heard his almost imperceptible sharp intake of breath. Yes, it was a beautiful place even in the deadness of the cold season. She set the glider down on the landing area near the path leading to the entrance of the monastery. Niccolo slipped on the shirt, shoes and coat she'd brought for him and they disembarked.

Jade pulled her coat around her tighter as they made their way past the rows of prayer wheels and into the building. Smooth-headed monks filled the main chamber. Many different hallways arched from this room. The walls were of burnished gold and the domed ceiling was painted with a beautiful fresco of flowers and birds.

She inclined her head toward each tan-and-scarlet-robed monk she encountered and Niccolo took her lead, doing the same. As she passed Buddha Hall, she stopped and bowed deeply, showing her respect. Niccolo followed suit.

"Our entrance is at the back," she murmured at him. "We stay here under the generosity and request of his holiness the Dali Lama."

"Why here?" Niccolo asked.

"The prayers and the strength of mind of the monks make it nearly impossible for the Dominion to enter."

Niccolo shot her a look of puzzlement.

"There's a lot we need to brief you on, Niccolo. Haven't you heard? The Dominion have managed to physically manifest in this realm of reality."

Chapter Three

Niccolo stopped in his tracks. The Dominion were the deadly enemy of the Embraced and of mankind. The Embraced had evolved to provide a buffer between the Dominion and humans. It was a symbiotic relationship. The Embraced kept the world as safe as possible from the Dominion and in return the Embraced took their sustenance from humans.

At least, that had been the case until mankind had discovered that vampires were real. Now there were laws against taking blood from humans. These days, the Vampir were required to feed from other Vampir or the Demi, the half-Vampir who took nourishment from sex instead of blood.

Normally the Dominion lived outside the bounds of this reality. They were psychic vampires who lived in the dimensional plane just to the left of this one. They fed off humans, sucking out their emotions and their very will to live while they dreamed. From time to time, when the walls of the two-dimensional barriers grew thin, the Dominion could possess a human, but manifestation... That was far more rare. In fact, Niccolo didn't think he'd ever heard of such a thing occurring.

Jade turned toward him. "Come on. Gabriel will be able to explain it all better than I can."

A monk passed near him and opened a door set in a tableau depicting a spring scene. He motioned to them both to enter.

Niccolo followed Jade within and down a long flight of badly lit stairs.

"The monks like for us to remain in our quarters as much as possible," Jade said. "Out of sight."

He concentrated on the swing of her braid. His fingers itched to undo it and let that midnight length free. He wanted it covering him, brushing his bare skin. He wanted the light woody scent of it filling his nostrils as he ran the tip of his tongue down the nape of her neck. Niccolo's body tensed as he imagined doing that and a whole lot more.

Christ.

He wanted her stripped and naked beneath him on a bed. He wanted to slide into her tight, creamy little cunt and fuck her until she came. Just the thought of it made his cock hard. He'd gone too long a time without a woman and this one tempted him far worse than most.

They reached the end of the stairs and into a large common room. "I guess everyone's out," she said, surveying the empty space. There was a note of concern in her voice.

Niccolo stopped at the foot of the stairs and scanned his environment. Besides the kitchen, there was a sitting area to his left. To his right stood a long table upon which were strewn papers. Also to the right was a hallway. The place was decorated simply. The floor was polished hardwood and the walls were painted white and hung with Tibetan artwork.

She turned toward him. "Kitchen's there," she said, pointing to a large area to his left. "Plenty of synth-plasma. There aren't any Demi here, so get used to the bottled blood." She gave him a pointed look. "Unless you can get one of the *other* women to donate, that is. Don't get too comfortable. We probably won't be here for long."

"You are living here together now?" he asked. "Is this some kind of House of the Embraced?"

"No." She shook her head. "This is just a place for us to plan and discuss things. A safe place. One of many throughout the world. The Dominion have grown very strong as of late and the monastery provides protection against their telepathic powers. This is a home away from home. There are contingents of Embraced centered all over right now." She shrugged. "We picked a country close to China because that's where you were."

"We? You didn't even know me until this morning."

"Gabriel, Adam, Charlie, Aidan and Penny have known you a long time, Niccolo. I was assigned to work with them by the Order and they decided to come here for you. The Order and the Council demanded I deal with you. They sent me because I speak Mandarin." She gave him a pointed stare. "You're my job, nothing more."

"And for a moment I thought you cared."

She flashed a grin and turned. "Only thing I care about right now is a shower." She walked down the hallway. "Come with me. I'll show you where you sleep."

Niccolo followed her down a hallway and into a room decorated in dark blue. A fresco of a lake with cranes adorned the ceiling. A royal blue silk comforter covered the bed. It had been a long time since he'd slept on a comfortable mattress. He'd never been a materialistic person, so he hadn't thought he'd miss such things while he was in prison. Now, surrounded with luxuries provided to him by his friends, he felt very thankful.

Jade walked over and pulled the closet open. Clothes hung within and boots and shoes stood on the floor under them. Jade made a sweeping gesture with her hand. "Courtesy of Gabriel."

Jade walked past him, toward the door. He fisted his hands to keep from grabbing her and dragging her up against him. The mattress was good for more than just sleeping. But he sensed he'd end up with a pair of bruised balls for his effort if he tried anything right now. Watching her walk past without touching her was almost worse.

She turned in the doorway. "I'm going to take a quick shower. They should be back soon, Niccolo. They're anxious to see you." She smiled. "There is someone here to see you now, however."

Niccolo felt her before he saw her. Kara, his feline familiar, ran into the room. He scooped the large brown tabby into his arms, immediately burying his face in her fur. Her purring was almost enough to blow his eardrums. He staggered back and sat on the bed. He couldn't describe the relief he felt having his familiar back after all these years.

"Now that has to be the oddest sight I have ever seen," said Jade from the doorway in a wondering voice. "A man like you cuddling a cat."

He lifted his head but she'd disappeared down the hallway. Her light laugh floated back to him.

Niccolo lie back on the bed and let Kara take up residence on his chest. He was almost content in this moment. Seeing his familiar again was like having a missing part of his soul back. He breathed in deep and allowed the muscles of his body to relax. Kara's purr was a balm.

It was very rare for an Embraced to find their familiar. When they did, the animal became immortal, tied to them at soul level. Usually, the familiar was related in some way to a transformational animal. If a vamp turned into a wolf, his or her familiar was a dog. In Niccolo's case, his transformational animal was a panther. Feline to feline, canine to canine, bird to bird.

He relaxed back against the bed and slung an arm over his eyes, allowing Kara's heavy purr to rumble through his body. A sense of peace, something he hadn't had in a very, very long time, almost stole over him.

Almost.

He was relieved at being freed from prison, even though it had been his choice, ultimately, to allow them to arrest him. He'd wanted a rest, but he hadn't received it. Not even in prison. Agencies from all over the world had sought his aid for various initiatives. When he refused to help them, they'd threatened someone innocent, told him he had to do it or they'd die.

He seemed he would never find peace. Not really.

The sound of running water met his ears. He tried hard not to imagine Jade in the shower, naked and wet. He tried not to picture himself in there with her, taking the soap in his hands and washing every part of her body himself. He could imagine how her breasts would feel cupped in his hands, how warm they'd be and how pink and pretty her nipples would look. He could imagine fisting his fingers in her heavy fall of hair and sliding his hand down to her hip...lifting her leg so he could slide his cock into her aroused pussy. She'd be hot and tight around him.

Niccolo groaned out loud at the images dancing through his mind. He rubbed a hand over his face and opened his eyes.

This was fucking torture. He wasn't used to having to hold back. Hell, he wasn't used to having to chase after a woman this way. Mostly, they pursued him, not the other way around. He had no idea how to go about this. He had no capacity for seduction or finesse, and he definitely had no patience. Usually women tripped over themselves to fill his bed.

The water shut off. He pictured her toweling off. He could see the water droplets glimmering on her skin and how they'd taste on his tongue when he licked them off.

"Fuck," he muttered.

Kara had fallen fast asleep on top of him. He gently laid her on the mattress beside him and kissed her head. Unable to lie even one more moment on the bed while Jade stood completely naked just twenty feet away, he got up and went to the door.

She emerged from a steam-filled bathroom, wrapped in a large white towel. Not noticing him there, she turned and walked away from him, probably toward her room. Her wet hair hung loose down her back. As she walked down the hallway, she lost the edge of her towel. It fell open, revealing a sexy tattoo of a crow marking the small of her back, her gorgeous curved ass…and long, wicked-looking scars snaking their way across her shoulders and the backs of her thighs.

He stood there, stunned by the scars and turned on by the unexpected flash of her body all at the same time.

Jade turned to retrieve the edge of the towel and caught sight of him standing there. Intense emotions flitted through her light blue eyes and across her face, not the least of which was shame.

"You see how ugly I am now?" she spat at him and then gave a short, bitter laugh. "It's a sure-fire cure. At least you won't bother me anymore." She went toward her room.

Niccolo was there in the blink of an eye. She opened her door and he slammed the flat of his hand against it.

Jade made a low sound of anger in the back of her throat. "Let me go," she growled at the closed door.

"No. Not until we get something settled."

"There's nothing to get sett—"

He turned her around to face him. "What or who did that to you?"

She looked away, down to the hallway to the common room. "It was a long time ago and I don't…talk about it. *Ever.*" Her voice shook with emotion.

Fair enough.

He placed a hand on either side of her head and she looked up at him. In this position he could almost imagine they were lying in bed and he was about to slid his cock into her welcoming pussy. He could almost feel her silky thighs sliding around his waist. The look in her eyes destroyed the fantasy, however. They were like two pretty gun barrels trained on him.

"How could you think you're ugly?" he asked.

She made a scoffing sound. "You haven't seen me completely naked."

Niccolo curled his hands into fists. "Do you have any idea," he said slowly, "just how much I want to see you naked? I guarantee I'll like what I see."

"Why? How? You saw you saw my scars."

He nodded. "Yeah, I saw your scars. I also saw the sweetest curved ass I think I've ever laid eyes on, and a sexy tattoo at the base of an elegant, slender back that I want to trace with my tongue. I want to fuck you, Jade. I want a night of pure, down and dirty sex with you. I want to feel the muscles of your cunt milk my cock as I make you come over and over." He took a shuddering, shaky breath. "I want to hear you scream my name at the top of your lungs."

Her whole body went tense. He could scent the faint musk of her as she became aroused. His words had excited her, and they'd turned him on, too. His cock had swollen painfully in his pants. All he wanted was for her to relent, open his zipper and take it into her hand.

He dipped his head and brushed his lips over her silky bare shoulder, feeling the edge of a scar under his mouth. Jade shivered against him. "How could you think I wouldn't want you after I saw your scars?" he murmured. "You don't know how fucking wrong you are. All I want right now is you."

Her breathing hitched as he moved his hand to her nape. His fingers tangled in the long, damp skeins of her hair. Niccolo closed his eyes at the sensation and inhaled the fresh, alluring scent of her soap and shampoo.

Unable to resist, he pushed her hair away from the delicate shell of her ear and found a sensitive spot right beneath her earlobe. He kissed it lingeringly, then let the tip of his tongue taste it.

Jade's breathing and heart rate increased, and he felt her hands clench on the towel, holding it against her body like armor.

He dropped his hand down to the bottom edge of the towel and rubbed his fingers over her smooth skin. *Ah, God, it did feel like silk.* She let her breath out in a fast huff as he dragged his fingers upward, bringing the edge of the towel with it. He let his hand come to a rest high on her thigh, almost on her hip. She felt so sweet and soft, such a contrast to her tough demeanor.

He had to stifle the rising groan in his throat. A little higher and to the right a bit and he'd be able to sink a couple fingers into her pussy. He could imagine how hot and wet she'd feel.

"Why won't you just leave me alone?" she said in a voice that shook with several emotions, Niccolo suspected. Anger was definitely one of them.

He groaned. "No way can I do that. Sorry."

He knew that he might be pushing her too hard. He might end up with her knee in his solar plexus or his balls pretty soon, but he was willing risk it to touch her. It was like trying to tame a wild animal to take food from his hand. He never knew when he might be bitten.

He inched his hand to the right and up, feeling the soft glide of her flesh against his fingertips. All Jade did was clutch her towel tighter and closed her eyes. She didn't lash out at him, and he took her passivity as permission. He wondered at her apparent nervousness at his touch. The OtherKin Sidhe were a notoriously sexual race, and Jade didn't seem like the shy type.

Niccolo grazed her silken, smooth pubic area. He closed his eyes and tipped his head back. The Sidhe were virtually hairless from the neck down. Ah, God...he'd forgotten. "Hell, Jade, you feel so good." He dipped his head and kissed her throat. "Spread your thighs for me."

She whimpered a little deep in her throat and parted them a fraction of an inch. Niccolo slid his finger in to stroke her small, sweet clit. It felt swollen, wanting his attention, even if Jade wasn't sure she did. Niccolo shuddered, thinking about how it would feel against his tongue, or sucked between his lips. He rubbed it, feeling it grow larger and even more aroused under the pad of his finger.

Jade stiffened against him and let out a fast, hard breath. He lowered his mouth to hers, pressing her up against the door behind her, and kissed her long and deep. She'd tasted good, hot and needy. Her tongue was like velvet against his. Niccolo thought he could get drunk on her. He was already halfway there.

He pulled away a little to fight the urge to ease her down to the floor. "Let me make you come," he murmured against her lips.

She didn't answer and he didn't stop. He stroked her clit over and over until her breathing came faster and scent of her cream infused the air. Finally, she moaned low and sexily. Her body shuddered against his. Niccolo slanted his mouth over hers, consuming her sighs and moans and continued to caress her clit, extending her climax.

When the tremors had passed, he braced his hands on either side of her. Jade stood, her eyes open wide and seemingly unseeing. She looked stunned. Her hands were white where she gripped the towel to her body.

"Are you okay?" he asked.

Her eyes focused and flashed dangerously. "No."

Sounds came from the common room and Niccolo turned to look. When he looked back at Jade, she was disappearing through her door. It closed in his face.

Damn.

"Niccolo!" a woman yelled joyously. Penelope ran toward him and leapt into his arms. Niccolo grabbed her so she wouldn't land ass first on the floor. He hadn't seen Penny since he'd gone to prison. He hadn't seen any of the people who now awaited him at the end of the corridor with smiles on their faces. "Niccolo," she said again warmly with a fading trace of an English accent. "It's so very good to have you here." Tears glimmered in the depths of her blue-green eyes.

He set her to her feet, at a loss for words.

She looked much as she had when he'd last seen her. Her reddish-blonde curls were cropped short and fell in tumult around her pretty heart-shaped face. Penny had been Embraced in the late 1800s and had been an instrumental force, along with her mate, Aidan, in defeating a rising tide of the Dominion. It had been the battle that had revealed the existence of the Embraced to humankind. Niccolo remembered it well. He'd fought in it.

Penny grabbed his hand and pulled him into the waiting throng. Gabriel and Fate embraced him next. Niccolo found he almost couldn't speak in the faces of all his old friends.

"Did you find the peace you were looking for?" whispered Fate into his ear as she hugged him.

No. But he wouldn't say that out loud. "I heard you have Paris now," Niccolo said instead to them both.

"Yes," answered Gabriel smoothly, though his blue eyes were filled with emotion. "The Council gave me Paris and a good chunk of France about ten years ago. Vaclav and Monia are there now, watching things for me while I'm here."

"It's a fitting territory for you."

Gabriel inclined his head. "It's good to be home." He pulled Fate to him. "And she seems to like it there." Fate tipped her head up and kissed him. So, they were still in love after all these years. An unexpected pang of jealousy speared through Niccolo.

"I've kept all your investments and accounts in proper order over the years," said Gabriel. "You were wealthy before, of course, but now..." Gabriel trailed off and gave a loose shrug. He grinned. "You're way beyond wealthy now. I'll be turning over access to your accounts to you tonight."

"Thanks for seeing to it," he answered.

Niccolo knew he had enough money to do anything he desired. Those who lived as long as he had were truly foolhardy if they failed to amass a fortune. To him, the money was a symbol of freedom and no more. It was like the prized motorcycle he'd had so many years ago. It was a way to get around, access to things he wanted to do and see—freedom. He'd never been a greedy man and he didn't care about luxuries or possessions.

Charlie grabbed him next and hugged him hard, followed by Tiya. Tiya, Niccolo knew less well. She was an OtherKin Sidhe, like Jade. It had been when he'd rescued her from a group of vamps who'd desired her fae blood that the SPAVA and the Council had arrested him. Niccolo was happy to see Charlie and Tiya had stayed together after that traumatic incident.

The last news Niccolo had heard about Charlie was that the council had given him the Hong Kong territory. China had become the world's primary superpower during the time that Niccolo had been incarcerated. The United States was no longer the global power it had once been. Now the world looked to the East for protection and direction. Therefore, Hong Kong was a mark of honor. Charlie and Tiya were doing very well for themselves.

Aidan moved forward and shook his hand, a huge grin spread over his face and his brown eyes alight with happiness. "We missed you, Niccolo," he said. He'd lost most of his Irish accent, it seemed.

"I missed all of you, too," Niccolo answered and looked away. He'd never dealt well with emotion. Cold and focused, that was the state Niccolo liked best, the state to which he was most accustomed. This reunion scene was nice, but it also made him extremely uncomfortable. He'd never been a man of many words and he had no idea what to say now. A part of him wanted to leave, get away from their curious and emotion-filled gazes.

Last to hug him was Adam, one of his best friends. "Hasn't been the same without you, Nic," Adam said. "Damn, man, you've lost almost all your accent. It's weird hearing you talk."

Niccolo thumped Adam on his back. "Thanks for taking care of Kara and thanks for getting me out. I appreciate all that you've done, but I need to tell you something." He went silent for a moment, searching for the right words. "I will never hunt and kill rogues for money again. I will never again be an Executioner."

The room went silent.

"Niccolo," said Tiya finally, "will you do it for a more noble purpose than money? Because that what this work will be about. This goes beyond hunting a simple rogue. It goes beyond anything you've ever done before."

"Your release came because of our request of the Council of the Embraced," said Gabriel, breaking in. "The Council is working with both the Order of the Morrigan and the Federation. It was agreed unilaterally that we'd need you for what's coming. They deliberated for a long time, then finally acquiesced."

"What's coming?" asked Niccolo.

"How much did Jade tell you?" Charlie broke in.

Niccolo shrugged. "She said the Dominion have found a way to manifest and they've grown strong enough that we must seek holy places to strategize safely."

Gabriel nodded. "By the way, I'm sorry we sent someone you didn't know to gather you. It was at the request of the Council that we do so. They stipulated we include a Priestess of the Morrigan to...handle you."

Oh, yeah, she'd be handling him really soon if he had any say in it. "*Dio.* So, she's my keeper?"

"Yeah, I'm your keeper, bloodsucker. I'm your judge, jury and executioner, too," came Jade's voice from the hallway. Dressed in a pair of tan leather pants and a white spaghetti strap T-shirt, she leaned against the wall with her arms crossed over her chest. The thick scars on her shoulders were readily visible and Niccolo wondered for a moment if she'd done that on purpose.

She didn't look friendly. She didn't look pleased that he'd just stroked her sweet little clit to climax in the hallway. Hell, she looked downright pissed off.

The other thing he noticed was that her small breasts were currently braless and her nipples pressed a little through the fabric of her shirt. Her hair was unbound as well and fell like a black lacquer waterfall down her back. His fingers curled with the impulse to stroke both nipples and hair. Of course judging by the look in her eyes, if he tried that right now he'd draw back a stump.

"Your sexual charm aside," Jade narrowed her gun-barrel eyes at him, "I have direct orders to put you down like a dog if you turn out to be rabid."

Niccolo lengthened his time estimate on seducing her into his bed.

Adam failed an attempt to stifle a laugh. "I see you're already on Jade's good side, Nic."

Fate crossed her arms over her chest. "Well, finally a woman Niccolo can't charm at first sight. Interesting."

"Niccolo has to be briefed," said Gabriel, moving toward the long table. "We have one night here to relax and catch up. Tomorrow morning, we part ways. The Council has sent orders."

"Where are we going?" asked Tiya.

Gabriel glanced at her. "You and Charlie are going home until further notice, as are Fate and I." He looked at Penelope and Aidan. "Since we have Vaclav and Monia in Paris, you will accompany Charlie to his territory as backup for the time being. Niccolo, Jade and Adam are going to New York City."

"Why New York, Gabe?" asked Adam, then realization washed over his face. "You're suspecting Drayden of something, aren't you?"

A sour look crossed Gabriel's face. "Are we ever not suspecting Dray of something?"

Niccolo's stomach clenched. *Drayden fucking Lex*, born Dokomos Lovász. Niccolo had known him since Dray had been Embraced. Out of all the Embraced, Niccolo was the one who knew him the best since they'd been close friends once, although Dray was a vamp most of them had some kind of history with. He was a greedy son of a bitch, ruthless and cold. Niccolo wouldn't put it past Lex to throw in with the enemy if the rewards were great enough. He'd probably even throw in with the Dominion.

Gabriel glanced at Niccolo. "Drayden has managed to acquire two more territories since you went to prison. He owns most of the United States now and has a total of three council seats."

Niccolo ran a hand over his face. "He has what he's always wanted, power."

"But for him, it's never enough," said Charlie.

Gabriel collapsed wearily into a chair at the table. "We cannot locate the manifestation. Not even with Fate and Penelope, our two most powerful dreamwalkers, have we been able to pinpoint his location. The Dominion are hiding this creature well. If Drayden is working for it, he might lead us to it."

"So what's with this manifestation? Why do we care so much about it?" asked Niccolo.

"This thing plans to open a doorway to allow the Dominion through," Gabriel answered. "Do you remember the doorway in New York the last time?"

Niccolo nodded.

"This one would be a hundred times larger and there would be no ritual of the kind Penelope and Aidan performed to close it."

Niccolo remembered all too well the carnage on that cold winter night. If it hadn't been for the union of Penelope and Aidan, they well may have lost that battle.

"And," said Gabriel slowly, "it's already killed two council members. It wants to take out the leadership of the Embraced and eradicate us eventually. It wants free reign over Earth and the ability to feed off humans without us to hinder them."

That made sense, of course, since the Embraced were the natural predators of the Dominion. Of course they wanted them rendered useless. Niccolo closed his eyes. He was trapped, goddamn it. Trapped. He couldn't walk away from this. All he wanted was to try and leave this place, escape having to endure that slow, sick feeling of death that he knew would envelop him if he continued down this path.

He opened his eyes and regarded Jade. She'd sprung him for one reason and one reason only, because he was damned good at his job—damned good at killing those who needed it. He glanced at his friends, all of them looking at him expectantly. Didn't they understand what they were asking him to do? The kind of price he was going to have to pay for this?

"We suspect the doorway may be dependant on some kind of astrological confluence of events. We simply don't know when or where all this might be taking place," Gabriel continued. He pushed a hair back through his hair, looking tired. "We're working against a clock we can't see, Niccolo."

Fuck. Trapped. He might as well be back at Harcourt.

He nodded slowly, the concrete feeling of resignation curling through this stomach. "If Drayden knows where this thing is, we'll find out."

Gabriel smiled. "It's good to have you back, Niccolo."

Something hard settled in his soul.

Penelope went into the kitchen and came back with two bottles of wine. "Let's celebrate Niccolo's return. One of these is a nice red wine for Tiya and Jade. The other is a wonderful blood wine. They didn't have that two hundred years ago, did they?" She waggled her eyebrows and grinned at Niccolo.

Niccolo couldn't return her grin. He looked over toward Jade, but she was gone.

* * * * *

Niccolo awoke in the middle of the night to a sensation of *presence* running down his spine. Someone was in the room with him. Darkness met his eyes when he opened them. He sent his awareness out into the room, feeling first his cat…then a foreign entity.

Making no sound, he sat up and peered through the blackness. He had very good vision, even in the inkiness of the room. A man dressed in black reached down and scooped Kara into his arms. In his other hand, he held something long and pointy.

Long and pointy positioned itself against feline throat.

"Don't touch my cat," Niccolo snarled. Out of pure reflex, he reached under his pillow, sought the blade he always kept there and slung it across the room.

The man shrieked and dropped to the floor. Hissing, Kara bounded free of the man.

Niccolo flicked on the bedside lamp and crossed the room on bare feet. He'd embedded the knife in the man's chest up to the hilt, right in the heart, right where he'd aimed. The Chinese man's eyes stared up sightlessly toward the ceiling, his face relaxed in a familiar mask of death. A hawthorn stake, deadly to the Embraced, lay on the floor near his hand.

Adam and Jade reached the doorway at the same time.

"He was going to kill Kara," Niccolo said in a cold, neutral voice, one that didn't reveal his feelings at that moment.

Death followed him wherever he went. Hell, he *was* death. His worst fear was that one day he'd snap and kill the truly innocent. He walked the razor's edge of it now.

Adam looked at the dead man and then at Jade. "You don't touch that man's cat unless he knows you. Remember that, Jade."

Jade's mouth twisted. "So I see." She knelt beside the man. "An assassin," she observed. "He made a beeline straight for your room. Someone doesn't like you much."

Niccolo sank down beside the man, noting that he wore the dark robes of a monk. Without a doubt, that had been how he'd gotten in. Someone had to have tipped the man off about their location. It pointed to an Embraced.

"Hey! Niccolo's not the special one," Adam protested. "He was probably just the first. I'm sure this guy meant to take us all down in our sleep. The man probably knew to start with Kara, our resident watch-cat."

Jade glanced up at him, amusement flickering over her face. "You sound jealous that someone just tried to kill Niccolo and his cat, Adam."

"You just don't mess with that man's cat," Adam repeated, shaking his head. "Poor dickhead found that out the hard way."

Gabriel and Charlie entered the room. "Well," said Gabriel as he surveyed the scene. "It appears our morning has come a bit earlier. Someone knows where we are."

"Time to go," murmured Charlie. "They must've deduced we'd be somewhere within the radius of the monasteries around Harcourt and checked them all."

"Or it was Drayden," Gabriel answered. "He could've easily discovered our location."

Niccolo sat back on his haunches, feeling the post-killing malaise sink into his bones. He'd done it so often, he should've been used to it. Another man probably would've learned to take joy in it, if not simply grow numb. Numbness was a blessing he didn't have.

Adam, Charlie and Gabriel bore the body and the hawthorn stake away, leaving a bloodstain on the wooden floor. He stared at it wearily.

Jade's cool voice entered his awareness. "It must feel strange to kill an assassin when you've been one yourself."

He looked up at her. She really did know his history, didn't she? "I've played assassin many times."

"I know. You did it just five years ago on your last loan-out from Harcourt."

He held her gaze steadily. "It was the Federation."

Her eyes narrowed and she tipped her chin at him. "You killed a corrupt politician in Malaysia for them."

He nodded. "When I refused to do the job they kidnapped a child from the street in Kuala Lumpur and said they'd kill her if I didn't complete it." He closed his eyes briefly against the painful memories. "The child was innocent. The politician was not."

"They manipulated you. They knew your Achilles' heel." Jade held his gaze for a heartbeat longer and then stood. "Your weakness is a good one to have, but you are still a dangerous man, Niccolo. You're lethal." She paused. "I don't trust you not to combust."

He stood slowly. "Then I'm glad to know you're here to put me down like a rabid dog if I do," he said evenly and honestly.

Jade held his gaze a moment longer and then turned and left the room.

Chapter Four

Beside her, Niccolo made a strange noise in his throat as they set their bags down and surveyed the apartment that Gabriel had procured for them. Jade smiled. It was one of a series of strange noises he'd made since they set the glider down in New York City's aerial port.

Niccolo likely felt like he'd been asleep for the last two centuries and had awoken to a strange new world—Rip Van Vampire. Recovery from the Third World War had set technological advancement back quite a ways. It had practically leveled most of the major cities. The world had been lucky to survive it at all. One hundred and twelve years after its end, much of the world's major cities had rebuilt and recovered nicely. The world was much different than the one Niccolo had left.

The war had been costly in terms of life lost and infrastructure destroyed, but it had had an upside. It had taught the world's superpowers to play nicer together, since the war had produced no clear winner and a lot of hardship for all. It had also dampened the world's taste for new and interesting weapons, since the newer and more interesting the weapons, the more destructive the wars. These days, technological advancement focused more on medical research and exploration of the universe beyond Earth than it did on attacks on other nations.

All good lessons, although humankind seemed unable to learn things without half destroying themselves first.

Jade inhaled the scent of fresh roses on the large dining room table and surveyed her lush and lovely surroundings. Gabriel and Fate had excellent taste. They'd chosen an apartment in an older building, one that hadn't been destroyed in the war. It was set a few blocks in from the New Times Square, and had a very early twenty-first-century feel, complete with antique furniture. The Embraced tended to do that, surround themselves with things of the past.

The technology was all up-to-date, however, including a media wall made of cream-colored panels, which provided visual and informational entertainment of all kinds, the news and the weather. Jade knew if she walked down the hall to her left, she'd find the bathroom with a dry pulse wash. Personally, she preferred water. That was the old-fashioned girl in her, she guessed. She wondered if since this was an Embraced residence, there might be a water shower.

Jade examined the kitchen from where she stood. That was anything if not modern. It was huge and all gleaming metal, contrasting with the polished wooden floor of the rest of the place. The food storage unit was enormous and state-of-the-art. A radiant cooking element stood to the left of the unit. In middle of the kitchen was a huge stainless steel island, and above it hung a rack with wineglasses, utensils and old-fashioned copper pots and pans.

She frowned. This kitchen seemed far more suited to a five-star chef than a vamp who lived off blood. How strange.

She watched Niccolo lean down and open Kara's carrier. The tabby strolled out, unconcerned at the change in her environment. She sat down, licked a paw and then began to investigate the apartment. Niccolo walked to the huge window that dominated one wall and looked down at the busy street below. The burgeoning plant containers on either side of him looked extra green against his black pants and shirt.

His eyes were haunted. She'd noticed that about him at Harcourt, although since he'd agree to this little initiative, they'd grown more so. He had the look of a caged animal, almost.

And she intended to keep him that way.

He might not want any part of this, but they needed him. All she cared about in this world was bringing criminals to justice. Jade was sorry Niccolo didn't care about that anymore, but she'd still make him do it.

Adam grabbed an apple from a bowl near the flower vase and plunked himself rowdily down on the red watered-silk coach. He propped his cowboy boots on the mahogany coffee table in front of him. "Gabe does it again," Adam commented before taking a bite of apple. "He rented a damn nice place," he said around a mouthful.

"This place is mine," said Niccolo from the window. "He's been keeping it for me and had it refurbished in anticipation of my release. I kept many apartments before I went in. This was one of them." He turned to look at Adam. "It looked different back then, and I didn't have this much furniture." Niccolo turned back to stare out the window, looking a little lost.

Jade fisted her hand, feeling a jolt of empathy go through her. She shouldn't care about this man or how he felt. She shouldn't have loved the way he'd touched her and kissed her back in Asia. Most of all, she shouldn't have relived that moment in the hallway over and over in her mind. Goddess, the thought of how easily he'd pulled that climax from her made her wet every time she remembered it. She *definitely* shouldn't have been aware of every little move he'd made between here and Tibet and fantasized about him touching her even more.

Suddenly annoyed with herself and her apparent weakness for him, she picked up her bags and headed toward the back of the apartment to claim a bedroom. They had some time to relax and recover from the journey they'd made, and Jade wanted to settle in to her new surroundings. There was no telling how long she'd be here.

"Well, I have a place of mine not too far away. I guess that leaves you and Jade here…alone," said Adam from the living room. There was a world of male innuendo in the last word he spoke.

Jade's steps faltered. Normally, she would have simply rolled her eyes, except that she felt concerned about staying here alone with Niccolo.

After she'd put her clothes away and bathed using the absolutely enormous, decadent water shower, she wandered into the kitchen to find something to eat. She'd been happy to find any water shower, one big enough to fit five was like finding heaven.

Adam had left and Niccolo sat on a chair with his booted feet on the coffee table and his head tipped back with his eyes closed. He wore a pair of black pants, that she'd noticed nicely displayed his gorgeous ass, and a light gray T-shirt made of Aratex, a type of material that was thin, yet warm enough to wear in very cold temperatures. The material of the T-shirt had stretched taut, displaying hints of his chest beneath it. Jade let her gaze skate down the length of him before she averted her gaze.

She pulled open the heavy door of the food unit and examined the available selection in the frozen, chilled and heated sections. Gabriel had done well. The place was stocked with lots of excellent things.

"Hungry?" said Niccolo behind her. She instantly stiffened.

"Well, yeah, I haven't eaten in over twelve hours and I'm not on a liquid diet," she cast a look over her shoulder. "Like some of us."

"Do you have something against the Embraced, Jade?"

"Me? No, nothing," she answered honestly.

"Could've fooled me."

She sighed, closed the unit's door and turned. "*Really*, I don't."

"Are you willing to prove it?" he challenged.

Jade crossed her arms over her chest and glared at him. "I don't have to prove anything—"

"Let me make you dinner."

Forgetting to be pissed off for a moment, she gaped. Niccolo...cooking? Somehow the image just didn't jibe. "What? You can cook?" she said disbelievingly. She shook her head and grimaced. "Hold on, if it involves blood, count me out."

"The Vampir need blood for nutrients, Jade, but we enjoy eating regular food. Do you think all my life has consisted of has been drinking blood and killing people? I've lived long enough become a more well-rounded person than that."

She uncrossed her arms and relaxed a little as she considered him. An image of Niccolo in an apron suddenly filled her mind and she stifled a laugh. The sight of this man working in the kitchen would almost be worth any concoction she'd be forced to choke down.

"Okay, fine," she answered finally with a dismissive wave of her hand.

She took a seat and watched as Niccolo pulled various vegetables out of the unit, along with some beef. After searching through the cabinets, he came up with several different spices and a large wok.

Well, he certainly did appear to be comfortable, though it seemed beyond strange to have this man appearing at ease in such a domestic setting. It was almost as strange as seeing him cuddling with Kara. He grabbed a knife and cutting board and began slicing the beef into strips and parsing and washing the vegetables.

He looked almost content.

She leaned forward and rested her hand on her palm. "So, uh, it looks like you enjoying cooking," she ventured.

He glanced up at her. "There's a reason Gabriel paid so much attention to the kitchen in my apartment, Jade." He grinned a little and it set butterflies free in her stomach. She stiffened.

She stuck her hands in her lap, suddenly unsettled. "Well, don't worry. I have nausea medicine in my bags," she shot back sarcastically.

"Are you always this pleasant to be around?"

"Nah, sometimes I kill people," she shot back.

He turned and threw some ingredients into the now warm wok on the radiant. The beef sizzled and a delicious smell wafted to her nose. Her stomach growled. "You're the one who chose to enter the Order of the Morrigan," he said in a flat voice.

"Yes, I did. Back then, it was a refuge for me." Realizing she'd let slip more than she'd wanted to, she snapped, "We're birds of a feather, I guess...with the killing, I mean."

He turned. "I didn't choose to become a Council Executioner. Not really. I choose to *stay* one, not become one."

Jade reached across the island and grabbed a glass and a bottle of whiskey. She was going to need sustenance to get through this night, she could tell already. "What do you mean?"

"I mean that after Antonia, my *mere de sang*, was killed, I returned to my birthplace. It was Roman Empire no longer, by that point. There, I met others who were like me. They were being threatened by a rogue Vampir and I..." he shrugged. "I had a history of killing. To protect them, I hunted down the rogue and killed him. It was then the Council drafted me into being an Executioner. I was one of the first." He stilled for a moment. "At that time, I felt compelled to do it. I felt like one of the few with the ability to protect."

Jade took a sip of the smooth whiskey and studied Niccolo's broad back over the rim of her glass. A protector. Yes, Niccolo was nothing if not that.

He turned and speared her with his gaze. "I'm surprised you don't know this about me since you know everything else." His voice had gone dangerously flat.

She set her glass down and traced the rim with her finger. "I don't know every little detail about you, Niccolo. The Order doesn't have records that complete."

"If you knew every little detail about me, Jade, you'd know that the one time I felt close to *combusting,* as you put it back in Tibet, I voluntarily incarcerated myself." Niccolo grunted, having made his point, and turned back to his cooking.

Jade was suddenly without a comeback. She took a long drink of the whiskey and felt some of the tension leak from her shoulders.

He arranged the food he'd made on two plates and set them on the table. Seduced by the scent of the food, she sat down. He'd made a beef stir-fry with lots of crunchy-looking vegetables served in a large, shallow dark green bowl. Her stomach rumbled as she inhaled the spicy scent of the dish. It appeared he perhaps hadn't lost his touch in the kitchen.

She could barely boil water, herself.

Niccolo sat down and picked up his fork. "See, no blood."

She grumbled and picked up her own fork.

He speared a strip of beef, a pea pod and a sliced carrot and held it up to her mouth. "Try it."

She eyed it carefully, considering pushing his hand away, but the food looked and smelled so good. Her stomach rumbled again, giving her no graceful way out of taking the food. She took the food from his fork and closed her eyes briefly as the ginger and other delicate spices exploded in her mouth. It not only looked and smelled delicious, it *was* delicious.

"Niccolo," she said around a mouthful, "this is so good." She opened her eyes to find him staring intently at her.

His body seemed tense and a muscle worked in his jaw. Jade could see he was trying really hard not to push her...because he wanted her. *That* was clear. He sat back, the intensity bleeding out of his expression little by little, and set in to eating the meal. She relaxed a bit and did the same.

"So, what do you want, Niccolo?"

He stopped eating and looked at her. "What do you mean?"

"You know, besides me, what do you want?"

He stared down at his plate. "Freedom."

"You have that, or you will after this is over."

He remained silent for several moments. Finally, he grunted. "That's debatable. Anyway, it's not that kind of freedom I'm talking about." He glanced at her. "What do you want?"

"To bring the bad guys in," she answered quickly. "Every low-life scum-sucker that harms another... I want his balls."

His mouth quirked in a small smile. "Should've guessed that. Do you have the skill at necromancy like the other Priestesses of the Morrigan?" he asked.

She shook her head. "I'm a half-blood. I got the immortality, the strength and the hyper-awareness of my surroundings. I didn't get much magick. I can't talk to the dead." She shrugged. "The speed... I don't know where that comes from."

"You said your father was the human?"

She nodded, took another bite and chewed while she thought about her response. "The OtherKin are forbidden to mate with humans, but she and my father fell in love. He died so long ago I can barely remember him. My mother is still alive. She lives in London."

"How old are you?"

"I'm one hundred and five. An infant compared to you."

"So, what did you do before you joined the Order?"

She shrugged and took another drink of wine. That was a topic she didn't like to talk about. "I did what most everyone else did at that period of time, helped rebuild after the war. I was a half-breed, so..." she trailed off and took another bite.

"So what?"

"So my people didn't take to me very well," she snapped at him. Some of them had wanted to kill her. Several of them had almost succeeded.

Niccolo leaned forward. "Why do I have the feeling you don't like me very much, Jade?"

She set her fork down. "That's not true," she said honestly. "I haven't formed an opinion about you one way or another." Lie. Niccolo scared her down to the very fibers of her underwear, which seemed to be perpetually wet whenever he was near. That really pissed her off.

An expression she couldn't interpret passed over his face. He moved his chair closer to hers. She fought and barely beat her impulse to push her chair back away from him.

He leaned forward. "You're not being honest with me. Why is that?" He'd leaned so close his breath stirred the fine hairs around her face. "And why is it that I seem to make you nervous, Jade?" he asked softly. "You don't seem like the type prone to nervousness. You wanted me to touch you back in Tibet. I know you did. Yet you seemed scared by it. What's going on with you?"

What was she supposed to say...? *You're the first man who's made me want to have sex in close to five decades.*

Hardly.

She pushed her chair back, stood and walked toward her bedroom. Niccolo followed her and spun her around halfway down the hallway. "I know you're attracted to me, Jade. I'm not going to let you balk without some kind of explanation."

"You think I owe you an explanation?" She laughed. "What's the matter? Is your ego bruised by my rejection?"

He held her arm and cupped her cheek. A part of her wanted to pull away, but another part welcomed the heat of his skin on hers, the contact of it. She fought the urge, as she always did, to give in when Niccolo touched her. Most men would've given up on her by now but not him.

He was damned relentless.

"Ah, but there's this little thing you're forgetting. I can hear your heartbeat and the increased rate of your breathing. I can scent your arousal on the air between us and it is intoxicating. I know you're attracted to me, Jade. Those signals are far from a rejection." He lifted a brow. "So, why are you doing it now? You have a man somewhere you're committed to? Or a woman, maybe?"

"No."

He rubbed his thumb tenderly down her cheek. "Then what's stopping this? When I made you come back in Tibet? That was far from pushing me away."

She couldn't respond. All she could do was stare up into his dark eyes. "I haven't given you an engraved invitation to try and fuck me, either," she finally pushed out.

He rubbed his thumb on her skin. "I just want to know why you're pulling away from me so hard. I just want an explanation."

Her lips twisted in a bitter smile. "Not used to it, are you, big guy?"

His head dipped toward hers. "Not really."

She turned her face away. He turned it back and kissed her.

And she began to drown.

His mouth was hot and tasted of spices. She took a step back and he followed her until she was up against the doorjamb to her bedroom and didn't have anywhere to go, unless she wanted to make things *really* serious by bringing him closer to the bed.

He snaked an arm around her waist and pulled her up against his chest, even as he tangled a hand in her hair at the nape of her neck. She left her arms dangling awkwardly at her sides like some limp doll.

But she kissed him back.

How could she not? The man kissed better than she could remember most men made love. He nipped at her bottom lip and then pulled lazily away at before slanting his mouth over hers once more to allow his tongue to caress her tongue. His kiss was at once ferocious and tender and, like most things about this man, tended to take her breath away. She tentatively placed her hands on his upper arms, feeling the tenseness and bulge of the muscles there.

Oh, sweet, merciful Morrigan. She might lose this battle.

She prayed briefly to her deity for strength until Niccolo lightly fisted his hand in her hair and drew his sensual mouth down her throat.

She forgot her prayer. Forgot about most everything except his lips caressing the tender skin of her throat and every single erogenous zone it seemed to suddenly contain. Since when had her neck become so sensitive? The very worst part about it was that his breath wasn't affecting her when he was nipping and licking her throat. Her reactions were all her own.

Jade slid her hands up his broad shoulders to his neck and felt the silky brush of his hair against her fingers. He intertwined his fingers lightly in her hair and tilted her head to the side, exposing the long line of her throat. She felt the buss of his smooth lips and then the hard brush of his sharp fangs.

She stiffened. Now was the time to stop him if she didn't want to be bitten, but she simply couldn't find it in herself to do that.

Her cunt felt heavy and hot. His kiss alone had made her body ready itself for him. He'd hardly even touched her. She'd grown slick and sensitive between her thighs and her nipples felt like two hard little pebbles topping her breasts. Her body cried out for the touch of this man, for the invasion of his cock in her pussy.

Niccolo slid his thigh between her legs and pressed up against her sex. He groaned against her throat and Jade stifled a whimper at the intimate contact. Slowly, he moved his leg back and forth against her until her breath caught in her throat.

He pulled her head to the side, displaying the vulnerable column of her throat. With one hand at the small of her back, he dragged her up against him. The action made her shudder with the friction it exerted on her clit against his hard thigh.

Something in her mind went *tick*…and Niccolo's powerful glamour cloaked her. At the same time, his fangs came down and penetrated.

Jade's fingers clenched on Niccolo's shirt as pleasure poured into her body. She felt the draw of his mouth on her throat and it seemed to tighten a line straight down to her cunt. His glamour was so heavy and so skillfully wielded that she felt no pain at all from the bite. Only ecstasy.

Her climax hit her like a freight train. Jade cried out and felt her knees go weak. Niccolo broke the bite and pulled her up against him so she wouldn't collapse.

The next thing she knew she was flat on her back on her bed with no idea how she'd arrived there.

Niccolo's glamour eased from her and she reached up, feeling for his bite mark as the waves from her orgasm still skittered through her body. Two perfect punctures dotted her skin. Normally, an Embraced healed the wounds, or so she understood. Niccolo had not.

Niccolo pulled his shirt over his head. She gasped at the sight of his smooth, muscled chest. Jade sat up and laid her hands on him, feeling the warmth of him on her palms. She had to touch him, just *had* to. Feeling drugged and possessed by a woman who wasn't her, she kissed his stomach, making him shudder. The muscles there rippled under her lips.

He eased her back down onto the bed and unbuttoned his pants. "I'm not letting you get away from me this time, Jade," he said. "You're mine." He held her gaze as he eased his pants down and off. His cock was long, thick and hard as steel.

The sight of it shot apprehension through her. Memories threatened. She swallowed hard and pushed them away. She wasn't going to let the past rule her. It was time for that to stop. It'd been too long. She'd been held a prisoner by her past for too damned many years. Here was a man, the first in a very long time, who made her feel hot, made her long for the intimacy between a woman and man. Here was her opportunity to cast off the past and return to a place of normalcy.

Maybe Niccolo could break the hold the past had over her and she could get her life back again.

She felt his touch through every part of her body, every one of her pores. It was almost as Niccolo had somehow become connected to her. The sensation was nearly frightening in its intensity. Now he hovered over her, his gaze concentrated. She stared up at him with wide eyes. Her body felt aroused, but her mind was still ambivalent.

If there was ever a time to stop him, now was it. Soon, it would be too late.

But when he slid his hand to the waistband of her pants, she didn't say a word in protest. When he undid them and pulled them off, along with her boots, she found she couldn't even whisper. Instead, she sat up, drawing the shirt over her head and tossing it to the side. She felt so vulnerable sitting there nude while Niccolo's gaze roamed her body hungrily.

Suddenly remembering her scars—it was mind-blowing she'd forgot them even for a moment—she dropped her gaze and crossed her arms over her chest protectively.

"Don't." The one-word command, uttered in Niccolo's deep voice, seemed shockingly loud in the quiet room.

He moved down over her, gently taking her arms and pinning them to the sides beside her. She jerked away, flinching, her chest suddenly heaving in panic. He let her go with a quizzical look on his face. She laid there wide-eyed, slowly coming back to herself, reminding herself over and over that this man meant her no harm.

Memories. She squeezed her eyes shut, focusing hard on pushing them away. Her breathing returned to normal.

"It's all right, Jade," he soothed in a gentle voice. He leaned forward and pressed his lips to hers, pushing her back to lie flat on the mattress using only the pressure of his mouth on hers.

Jade's heart thumped in her chest and her anxiety ran high. She couldn't remember how to act with a man in an intimate situation. She could defuse a bomb, hack a computer system and plan an assassination, but she didn't know how to touch a man. Not really. It had been so long.

Niccolo didn't seem notice or mind her hesitation. He kissed her deeply, his hands roving her body in a territorial way that was surprisingly arousing. His smooth yet hard body brushed across her skin, making her tremble. His hands eased their way over her arms, stomach and outer thighs, rubbing and massaging, until Jade felt breathless.

She twined her arms around his shoulders as he deepened the kiss, greedily slanting his mouth over hers. He brushed his palm over one of her breasts and she arched into him, a moan caught in her throat.

"You like that?" he murmured against her mouth. "Do you like it when I touch you, Jade?"

She nodded shakily.

With sure hands, Niccolo turned her over onto her stomach, kissing and licking his way across her skin as he went. Settling her on her stomach exposed all the vicious scars she bore. She allowed him to do it, feeling unaccountably relaxed. The way he touched and kissed her with such reverence eased her discomfort with the situation.

Niccolo gathered her hair up and draped it over the mattress on one side, then leaned down and kissed the nape of her neck. The action seemed to tighten her body in places that were much farther down. Her pussy felt hot and needy from the mere brush of his lips. His tongue flicked out and tasted her skin, then dragged the tip of his tongue down along her spine, slowly.

She writhed a little and moaned. It was an exciting sensation, but it was also a tease. She wanted more.

Finally, he reached the base of her spine.

"I told you I wanted to trace this tattoo with my tongue," he murmured as he scattered kisses at the small of her back. He groaned. "This is my favorite place on a woman." He palmed her buttocks and the base of her spine with a broad hand. "The curve right here is so beautiful. Especially on you."

Jade closed her eyes and sighed, enjoying the feel of his lips on her skin and the intimacy they now shared. It was a solid reminder to her that sex could be good thing.

She'd forgotten that.

Niccolo made it seem like a very, *very* good thing. Her body hummed with anticipation and pleasure. She felt breathless, boneless, and more cherished than she ever had in her life.

She pushed up and turned over, wanting to touch him in return. Almost of its own accord, her hand went to his chest, where she traced her fingers over the definition of muscles and the ripple of his stomach. She touched him in a curious way. Goddess, he probably thought she was a virgin because she acted so innocent.

He shuddered in pleasure at her touch and kissed her. She returned it greedily, pressing her body against his and wanting to even feel more of him. She twined her fingers through the hair at his nape, feeling the silky tendrils brush her fingers.

"You're gorgeous," he murmured against her lips in a strained voice. "You're the woman I dreamed of for the entire time I was in Harcourt."

Jade couldn't respond. She never expected this degree of tenderness from a man she'd watched snap a man's neck with one hand. It was jarring. She never would've thought that hands that could bring death so swiftly and surely could also bring pleasure and comfort.

Niccolo drew his fingers down her stomach and over her mound. He urged her to part her thighs and she did so, but her body stiffened as bad memories rose up once more. She closed her eyes shut, willing them away.

"Jade?" he murmured.

She couldn't respond for a moment. She opened her eyes and held his gaze, but it was hard. Her breathing grew heavier, but this time it wasn't from arousal. It was from anxiously fighting the edge of fear that threatened her.

"You're so tense. Relax," Niccolo soothed her. He stroked his index finger over her clit and pleasure shot through her body. "I'm going to make you feel good, Jade. There is nothing to fear when I'm touching you." He caressed her clit over and over, skating her to the razor's edge of a climax. "My hands will only bring you pleasure."

"Please," she pleaded breathlessly. His touch made the fear disappear, leaving only longing in its wake. She closed her eyes again.

"Do you like that? Do you want to come?"

"Yes," she gasped.

"Look at me, Jade. Open your eyes and look me."

She opened her eyes and locked her gaze with his.

"You see me? I'm the one giving your body pleasure and that I will not hurt you."

"Please, let me come!"

He eased the pressure on her clit a little, controlling when she'd climax. It made her crazy. "I want you to know it's me doing this to you, Jade. No one else."

"Niccolo," she breathed. "Please."

He smiled. "You are aroused and ready for more, Jade."

She wasn't so sure about that, yet didn't protest when he dipped his finger down, skimming through her dampness, and slid one finger very carefully within her.

Jade's body tensed in a combination of yearning, wonder and fear. Niccolo withdrew his finger, and Jade felt a mixture of relief and regret. Instead, he used her cream as a lubricant and caressed and stroked her clit over and over.

The sensation of it bloomed through her body, rose like heat up her spine. The shiny crystal edge of a climax taunted her, but with the pace and pressure of his caress Niccolo controlled whether or not she would feel it.

"Come for me," he growled. Knowing just how to push her over that edge, he deepened and lengthened his strokes.

A second hard climax claimed her. Jade cried out, her fingers finding purchase in the blankets. She held on for dear life under the racking spasms of pleasure that shook her. It stopped her thought, stopped her memories. It stopped everything in the whole world for a blessed time.

While the tail end of the pleasure still held her body in its thrall, he pulled her against him, parting her thighs. He set the head of his cock to her entrance.

And memories rushed back and overwhelmed her.

Terror infused every pore of her body. Jade scrambled back away from him, breathing heavy. Her hair fell into her face, forming a curtain across her eyes. She squeezed her eyes shut as the images assaulted her.

Tied. Unable to move. Unable to see. Men pounding into her over and over until she bled, until she went numb. Then the lashes of the whip, the fists, the flash of a sharpened blade.

"No." She said only the one word, softly, but to her own ears it sounded harsh and agonized.

Silence.

Stillness.

She felt the brush of a strong hand on her leg. She flinched, but Niccolo didn't withdraw. Instead, he carefully pulled her stiff, trembling body toward him. He didn't say anything. He only held her and stroked his hand through her hair.

"What happened to you, Jade?" he asked. Curiosity and emotion tinged his words.

She didn't answer and he didn't push. Jade was grateful for that. She felt drained, saddened and humiliated. She lay stiff, suddenly cold and shaking.

She'd tried. She'd tried to break free of the past, the memories and the nightmares. Sorrow rose up, choking her, but tears wouldn't come. As Niccolo was a prisoner of his life, his talents, she was a prisoner to the ones who'd hurt her so long ago. The past was her prison.

She shuddered against Niccolo and let him soothe her. Much later, after listening to the steady beat of his heart, after she had calmed, she drifted to sleep.

* * * * *

After Niccolo had covered Jade with a blanket, he stepped out of the room. Touching her had made his cock hard and primed his body for sex. God, he'd wanted her almost more than anything, but what happened after she'd come, when he been finally ready to slide inside her, that had doused his desire faster than a bucket of cold water.

Over the years he'd seen women traumatized by men. The signals were all there in Jade. Something truly bad had happened to her. Whatever it had been, it had been life-changing. Earlier, he'd suspected that something had happened to her because of the scars and because of the way she reacted whenever her wrists or arms were restrained. But what she'd just done... It had been like she'd been trapped in a waking nightmare.

He wanted this woman with an unreasonable fervor, and yet he wouldn't be able to take her like he took other women. Jade required special handling.

After such a long life, he'd learned the art of restraint. He gritted his teeth. That didn't mean he liked it. It had been a long time since he'd had sex, but Niccolo understood it had been *far* longer for Jade. He had to know why and she didn't seem willing to tell him.

He headed toward the living room, having made his decision. Jade had snooped into his past and discovered a secret he didn't want anyone to know. He would snoop into hers.

There was something about this woman that stirred his blood, something about her that kicked every emotion he thought he'd lost into high gear. She touched him in a way that no one else had in a long time. It was her strength and her vulnerability. It was her need to protect and do what was right. It was that look in her eyes, like a lost little girl trying to find her way back home.

It made him want to cherish her, protect her, make her his. More and more he found he coveted this woman, wanted to get to know every part of her. If he had to delve into her past to find out her demons, he'd do it. He wanted to help her slay the monsters that lived in her light blue eyes. Niccolo found he wanted to do it no matter the cost.

Jade was a woman who seemed to share a part of his soul. They had more in common than Jade knew. By helping Jade, he would also help himself.

Adam, Niccolo queried telepathically.

Adam took more than a moment to respond. *Aw, Niccolo, what? I'm kind of busy.*

Niccolo suppressed a chuckle. Adam had been in the city not even twenty-four hours and he already had a woman in his bed. That was pure Adam.

I need every file on Jade that I can get. Where can I find those in this city?

Adam took a moment to answer. *The Council has some, but I'm betting they're not in-depth enough to satisfy you. There is a record keeping of the Order of the Morrigan here in New York City, but, Nic, man, they're not just going to let you in there to take a peek at their files.*

Leave that part to me. Just tell me where they're located. He paused. *I just need transportation.*

Adam told him. *Oh yeah, Nic, I almost forgot to tell you. We got together and bought you a little homecoming present. It's in the garage of the apartment building, slot twenty-five. There's your transport.*

Thanks, Adam. He severed the connection.

Niccolo grabbed his coat and checked one last time to make sure Jade was sleeping. Then he exited the apartment and made his way to the parking garage and the gift that awaited him there.

Niccolo opened the door to slot twenty-five and stopped dead in his tracks.

His Harley.

It was the one he'd had before he'd gone in. He walked to the fine black and silver machine. It had been his pride and joy. As he approached the machine, he noticed that it wasn't the same bike he'd had before, but it was a very close replica. There were some modifications to the engine and the exhaust system, and the bike was solar-powered, as most vehicles were these days.

It sat next to the boxy, nondescript silver preset transport vehicle, called a *PTV*. That thing didn't even need a human driver. The passenger simply logged his itinerary into the PTV's computer, sat back and let the computer get him where he wanted to go. Niccolo understood that most of them came equipped with holoscreens for entertainment and minibars for refreshment.

Niccolo straddled the bike and felt the knowledge of how to maneuver it pour back into his body. He hadn't forgotten. He'd driven it in his mind almost every night in Harcourt, the wind blowing through his hair and the sound of the engine thrumming in his ears.

He started the bike, and heard the near purr of the engine, instead of the loud roar. He frowned, and then shrugged. Times changed. He knew that well enough.

Niccolo used the remote in his pocket and signaled the garage's slot door to open. PTVs on preset travel paths whizzed past the slot door's entranceway.

Yeah, times *really* changed.

Niccolo took a moment to take in the scene before him. Beyond the busy thoroughfare rose the shiny steel and glass city. The buildings were much taller than he remembered them being at the beginning of the twenty-first century. The sky above was a brilliant blue and white clouds scudded through it. All vehicles were solar-powered now, so Niccolo understood, making the skies above the cities incredibly free of smog.

Soon it would be evening. By the time he reached his destination, it would be well past the time the workers should have gone home for the day.

He gunned the bike's motor, hearing a most unsatisfying purring rev come from the engine. Then he eased the throttle forward. The bike jolted forward at nearly the speed of light, and Niccolo barely gained control of it before it slid right out into the steady stream of traffic. Euphoria filled him as he whipped the bike around and gunned it up the entrance ramp to the freeway. The word freeway had an entirely new meaning to him now since it was literally *free* of PTVs and their preset tracks.

The bike had lost its growl, but it had gained a hell of a lot of power. Tradeoffs could be good.

There were only a couple other vehicles using the freeway, a sleek black car carrying about six passengers and a cargo truck. Niccolo passed them both in blaze of speed, truly reveling in his freedom for the first time since Jade had sprung him.

Chapter Five

Jade sat on the couch with her knees pulled up to her chest. She'd awoken to an empty apartment. She was glad Niccolo wasn't here since she had no idea how to act around him now. Jade bit her lip, shame infusing her at the memory of her reaction. It was weak of her to allow the past to control her this way. It had happened so long ago. She'd survived. The men who'd done it had been punished. It should be over for her now.

Even though she continually reminded herself of these facts, the nightmare persisted. She'd spent the last fifty years immersing herself in the job of bringing more men like them to justice, and yet it appeared she still hadn't healed.

When would it stop?

She closed her eyes. The nightmare for the men who'd done it to her had ended long ago. They were dead. For her, it went on until she could get past it. That struggle was all her own. She thought she'd been ready to face it head-on. She'd allowed Niccolo to touch her intimately, bring her to climax twice, but the touch of his cock against her had brought everything back in a tumult of images and painful emotion.

Morrigan, she wanted to be free of this curse.

Hell, she *wanted* Niccolo.

Who wouldn't? The man was like a wet dream come true. She wished could say she wasn't attracted to him. She wished she could push him away and not look back. However, that wasn't going to happen. And perhaps that was a good thing. Maybe she could use him to help her get over this fear of hers. Jade doubted Niccolo would mind being used in such a carnal fashion.

Jade picked at a pilling on her black pajama bottoms. She still couldn't believe she'd fallen asleep in his arms. It was undeniable. Niccolo made her felt safe. Protected. Some small part of her acknowledged this fact.

She couldn't remember the last time she'd felt that way in the presence of a man. Jade glanced up and out the window, seeing the world swathed in full night. She'd determined long ago that she had to make her own safety. There was no one there to back her up. Niccolo was the first man—*person*—she felt could back her up since the brutal rape and torture that had nearly killed her.

He was muscular. Physically, he was the most powerful person she'd ever met, and she couldn't help but like that. She liked that he was stronger than her. She liked that he could protect her if need be. She'd spent the fifty years trying to do that for herself and she felt so tired.

At the same time, she felt mad at herself for enjoying his strength.

The front door opened. Niccolo's steady tread sounded in the hallway. She considered making a dash for her bedroom to feign sleep, but she wasn't going run from him.

Niccolo walked into the dining room and glanced at her before dropping his keys on the mahogany table. He turned toward her, his eyes deep and dark, his face serious. "Okay?" he asked.

She tried to look him in the eye, but had to glance away. "You know, jet-lagged."

He nodded.

"Where were you?"

He gave a careless shrug and walked toward her. "Enjoying my freedom. I took a little ride on the bike Gabriel and the others bought me."

Yes, the bike. They'd seem to know the perfect homecoming gift for Niccolo. It was true the bike fit his personality well. "Where'd you go?"

He shrugged again and sat down. "Around the city."

Why did she have the feeling he wasn't telling her the truth? At least, he wasn't telling her the *whole* truth. The look in his eyes appeared more haunted than usual. Something other than this small talk seemed to be on his mind, but Jade made a guess he didn't want to share it. He glanced at her. "Checked out Lex's house from afar."

Jade swung her legs over the side of the couch and sat up in sudden interest. "Oh, yeah? See anything interesting?"

Niccolo's gaze traveled over her torso and she realized belatedly what she was wearing—a thin white T-shirt and no bra. She hunched her shoulders involuntarily, trying to conceal herself from his hot gaze. Goddess, that seemed ridiculous. The man had already seen her naked.

Niccolo looked away, and ran a hand over his tired-looking face. Stubble graced the strong jut of his jaw. "No. His house is as I expected for an egomaniac like Dray."

"It's huge," she agreed. "Makes you wonder what he's trying to compensate for, doesn't it?"

He flashed her a grin full of white teeth at her comment. It made something tighten in her chest. "Lots of servants coming and going. Human and Embraced alike. Dray always wanted to be treated like a king."

Jade tipped her head to the side, studying him. "You've known him a long time, haven't you?" She was grateful to have something work-related to talk to him about at this point. Leaning back against the couch, she drew her knees up protectively against her once more.

Niccolo leaned back also, and blew out a hard breath. "We were friends once, a long time ago."

"In Italy."

"Yes. We were friends until he betrayed me for money to a rogue Vampir I'd been hunting."

Jade nodded. It had been one of the few times in Niccolo's life that he'd almost been killed. "I read that in your file."

Something flickered through his eyes. Was he still upset about that?

"He fled Italy after that incident," Niccolo answered.

She rested her chin on her knee. "I always wondered why you never went after him."

Niccolo shrugged. "He'd been a friend for a lot longer than he'd been an enemy." His gaze hardened. "But times change and years pass. He's nothing but an enemy now."

Jade sighed. "That's good. I like to hear that, because he's under a lot of suspicion. We need to break into both his sys files and his security, Niccolo. I can do the security, but I don't know about the sys files. Normally, I could it without a problem, but Drayden's files are encrypted with state-of-the-art technology. Does Adam know any really good hackers in this city?"

"He lives here a lot of the time, so I'm sure he does. I'll ask him in the morning."

They fell into silence. Outside, large flakes of snow began to fall in the darkness.

"You sure you're okay, Jade?"

Instead of answering, she reached up and touched the puncture wounds on her throat. They felt sore, but not painful. She looked away and said softly, "You didn't heal them."

Niccolo remained silent.

She looked up and locked gazes with him. His body language was hard to read. His shoulders were hunched, and he wore an intense expression on his face and in his eyes. In fact, his entire body looked rigid. His hands were nearly white from gripping the arms of the chair.

"No, I didn't," he said finally.

She tipped her chin up and narrowed her eyes. "Why?"

She watched as his lips parted and that slow ache between her thighs began. She was growing used to the sensation. "I wanted to mark you as mine," he answered evenly.

Jade almost snapped at him, accused him of being a dog marking his territory, but she knew that it was almost exactly that. Vamps marked people they wanted to protect or keep. They marked them in a visible place and with their scent to tell all others to back off.

It took several heartbeats for Jade to find the ability to speak. A mixture of emotions—outrage and a curious blend of happiness and anticipation—swirled through her. "I'm an OtherKin Sidhe, Niccolo. I heal fast."

Niccolo leaned forward. He spoke in a low, steady voice. "Then I guess I'll have to mark you again. After that, maybe again."

Jade took a moment to relearn how to breathe. Then she leveled a steady stare at him. "Do you always expect women to just fall at your feet?"

"Usually, they do. You're the first one I've had to work for."

She snorted, her temper flaring. "You're so fucking arrogant," she shot at him.

Niccolo stood and walked toward her. She resisted the urge to bolt from the couch. Instead, she tried to appear as if his proximity didn't affect her, didn't make her heart beat faster and her cunt ache. Niccolo braced one hand on the arm of the couch where she reclined, the other on the back, and bent over her. His sweet-scented breath bathed her cheek.

Jade deliberately kept her gaze fixed on his eyes and an unreadable expression on her face.

"So are you," he murmured, and then kissed her.

Being kissed by this man was like being assaulted with pleasure. She never knew if she should run screaming or completely give in. Her hands fisted on either side of her as she fought not to touch him. Niccolo's lips worked magic over hers, making love to her mouth and to her tongue with the same skill he'd likely employ to her entire body.

The thought of how he'd command her body, the image of him working over her, driving into her, his breath hot against her skin... That image combined with his masterful kiss was almost enough to send her over the edge.

How great that would be for his ego, if he could make her come with a kiss.

Niccolo made a sound deep in his throat, snaked his arms around her and dragged her up against his chest. Jade gasped at the ease with which he hoisted her. Vampiric strength never ceased to amaze her. She grabbed his shoulders, feeling his muscles work as he moved, because she didn't trust him not to drop her. She didn't trust anyone.

He slanted his mouth hungrily across hers and greedily stroked his tongue against hers over and over until she moaned in spite of herself. Every little movement he made rasped her shirt across her stiff, sensitive nipples. The ache between her thighs intensified.

Niccolo slid his hands down her back and cupped her buttocks. Without even thinking about it, she wrapped her legs around his waist, grinding her needy pussy against his rigid cock, and pressing herself up against him as if trying to climb his body. Because of his size, he made her feel light and delicate.

Niccolo broke the kiss and tipped his head back. "Jade, you're killing me," he groaned. "You don't know how much I want you." He let out a series of soft curses under his breath, and then kissed her deeply again.

A part of her wanted to push him away, stalk out of the room, prove to this man that she wasn't one of those women who'd drop at his feet just with a kiss...but all she wanted was more of him.

Sweet Morrigan, she wanted *so* much more from him. She couldn't help herself. He was like a drug.

Niccolo slid his hand past the elastic waistband of her pajama bottoms, and cupped her bare buttock. She felt the rasp of his calloused palm against her. Her pussy seemed to grow hotter and wetter, anticipating the feel of him touching her more intimately.

It came.

He rasped his finger along her exposed, swollen labia and over her anus. She tensed and shut her eyes, trying to get past the fear and more fully into the pleasure.

"You feel like silk," he murmured. "I need more of you, better access. Okay?"

"Okay," she answered breathlessly.

He lowered her to the couch and eased her bottoms off. His gaze was focused as he ran his palms up her thighs and hips. Barely thinking about it, she spread her legs for him. Her breasts had seemed to grow heavier in her arousal and her taut nipples pressed against the fabric of her shirt.

Niccolo's gaze ran over the picture she made. "You're beautiful, Jade. So fucking irresistible. I want to make you come. I want you screaming my name again." He slid her hips to the edge of the couch, spread her thighs, lowered his head and licked her.

"Niccolo," she breathed in surprise. She hadn't known what he'd do, but she hadn't expected him to go down on her. She grabbed on to the cushion beside her and held on under the swell of a near climax that rippled through her body.

Niccolo groaned. "You're so sticky sweet. You taste so good." He toyed with her sensitive clit with the tip of his tongue and then slowly licked her labia, easing into every fold and teasing every sensitive centimeter of her sex.

She arched her back and moaned. His hands clamped onto her hips, holding her in place. His thumbs pulled her labia apart, revealing the heart of her to his eyes and tongue. She watched the erotic sight of his dark head between her thighs, his strong hands gripping her and the muscles of his shoulders working as he licked and sucked her.

He laved her anus with his tongue and she jerked. He shushed her and laved it again. She felt skitters of pleasure jolt up her spine. It felt good, but it was so intimate, almost more intimate than she could take. She closed her eyes and turned her face away.

"Look at me, Jade," he murmured.

She tipped her head forward and let her eyes flicker open. She felt drunk on him.

"Look right into my eyes while I suck your sweet clit. Know it's me giving you pleasure and no one else. I want you to know it is pleasure I'm giving you, not pain, not fear."

Her eyes widened. She held his gaze as Niccolo lowered his mouth to her clit and sucked it between his sensual lips. Pleasure skittered through her body as he teased it, driving her to the razor's edge of a climax. She moaned and her eyes fluttered shut.

"Look at me, Jade," Niccolo commanded in a low voice.

"Let me come," she moaned.

"Look at me and I will."

She stared into his eyes and felt suddenly mesmerized. He held her gaze steadily as he sucked and licked her clit. With his finger, he stroked her entrance, massaging the sensitive nerves around her labia until she thought she'd scream for a want of a climax. He controlled that with the pressure of his mouth. He controlled when she'd reach orgasm. The whole time, he held her gaze—dark brown eyes to light blue.

"Come for me, Jade," he growled. "I want to hear you scream." He eased his skillful tongue up into her and thrust in and out. At the same time, he stroked her clit with the pad of his index finger.

Jade's climax enveloped her body. She gripped the couch and cried out his name as the waves of it washed through her body, driving all cognitive function away. Niccolo drew it out by gently caressing her clit and easing his tongue in and out of her.

The climax left her limp, breathless. "Niccolo," she breathed again.

He climbed up her body with a feral look in his eyes, pushing her T-shirt up and over her head and latching his mouth onto a nipple. He pulled and licked at it, stroking the other with the pad of his thumb and making low sounds in his throat. Jade arched her back and wrapped her legs around his waist.

Holding her that way, he slipped her from the couch and onto the floor with his almost unnerving strength, and settled himself between her thighs.

Niccolo reclaimed her mouth hungrily and thrust his pants-clad pelvis against her cunt, rasping the rough fabric that came between them against her aroused clit in a way that made her moan and see stars. She could feel the jut of his rock-hard, huge cock against her tender folds.

"This is close to how I want to take you," Niccolo murmured near her ear. "Except I don't want anything separating us." He gently dragged her earlobe between his teeth, making her shudder. "I want to ease my cock inside your sweet pussy, Jade. I want to feel all those slick muscles clamp down on me. I want to thrust into you again and again until you come all over me. Then I want to do it some more."

His words pushed her toward another climax. Skitters of pleasure shot up her spine and through her body. He grabbed her ass and held it while he thrust up against her in a semblance of the actual act. Jade spread her thighs, wanting and needing the contact. Her second orgasm washed over her and she cried out. He kissed her deeply, swallowing her sounds.

Niccolo broke the kiss and groaned. "Jade, fuck, I want you so much." He sounded agonized.

She went still, understanding his hesitation. Niccolo knew something. He had to suspect something bad had happened to her because of how she'd reacted that afternoon. She snaked her hand between them and undid the buttons of his pants. "I want you, too," she breathed. She needed him...in more ways than one.

He raised his head. "You sure? Are you absolutely sure, Jade?"

She held his gaze for a moment before nodding. She lifted the edge of his shirt, pushing it up and over his head. Oh Goddess. *Beauty.* Every time the man's shirt came off, her IQ dropped about twenty points and she became momentarily unintelligible. Unable to form a thought, let alone actual words.

She pushed up, pressing her bare breasts to his chest. Jade kissed and licked and bit his chest and shoulder. He pressed her to him with a groan, his fingers tangling in her hair, and running down over her back. He pulled her up so she straddled him, her bare pussy spread and vulnerable to him. The material of his pants rasped over the sensitive skin of her inner thighs. The buttons of his pants were undone, revealing a tantalizing glimpse of the narrow line of dark hair leading to his cock when she glanced down to see how intimately her pelvis pressed against his.

Niccolo placed his mouth to her ear at the same time he slid his hand between them to cup her exposed sex. "I only want to give you pleasure, Jade. Nothing else. I want you to relax, okay?"

"Uh-huh," was all she could manage.

He slid the length of his middle finger over her pussy. Her labia were swollen and her clit was pulled from its hood and begging for more attention. He eased his finger slowly inside her and Jade bit his shoulder gently at the sensation.

"You're so damned tight," Niccolo breathed.

He thrust up inside her slow enough to make crazy. Her muscles clenched around him, and she moaned low and long. He pulled his finger back out and did it again. She felt herself gush for him in response, making the slide of his finger in and out of her body easier.

"That's it," he murmured. "Is it good?"

"Yes."

"You want more?"

"Yes," she breathed.

He added another finger, widening her, stretching her muscles. She gasped at the invasion and felt her pelvic muscles relax. Her eyes practically rolled back into her head, it felt so good.

"I can't wait to slide into you, Jade." He groaned. "It's going to feel so damn good. You're going to come hard all over me when you feel me easing in and out of you." He rubbed his fingertips back and forth against a sensitive knot of nerves inside her.

Jade cried out and a climax suddenly overwhelmed her. She sank her teeth into his shoulder and scored his back with her fingernails.

"There's a good girl," Niccolo murmured. "You're so fucking sexy when you come. I'm harder than a rock for you right now." He kissed her throat. "Are you ready for me?"

Her body stiffened and she nodded tentatively.

He laid her back onto her back and stared down at her while he eased his pants down enough to allow his cock to spring free. She watched as if drugged.

"Touch it," he said.

Jade bit her lower lip and reached, wrapping her hand around the base of his cock. Niccolo tipped his head back and he groaned. She pumped him up and down, exploring the hard softness of him and the veins running down the length. It was gorgeous. It was...

Memories flashed through her mind and she jerked her hand away with a gasp. No. No, goddamn it! She was not going to allow those events to rule her reality.

Niccolo paused for a moment. Then he backed away from her a little and pulled up his pants.

"You're so honorable," she muttered.

Niccolo sighed. "Honorable is the last thing I want to be. I'd rather have you begging for me instead of pulling away in sudden horror."

"I know." She reached out and ran her fingers up his length. He was so beautiful. She wanted him inside her. Desire pooled between her thighs for him, pushing away everything else, momentarily pushing away the fear. "I *do* want you, Niccolo. I want you so fucking much." Her voice shook with wanting. "I just...just... I wish there was some way..."

She didn't want to say too much, didn't want to reveal what was hindering her. Though Jade suspected Niccolo had discovered the nature of her problem.

Lust flared in his eyes. "I'm going to use a little glamour on you, just a little to take the edge off. All right?"

She nodded slowly. That might work. It might calm her down enough that she could get past her memories. "Okay."

It cloaked her immediately, rolling her eyes back in her head. It was just a little bit of magick tingling through her body. She still had full awareness and free will, but she felt relaxed. The tension had disappeared from her shoulders. The throbbing between her thighs seemed more forceful now that the edge of her fear was gone. She felt needy. Goddess, she wanted him so much, she could barely stand it.

Jade spread her thighs and slicked a finger through her folds, feeling how hot and swollen she was. Niccolo watched her with an intense gaze. Every muscle of his body appeared rigid. She flicked a finger over her sensitized clit and cupped her breast with one hand, feeling her pebbled nipple against her palm. Pleasure shot through her body, making her writhe and moan.

He came down over her body, covering her hand with his. "I'm going to fuck you senseless, Jade. You know that, right?"

Ah, she hoped so.

He guided her hand over her pussy, making her caress her own clit, skim over her creamy labia and finally sink her own fingers into her cunt. She gasped at the sensation of all those gripping muscles, the wet heat of it.

"That's what I'm going to feel," Niccolo murmured hoarsely. "It's like heaven in there."

He eased her hand away and brushed the head of his cock against her. She tensed, but the glamour kept her mostly relaxed. No memories rose up to slap her in the face. No fear strangled her. Only powerful lust.

"More," she breathed.

Niccolo slid the smooth crown of his cock past the entrance of her cunt and Jade though she'd come right then. She arched into him, pushing her hips at him, wanting more. The way he stretched her muscles felt exquisite. Jade was sure she hadn't ever felt anything better. She felt impaled and possessed.

Niccolo groaned and pressed his hips toward her, sliding in another few inches. She writhed against him and he grabbed her hips, holding her in place. "More?"

"Uh-huh," she barely managed to respond.

He pushed in another couple inches and an orgasm flirted hard with her body, making her pant. "You feel so fucking good," he said drunkenly.

"Give me all of you."

Niccolo pushed in until he hilted. She felt the press of him against her cervix. He pulled out and thrust in again so slowly she could almost memorize every vein of his cock as it glided inside her. He held her hips, keeping her from writhing as he shafted her slow, then even slower.

Jade felt the edge of a climax growing. "Faster," she gasped.

Niccolo pulled back and impaled her hard to the base of him and Jade came. She arched her back and almost screamed. Her muscles milked his now pistoning cock and she felt her come bathe him, easing the slide of his shaft in and out of her body.

Niccolo came down over her, thrusting into her and pressing her hips down on the floor with every thrust. He suckled and licked her neck, groaning out her name. His big body tensed and she felt his glamour intensify. He thrust all the way up inside her and bit her throat as he came.

The glamour and the pull of his mouth on her vein, coupled with the feel of his climaxing cock way up inside her pushed Jade over the edge again. She wrapped her legs and arms around him as they shuddered and groaned together.

They stayed that way until the waves passed, then Jade unwrapped herself from his body and he eased to the side, rolling to his back. Now that the glamour was gone, she felt tension leak back into her shoulders, yet she didn't feel panicked. Hell, she didn't feel anything except sated and exhausted...and ready for more.

Amazing.

Her body felt sore in places, but it was a delicious soreness. She cupped her breast, feeling the press of her hardened nipple against her palm.

She'd finally allowed a man in after fifty years.

"Oh God," he groaned.

Jade looked over at him. His cock glistened with her juices and was still hard as a rock. He glanced at her, noticing where her gaze had landed. "It's been a long time," he explained.

"Been longer for me." Her voice was husky with unshed tears as she realized she broken though some kind of invisible barrier. She'd had sex. Finally. And it had been good. So unbelievably good. There hadn't been pain or fear…only sweet pleasure.

She laughed, feeling a tear roll out of the corner of her eye. She dashed it away. "So that's what I've been missing? Hell, can we do it some more? I have a lot of making up to do."

Niccolo's warm arms pulled her close. "I'm ready right now," he murmured into her ear, and eased his finger through her folds. She was dripping wet with their combined come. He slid a finger into her and gently, slowly fucked her with it until she moaned. "Are you sore?"

She took a shallow breath and spread her thighs a little farther, giving him better access. "Yeah, I am a little." She didn't care, though.

He leaned over and slanted his mouth over hers. He kissed her possessively before pulling away. "Give the care of your body to me for a while, Jade. Give me your trust. I can show more of what you've been missing. *Dio*, it would be my pleasure. I love the way you feel."

He relentlessly stroked his finger over and over that knot of nerves inside her. He knew exactly how to touch her, the right pressure, and the right place.

"Uh," she said, her eyes fluttering shut. He'd asked her a question, hadn't he?

He nuzzled her throat, his fangs scraping the soft skin there. He did something, changed the angle of his entry a little and the pace of his thrust. A slow, steady, overwhelming climax overtook her. Just when she thought her body wasn't capable of coming anymore he brought her again. This one was easier and longer, almost gentle. Jade moaned and Niccolo kissed her, eating up the sound, as he drew the climax out longer and longer.

Finally, it came to a shuddering halt and Jade felt every muscle in her body relax.

"I want to show you how good sex can be, Jade," he murmured against her lips. "We've just gotten started. Let me. Just for the time it takes to complete what we're doing here. After that, we'll go our own ways."

She lay panting in his arms. Finally, she nodded. "Okay."

Niccolo made a satisfied sound in his throat and kissed her. He felt very satisfied at her answer, even if he did hear a note of apprehension in it. "You're mine," he murmured. He'd marked her again and hadn't healed it. He meant what he said when he'd first come in that night.

She was his. At least, for a little while.

Breaking into the Order of the Morrigan here in New York City hadn't been as easy as he'd assumed, but he'd managed it. It had taken him nearly all evening to locate her records. Finally, he'd found them…and had discovered the trauma in her past.

Four OtherKin Shifters had cornered her one night on the streets of Edinburgh. They'd been stalking her because they knew she was a half-blood. That disgusted them. They'd wanted to punish her for it.

And they had.

The account of what had befallen her had made even his stomach roil and he'd seen many ugly acts in his lifetime. They'd raped her repeatedly…in all their various shifter forms. They destroyed her reproductive system and made it so she'd never bear children. They'd whipped her and beaten her to within an inch of her life and then left her for dead.

The doctors who had treated her had been amazed she'd survived. Three reconstructive surgeries later and most of the damage had been repaired.

After she'd healed enough, she'd gone straight to the Order of the Morrigan. She'd trained like a woman possessed, catapulting herself into their top ranks, despite the fact she lacked the psychic abilities of a full-blood OtherKin Sidhe. She'd made up for that with her will and her strength.

Then she'd gone out and systematically hunted down and executed every one of her attackers.

On the surface, Jade was the perfect woman for him. Except for one thing—she still had a burning desire to bring justice. His passion for that had burned out long ago.

* * * * *

When Mr. Jones became quiet, he was at his most dangerous.

Dray resisted the urge to back away from the man when he turned toward him. Mr. Jones' soulless eyes, the eyes of a mannequin, stared at him from an elegant face. It was the face of an English college professor, narrow, close-shaven, tight-lipped, topped with short salt-and-pepper hair. Mr. Jones looked unobtrusive on the outside, a person someone would not look at twice. If they did, they would think he was a well-bred, civilized person. Courteous. Educated.

But anyone with a flicker of psychic ability could tell differently.

He was an *it*.

Mr. Jones, bereft of soul and all emotion except the ones it feigned to get what it wanted, was not of this world. It was but a shell, projected onto this plane of existence by the concentrated power of the Dominion. Behind Mr. Jones' dead, empty eyes was a merciless and insatiable hunger stretching into the astral realm. It was an anchor, a gateway and a telephone to the power that was the greatest enemy of both the Embraced of humankind.

And Dray was helping it. He glanced away from Jones' eyes.

Dray was not without conscience, silly, stupid thing that it was. He wished to be free of Mr. Jones. Free of its power and its thrall. It was too late for that, though. He was going for the ride he'd signed up for. Hopefully he'd at least get paid for it in the end.

"Drayden," Mr. Jones drawled in a dangerously quiet and cultured-sounding voice. "We contacted you because we thought you were capable." He lifted a thin gray eyebrow. "Were we incorrect?"

Drayden straightened his spine. "No, of course not. Of all the vamps you could've chosen, you chose the best."

Mr. Jones stared at him for a full five seconds before answering. Dray forced himself to keep its gaze and not shiver with revulsion. "So far you have not proved this."

"I will."

"Yes, you will. You will find this *Niccolo* and kill him before he has a chance to thwart our plans. The fae woman and anyone else helping him must be destroyed as well. Understand me? I want you to do it personally. No more middlemen. *Kill* them all and do it with your own two hands so you know it gets done."

He nodded, even though a twinge of regret passed through him. He wasn't a killer, not really. Yeah, it happened once in a while, but he was a thief and con artist by trade, not a murderer. It went against his basic nature. "What about the rest of them, the other Vampir in positions of power within the Council?"

Mr. Jones smiled, showing perfect, straight white teeth. Still, it was a smile that chilled Dray to the center of his bones. "We have them under control. Your job is Niccolo, the fae and the Vampir called Adam. They are the ones in your city." Mr. Jones reached up and plucked a bit of lint from the lapel of its expensive gray suit. "I trust this *Niccolo* won't be too much for you to handle?"

Dray gritted his teeth. "No."

"Good, I'm glad. However, I do think you need a reminder of the hell we can thrust you into should you fail."

Drayden took a step back. No...not again.

Mr. Jones snarled with an otherworldly vehemence and grabbed his wrist. It wrenched his arm to the side with the power born of the thousands of Dominion infusing it, and Dray heard something crack. Pain shot through his shoulder in a blinding wave and Drayden collapsed to his knees in front of it.

Images, memories filled Dray's mind, blocking out his sight of anything in the present. And then he was there, there in his past. In the place of his worst fears…

Hunger cramped his belly and thrummed through his head until he could hardly think. The distraction was a blessing from the events unfolding in the other room of the grimy two-room flat where he lived with his mother. Dokomos rolled to his opposite side on the filthy, flea-ridden mattress and covered his ears with his hands.

Every week it was the same thing.

The sound of Istvan slamming his mother up against the wall made Dokomos start and squeeze his eyes shut. The sounds of their arguments grew more strident.

Istvan managed his mother, finding men to pay to fuck her. He took most of the money she made, leaving only a little for them to survive on. Most of the time they went hungry and shoeless, cold and miserable in their unheated flat. When his mother dared demand more from Istvan, she got a beating that would keep her black and blue for days, and still Istvan would work her while she healed.

Dokomos fisted his hands and fought the rising scream of rage within his throat. If only he was older, stronger, he'd kill Istvan. He'd protect his mother, work hard to make money to feed and clothe her…and he'd send the stream of her cruel, unwashed customers to hell.

The sound of his mother's sobbing in the other room intensified and Dokomos wrapped his thin, useless arms around himself and rocked back and forth.

Too young. Too weak. He couldn't protect her.

Tonight the argument wasn't over money. It was over the fact that his mother had contracted syphilis. She was getting so bad that she couldn't work anymore at all.

A stream of loud obscenities punctuated the argument beyond the walls of the room. A loud crash met his ears and then...silence.

Had he beaten his mother to unconsciousness again? After a moment, Dokomos scrambled to his feet and raced to the door just in time to meet Istvan coming through it.

Istvan grabbed his collar and pulled him toward the door. "Your mother's dead, boy," he growled.

Dokomos' heart rushed up into his throat with words. Bile rose. Nonononono.

He'd never had the chance to protect her, to save her.

Dokomos caught sight of her before Istvan dragged him toward the front door. She lay in an awkward sprawl with her skirts tangled around her waist. Her eyes were open and sightless and blood streamed down her face from a wound on her head.

Dokomos exploded in fury and hatred, kicking and clawing at Istvan. Istvan hung on to him, cursing, and punched Dokomos twice in the face. Pain overwhelmed Dokomos' body, followed swiftly by despair.

If only he were stronger, more powerful...

Istvan slapped him once more for good measure and Dokomos tasted blood in his mouth and smelled it in his nostrils.

He looked up at Istvan with hatred burning in his eyes. He'd never had the chance to protect or save his mother...but he'd avenge her. One day, he would.

"Your mother's dead, but there's plenty of men who'll pay for a boy." Istvan dragged him out of the flat. "Especially one as pretty as you."

Mr. Jones snapped his fingers and Drayden jerked out of the real-as-life memory. He scrambled unseeing across the floor on his hands and knees before collapsing on the ground. His breath came harsh and heavy.

The years that had followed had been even more hellish. It was a time that Drayden never, never willingly remembered. The only pleasurable memory he had from his childhood had been when he'd finally grown up a little, become stronger, had gained a measure of power…and had slit Istvan's throat one night as he slept.

Footsteps sounded on the polished wooden floor. "Do your job and we'll make you richer and more powerful than you can imagine." Mr. Jones' shoes came into view. "Don't do your job, Drayden, we'll drag you into our dimension and make you relive your childhood over and over for an eternity."

Chapter Six

✺

Adam had been able to locate a hacker in a short amount of time. The woman seemed to live and breathe complicated computer code. She seemed to see it in her mind's eye as she worked; her fingers flying almost preternaturally fast over the keyboard. The mental interface attached to her forehead clicked over pages of code just as quickly. Jade could hardly follow it, let alone perform the actions herself.

From her perch on a couch near the wall, Jade watched the woman work in Niccolo's mahogany-bedecked office.

Niccolo paced the room like some caged wild thing. Every once in a while he'd look at Jade, his eyes dark and filled with the memory of the previous night and the promise of what else he wanted to do to her.

Every time he did, Jade shivered. Her body seemed sensitive to his every movement. Even though her cunt felt sore, she wanted him filling it again. He'd seemed to unlock some unknown floodgate within her. Niccolo had made her realize how much pleasure she'd been denying herself.

She hurt because last night had the first time she'd had sex in a very long time and also because Niccolo was not a small man, not in any way. She'd blocked most the sexual encounters of her life out, even the ones before her rape, but she couldn't recall ever being with a man like him. He was possessive and dominant, yet also caring. He wanted her pleasure before his own with a selflessness that she didn't think many men possessed.

Hell, he simply made her horny. She'd never thought she'd be horny ever again.

Adam stood against another wall, leaning back with his arms crossed over his chest. He'd taken one look at them both this morning and had known what was going on. Manly, knowing looks had been exchanged. Perhaps he figured she wouldn't be able to refuse Niccolo's obvious sexual charm, maybe he'd smelled them on each other. Or maybe the prominent fang marks on her throat, declaring his ownership of her, were what tipped him off.

Adam had always been interested in her, but now he seemed to be deferring to Niccolo. Perhaps Adam was honoring Niccolo's "territory".

Yeah, she'd allowed Niccolo to mark her. For now. Only because she understood it was deeply engrained in Vampir culture and Niccolo was too ancient a dog to learn new tricks.

Anyway, it was clear her body approved of the tricks Niccolo knew. He'd had a long time to learn how to please a woman. Her cunt twitched and tingled at the thought, at the memory of him inside her.

She wanted more.

She watched Niccolo pace back and forth across the floor once again. The man was an enigma. At first glance she would've taken him for a Neanderthal, an animal who didn't think much and was valued by others only for his brawn. Those around him, even his closest friends, thought he was dangerous, and on the edge.

On the edge? Perhaps he was, or had been when they'd incarcerated him. Dangerous? Yes, to the right people. Very dangerous. Not to those who needed his protection, though. Never them.

Jade shuddered a little remembering how well he'd loved her. There was a tender side to him no one else seemed to see. How patient he'd been with her when she'd balked the first time was a testament to the subtle depths he could perceive.

Unfeeling? No, Niccolo was anything but that.

He'd gentled her to his hand and touch. He'd waited until she was ready to accept him. He'd understood without being told that she'd needed to be treated that way. These were hardly the actions of a Neanderthal. She studied him, the confident set of his shoulders and his easy, confident gait. Yes, Niccolo Romano was a man who perplexed.

"Bingo."

Jade's head snapped from Niccolo to the hacker, Emily. Niccolo and Adam went to stand near her.

"I got in to his personal files," Emily said in a smug voice. "Bastard had them encrypted really well, but I found a back door."

Jade unfurled her legs from beneath her and walked across the room to stand by Niccolo. The computer screen looked a mess of white code, flickering now and again with the hacker's brain wave patterns. Jade knew enough of computers to understand more or less that what they were seeing was a corridor of doors, each one leading to a certain portion of Dray's personal files.

Adam leaned forward. "I can't make sense of it."

Jade pointed to a series of code. "That's his banking file, isn't it? Let's go snoop in there."

With the right mathematical sequence from Emily's hacker mind, the doorway opened.

"Hell," breathed Adam, taking a step back.

Jade raised an eyebrow. The man had more money than the U.S. government...not that the U.S. government was very rich anymore. Still, it was a lot.

"And that's just one account," said Niccolo. Emily turned with a mischievous look on her face. "If you want, we can divert some of this."

"No," Niccolo answered. "For now I don't want him to think anyone's investigating him. Can we see a date book or something? A list of his appointments?"

Emily went back to the "corridor" and selected another door.

A fancy computerized date book popped up, probably the same one on Dray's handheld computer. Apparently Drayden was a meticulous note taker. All his appointments for the next month were listed. Jade scrutinized the list along with Niccolo and Adam. Nothing blatantly suspicious caught her eye.

Niccolo rocked back on his heels and passed a hand over the dark stubble on his chin. "Can you download this for us?"

"No problem." Emily downloaded it. Then she swung around and took the headset off. "I need to get out for a while. I don't want to risk Drayden's security sweepers catching me in there, but I set that back door I talked about ajar a bit. I can get back in easily, whenever you need me to."

"Thanks, Emily," said Adam. "His schedule was mostly what we were after for now." He winked. "Maybe we'll call you back later to do a little funds transferring."

Emily stood, her brown eyes sheened with excitement. "Anytime. That was fun."

Jade could tell she lived for this. She wondered how much she charged for it. Her skills were highly refined.

They accompanied her to the door. Jade leaned against the wall, watching Adam help Emily with her coat. His hand brushed the woman's ass and Emily smiled coyly at him. Jade revised her cost estimate. Maybe they were getting a deal since Adam was clearly fucking her, or was trying to fuck her.

"Thanks, Emily," Jade said. "We'll call you when we need you again."

"No problem," Emily said as she exited the apartment. "Like I said, anytime."

Adam turned to them after he closed the door. "So, we're on Drayden detail for a while."

Niccolo nodded. "We'll have to tail him. He's got a lot of influence on the Council at the moment. I want to make sure he's into something before we approach him. That means surveillance, but we'll have to be careful. Drayden isn't a weak vamp. He has gained power for a reason."

Jade leaned against the foyer wall behind her with a sigh. She hated surveillance. It meant a lot of following and waiting and little actual action. "When do we start?"

"Tonight," answered Niccolo.

"Tonight?" Adam smiled. "That mean we have the day to ourselves, boss? I might go see if Emily made it home safe, then, if you don't mind."

Jade crossed her arms over her chest and said dryly, "How chivalrous of you."

Adam cast her a glance. "Hey, it's a big, bad city. Woman as pretty as Emily might need some protection." He gave her a slow smile. "Anyway, I'm sure you and Nic have lots to do today, yourselves."

Jade looked away from him, flushing.

Niccolo turned his gaze to her and his eyes gained an appraising light. "Go on, Adam. Be back here before twilight."

As soon as the door closed behind Adam, a tension immediately filled the air. She turned and looked at Niccolo who watched her with a hungry look in his dark eyes.

"Come here," he said in a low voice.

She bristled. They'd had sex once. That didn't mean he could command her.

"Hell no," she responded automatically.

"Adam was right, you know. I have a lot to do today…to you." A trace of a smile crossed his mouth. He started across the floor toward her. "I've been thinking about you all morning, Jade."

She straightened and uncrossed her arms.

"*Dio*," he groaned. "I've been thinking about stripping your clothes off, *cara mia*, kissing every inch of your body until you cream for me." He stood in front of her. "I want to take you from behind, Jade. I want to bend you over a chair and slide my cock into you."

The words went straight to her pussy. She imagined just that scenario, his big body slamming into hers from behind, her legs spread far enough to take him that way. She felt her body respond to just his words alone. He hadn't even touched her yet.

Niccolo grinned and it sent a frisson of lust straight up her spine. "You like it when I tell what I want to do to you, don't you? It excites you to hear me say the words."

She couldn't deny it.

He reached out and brushed her hair to the side, off her shoulder. She shivered. "Do you see it in your mind? Can you see me taking you from behind? I'll make you feel good, Jade. I promise." He rubbed the pad of his thumb slowly over her collarbone. "Do you believe me?"

She sighed and closed her eyes for a moment. "Ah, yes." She swallowed hard.

"Jade, you're ripe for all kinds of things. I want to be the man to show you just what." He stood a breath's space away from her. She could feel his body heat radiate out and warm her. "You want me to show you those things, Jade?" he asked in a low voice. He reached out and took a tendril of her hair between his thumb and index finger and rubbed it back and forth.

Jade's breath came faster. Well, hell, why not admit she did? They were both in this for their own reasons. She was using him to get past her fears so she could start her life again. He was using her because he'd been in prison the last two hundred years. It was a mutually beneficial deal.

She cleared her throat so it wouldn't come out all breathy and feminine sounding. She hated that. "Yes. Yes, I do."

Niccolo dropped the tendril of her hair, turned and headed down the hallway. "Then come here."

Anger trembled through her and a vehement curse poised on the tip of her tongue. He wanted to play games. She hesitated. But what if she liked the games he wanted to play? So far, she had.

Shit.

She watched him disappear through his bedroom doorway.

Double shit.

Jade allowed her newfound sexual curiosity override everything else and headed after him.

He'd taken off his shirt, an occurrence guaranteed to make her mouth dry. He reached for the buttons of his pants, but she crossed the room and set her hands over his.

She captured his gaze and undid the button, letting his pants slide down his legs. He'd already kicked his shoes off.

He reached up, grabbed the edge of her shirt and pulled it over her head even as her hands fumbled for his cock. When she could, she grasped him at the base and pumped him against her palm, making him groan low in his throat. She loved the sounds he made, loved the feel of him so heavy and aroused in the palm of her hand.

Jade couldn't resist the way his chest beckoned and she leaned in and scattered kisses along his heated flesh. She licked and sucked her way over the expanse and made her way down.

Her breasts felt heavy and her nipples had pebbled in her excitement. He palmed them once before she slid them out of his reach. Fascinated, she came eye-level with his cock. It was a beautiful organ. She wanted to lick it, suck it. She laved the smooth head, wanting nothing more than to feel it against her tongue.

Niccolo's body went stiff. She licked again, this time tracing her tongue up the full length of it. "Goddamn it, Jade," Niccolo groaned. "Don't tease."

He didn't want her to tease, so she wouldn't. She wrapped her lips around the head of him and sucked him into the warm recesses of her mouth.

Niccolo's breath left him in a rush and he fisted his hands in her hair. "Ah, *Dio*," he groaned. He let loose a string of soft murmurings in Italian.

She could barely get the whole of him in her mouth, but she did her best, letting her tongue explore him from the base to the crown. Niccolo groaned and his hips thrust forward, letting her know that he enjoyed what she was doing to him.

"Ah, that feels so damn good, Jade," he rasped. He placed one of his big hands to the back of her head and stroked his fingers through her hair.

She enjoyed it, too. Not only did she love giving Niccolo pleasure, she found a measure of control in this act that she liked a lot. Every suck, every touch of her tongue against him, made him react. He was at her mercy in this moment. She held all the power now.

She drew on him, fondling his balls as she sucked him deep into her mouth and pulled him back out over and over. His cock glistened with her saliva. He seemed especially sensitive in the area just under the head of his cock, so she tongued it, drawing groans from his throat. Then she nibbled gently down the length of him and licked the flat of her tongue against his tight balls.

"Fuck, Jade, you're going to make me come," Niccolo rasped. He pulled her up and crushed her to him, kissing her deeply.

He let his hand slide down, over her smooth mound, to stroke her clit until she gasped his name into his open mouth. He caressed her until she throbbed, until a trail of cream marked the inside of her thigh, until all she wanted in the whole world was Niccolo's cock inside her.

He moved her to the side and motioned at a long mirror hanging on the wall of his room. It showed them both to head to toe. Niccolo positioned her in front of the mirror and came around behind her. An ottoman stood near her. He glanced at her via the reflection and nuzzled her throat. Her eyes fluttered shut and she tilted her head to the side, giving him better access.

In the mirror's reflection, she appeared drugged and bed-tousled and already well loved. Her nipples were reddened and hard. When she parted her legs she could see her pussy — pink, excited, swollen, in the mirror's reflection. The image of herself, her body so aroused, was strangely erotic.

"Beautiful," Niccolo murmured near her ear. "I've never seen anything so gorgeous in my life." He stroked her nipples softly with the pads of his fingers until she moaned, deep and needy sounding.

Niccolo cupped her breasts. She watched him roll her nipples between his strong fingers and pleasure shot straight to her cunt, making it feel wet and heavy. Her hips thrust forward a little of their own accord, her pussy seeking something to fill it.

"You're going to watch me fuck you, Jade," he murmured into her ear. "I don't want to see your gaze move from that mirror. Understand?"

Feeling drugged, she nodded. Only Niccolo seemed to have the ability to do this to her, make her so needy for him that she'd be so agreeable.

He moved his hands down her body, over her abdomen to her cunt. "Come on, baby, spread your thighs a little farther for me," he whispered, urging.

She eased her feet apart a bit more, giving him greater access to her sex.

He pulled her lips apart, exposing her needy clit that had extended out completely from the hood. He dipped his finger down, gathering her cream on his index finger and then slicked it over her extended, throbbing clit. "I want to suck it," he murmured, stroking the pad of his finger over it, soft and slow.

"Oh," she moaned. Jade's hips jerked, watching him caress her so intimately in the mirror's reflection. His hand looked huge and dark against the delicate paleness of her skin. Over and over, he teased it. She watched his finger move up and down as though hypnotized.

"I want to take it between my lips, but there will be time for that later. Right now I want you to put a foot on the ottoman and cant your hips forward a little so you can see what I'm doing better."

She did it. Now she could really see her sex and how aroused it was. It hung reddened and glistening with her cream between her thighs.

Niccolo groaned near her ear. "Perfect. God, you're pretty. Now I can touch you easier." He ran his fingers over her labia, making her shudder. "Do you want me to touch you more?"

"Yes," she managed to respond.

"Watch me, Jade," he said. He pushed two fingers inside her cunt from behind and fucked her with them. She watched, moaning low as they disappeared into the depths of her and then reappeared over and over, glistening with her juices. Within her, her muscles clamped down around them, milking them. Her pussy pulsed and quivered at the invasion.

"You like that?"

"Yes," she said breathlessly.

"Is it going to make you come?"

She paused before speaking, breathing heavily. "Probably."

Something rumbled through her back and it took her a moment to realize it was Niccolo's rich, low laugh. He stroked her clit with the thumb of his other hand. "How about now?" he whispered silkily in her ear. "Is that good? Good enough to bring you? Good enough to make you scream and drench my hand?"

"Uh." She couldn't utter anything else. She watched his skillful fingers work to pleasure her pussy in the mirror as intense waves of ecstasy stole her words.

"Come on, baby," he purred. "Give in to it."

Her powerful climax poured over her, stealing her breath so she couldn't moan. She watched her body in the mirror. Her eyes widened and her face flushed. Her body shook with the spasms and still Niccolo plunged his fingers in and out of her cunt and teased her sensitive clit.

Her gaze locked with Niccolo's as she orgasmed. His brown eyes flared hot and she became aware of the erection he pressed against her ass.

Once the waves of her climax had passed, but before they were completely over, he eased her down so her hands were palm-down on the ottoman and her feet were flat on the floor. He brushed her ass with his cock. She was a tall woman. They lined up well this way.

"Watch, Jade," Niccolo said and she realized she'd allowed her gaze to stray from the mirror.

She looked to the side, at the mirror. Her breasts hung like ripe fruit in this position. He palmed her breasts with both his big hands, teasing the nipples back and forth and lightly pinching them. Her hair fell over her shoulder, where Niccolo had gathered it up so it would be out of her way.

He touched her hot, wet pussy, caressing her labia and stroking her anus until she moaned. Her hips jerked, but he held her in place.

Bad memories threatened to rise, but she willed them down and away. He stroked her again and again until she stopped jerking away, like a trainer gentling a skittish horse. Then, after the fear receded, the promise of pleasure rose. Niccolo awoke nerves there she hadn't known she had. Heat flared anew in her cunt and she felt a drop of her come dribble down her inner thigh.

"Niccolo, please," she whispered.

He caught her gaze in the mirror. "What, Jade?" His voice sounded strained. "What do you want?"

"Your cock. Please." Her voice had that breathy quality she hated, but now she hardly noticed it. Her body had taken over for her.

He teased the entrance of her aching sex, rubbing the delicate skin there until she shook with need. "You want me to slide into this tight little pussy? Are you going to watch me do it?"

"Yes." She spread her legs and pressed her hips up at him. She was going to die soon if she didn't feel him filling her. "Please."

He groaned and grabbed her hips when she rubbed her hot sex against him. Niccolo pressed the head of his cock against her hungry entrance and thrust the head inside.

Jade's breath hissed out, watching his big body moving behind her. He tipped his head back and groaned as he pressed into her farther, stretching her muscles so exquisitely. He pushed in and in until he was seated to the base of his cock within her.

Niccolo lowered his head and caught her wide-eyed gaze. Their intimate connection right now made her pant. "I'm going to take you until your knees go weak," he promised.

They were already weak just from having the full breadth and width of him filling her cunt. Her legs were spread and his broad hands braced her hips. She felt possessed by him. Before today, she thought she'd running screaming from a sexual situation like this, but she only craved more it from Niccolo. The most amazing part was that Niccolo hadn't used a bit of glamour on her this time. She'd allowed him to get her into this position completely on her own. It was a testament to both her growing trust of him and her growing libido.

She was healing. Finally.

She met his eyes in the mirror. "Do it, Niccolo. I want to feel you."

He pulled back out of her slowly, making her feel every ridge and vein of him. She closed her eyes and bit her lip for a moment. "Oh Goddess, yes," she moaned.

"Like that?" he rasped.

"Deeper and harder," she panted.

He pushed back into her slow enough to blow her mind, as deep into her pussy as he could. Her cream coated him, making his thrusts easy.

"Faster," she demanded.

"Deeper, harder *and* faster?" he asked.

She slammed her fist against the ottoman. "You're teasing me. You're trying to drive me crazy."

"Oh, yeah, *cara mia*. I'm definitely teasing you."

His accent when he said *cara mia* just about undid her right then. His accent had grown thicker with his arousal.

"I'm not made of glass, Niccolo," she panted. The muscles of her pussy convulsed around his length and she moaned. "Please."

He grabbed her hips and began to shaft her just the way she wanted. She grabbed on to the ottoman with both hands, feeling the relentless, hard slam of him into her body. With every thrust, the head of his cock brushed up against the secret bundle of nerves within her, sending skitters of pleasure up her spine.

As a climax built to a fever pitch within her, she watched Niccolo in the mirror, watched the muscles in his shoulders and chest and arms work, and watched his hips thrust back and forth with the glide of his cock in and out of her. His balls slapped at her with every thrust. She could see how his cock shimmered wetly on every outward stroke.

In the end, it was his eyes that made her come.

Niccolo met her gaze and held it, making this liaison about so much more than sex. It made it far more intimate, far more meaningful. Like they both added a bit of their soul to the act, instead of just their bodies. His gaze was so compelling she couldn't look away, even though the soul-level intimacy of it frightened her.

Just then it was as if their minds locked and she could feel the squeeze of her muscles around his cock, how hot and tight she was. She felt his pleasure at knowing how much ecstasy he was giving her, felt the climax building up in his balls and his anticipation of filling her with his ejaculate.

Her climax overtook her body, making her break his gaze. Shuddering, moaning and shaking, she grabbed on harder to the ottoman and let her orgasm take her body over. Spasms of pleasure rocketed through her cunt, causing her muscles to clamp down and milk Niccolo's still pistoning cock. She felt her cream surge out of her, making Niccolo's penetration even slipperier.

He gathered some of it up and stroked her anus, teasing the entrance of it with his fingertip. The action lengthened her orgasm, making Jade feel like she wanted to scream. She bit her lip against the waves of pleasure and closed her eyes, enjoying every moment of it.

Behind her, Niccolo let several sentences free in rasping Italian. He closed his eyes, tipped his head back and groaned. Jade felt his cock jump inside her and his hot come fill her.

Jade's knees did go weak then, watching him as he came inside her. He scooped her up, helped her to the bed and lay down beside her.

Jade felt limp. Niccolo kissed her and let his hands skate idly over her body. He pressed her close to him, murmuring her name over and over, and slipped his fingers between her thighs, idly using their combined come as a lubricant over her clit and the folds of her pussy. He stroked her opening, her pussy and her clit over and over like he just couldn't stop touching her.

All Jade could do was lie there for him. She could barely move. She moaned out his name, feeling drugged with pleasure and the feel of him. Jade sprawled nude on the bed, her thighs spread wide for him, uncaring how much access she'd given Niccolo to her body.

Niccolo seemed insatiable for the feel of her. He touched her silently and methodically. His fingers slid between her sticky, wet folds, toyed and stroked her clit.

Over and over. Relentlessly. Masterfully.

It seemed like it went on for hours. His kisses and intimate, possessive caresses making her feel drunk. She was lost in a labyrinth of lust. She became only her body, her job only to lie and allow Niccolo to pet her. She felt like a slave to him. Her body was his plaything, and she didn't want to be anything else in that moment. She felt like he worshipped her, cared for her.

Her soft moans filled the air, combined with his murmurings in Italian and the gentle, wet sounds of his fingers sliding in and out of her and around her aroused sex.

He brought her two more times in long, slow, easy, shuddering climaxes. Jade shook from the force of them, tossing her head back and forth on the bed and whispering his name.

While she came down from the waves of pleasure that had racked her body and he finally seemed satisfied with the amount of come he'd drawn from her body, he tucked her against him. She tried not to enjoy how good he felt but her bones felt like butter. She felt incredibly sated.

"How do you do that?" she murmured sleepily. "You know my body better than I do."

"Lots of practice."

"I don't remember anyone ever being so..." she trailed off, realizing she was letting far too much of herself slip in her lassitude.

Niccolo remained silent for several moments, and then asked, "You haven't been with many men, have you?"

She stiffened. "Of course not. I know that's obvious enough." She relaxed a little. "I had this thing...happen." Jade paused.

She almost felt like telling him, finally getting her awful secret off her chest, but why she felt Niccolo worthy of that secret she didn't understand. Hell, worthy? What was she thinking? It was a burden to bear, not some kind of honor.

"This thing," she continued, covering over what she'd said. "You know, I've been busy...working, studying with the Order. There just hasn't been time for sex." She trailed off again, settling into her lie. Her secret was best left in the dark where no one could see it, least of all her. It would be something she went to her grave with.

"So, you've never been in a steady relationship?"

She raised her head a little. "What do you mean? Like a boyfriend as opposed to the series of one-night stands the OtherKin and Embraced usually have? Yes, I once had a serious relationship...a long time ago."

She found the strength to move and rested her hands on his chest and set her chin on the backs of them. "What about you?"

Niccolo shrugged and looked away. "You should know better than me, shouldn't you?"

"Your *mere de sang*. Antonia."

He rolled his eyes. "*Dio*, what a surprise, you know."

Jade rolled over onto her back. "So, was she your one big love? There wasn't anything else in the records about any other women being significant in your life."

"No. After Antonia there were many women, but no one special."

"Strictly a one-night stand kind of guy, hmmm? True to your heritage as an Embraced."

He rolled onto his side and stroked her nipple until she squirmed, molten pleasure warming her pussy once more. She sighed. He touched her like her body was completely owned by him.

For now, maybe that was true.

"Yes," he said finally. "You could say that. You're going to be a little longer than one night, though, Jade."

"I am?" she breathed.

He lowered his mouth to her nipple and laved over it until her cunt twitched. "Mmmm, yeah," he finally said. "You taste good to me, Jade, in more ways than one. I'm not sure I'll ever get enough of you."

He settled back against the pillows. His cock had grown hard again. He reached down and stroked himself. She watched his huge hand move over his erection with fascination.

Jade covered his hand with hers and took over stroking him. He groaned and his hips thrust up.

"I'm yours until this Drayden thing is over with," she answered.

"Drayden...he's got a history, Jade. I'm probably the only one who knows it. Bad shit, really bad shit has befallen that man. You know how sometimes people have brutal things happen to them and they can overcome them, turn them in to something positive?"

Her hand stilled for a moment. Like her becoming a Priestess of the Morrigan so she could bring the bad guys in — the guys like the ones who'd almost killed her. Like how Niccolo had allowed himself to be incarcerated when he felt he was going to lose it. "Yes."

"And you know how other times it twists people into doing cruel things themselves?"

"Yeah."

"Dray's in the second category."

He pulled her up to straddle him, and ran his hands over her body. The touching now seemed more for contact and comfort than anything born of lust. Niccolo's face looked suddenly ashen in the dim light of the room. His cock had started to go flaccid where it touched her.

Niccolo reached up and touched her cheek. "He was raped when he was growing up, over and over. His mother's pimp took him as a child, after he killed Drayden's mom, and sold him to men who liked little boys."

Jade grimaced. "That's beyond horrible."

"He's had a really harsh life. I'm just telling you this so you understand why he might be helping the Dominion. His search for power and control comes straight from his lack of it as a child."

"Yeah, okay, I get that. It doesn't mean we should feel sorry for him or go easy on him," she answered. "It's terrible what happened to him, but it doesn't give him the right to harm others."

Niccolo nodded. A brutal expression overtook his face, and his eyes went gunmetal cold. "When the times comes, if Drayden is guilty of collaborating with the Dominion, I'll kill him, Jade."

She nodded, her body going stiff at the look in his eyes. She believed him. His demeanor changed so fast that it could be frightening. He'd gone from passionate lover to cold-blooded killer in zero to sixty.

"I just thought you should know," he finished. His eyes and expression returned to normal. The coldness bled out of his eyes, replaced by warmth.

"I don't have sympathy for people who let vicious occurrences in their life be an excuse for being cruel," she answered. "You've had bad things happen, and you're still a protector. You never slipped to the dark side."

He reached up and brushed her long hair away so he could stroke her nipples. "You don't think I'm cruel, Jade? You haven't been around me long enough to understand just how ruthless I can be. I hope you never see it."

Jade closed her eyes as her cunt pulsed. She felt sore and sticky between her thighs, but his touch could still excite her. It could make her forget that her pussy hurt from his already thorough attentions and crave even more of it. "Not to innocents," she managed to gasp.

His calloused thumbs caressed her breasts and nipples until she creamed for him. He ran his hands down her stomach to her sex, where she straddled him. He spread her, examining her clit. Jade felt his cock twitch back to life and grow hard where it rested against her buttocks.

"Damn it, Jade. I could make love to you forever," he growled softly.

She winced at the words *make love*, but he was gently, so very, very gently teasing her clit. It made her forget the offensive words, made her moan his name instead. That now familiar hot, fluttery feeling consumed her sex, made her needy for his touch and the feel of him.

He rolled her over and pulled her under him, so she could feel the press of his cock against her cunt. "What if I want to keep you longer than we've agreed?" he asked. He passed his index finger over the bite marks on her throat, noting his possession of her.

Jade went still, staring up into his dark eyes. Fear tightened her stomach. All she wanted was sex from him, nothing more. Something *more* lingered in his eyes right now and she didn't like it.

"I have other jobs to do," she replied. "When this is over, I'm leaving." She'd been alone for too long to contemplate the idea of twining her life with someone else's, even for just an extended period of time. She would've assumed that Niccolo would feel the same way.

Something that looked uncomfortably like a denial of her words, a challenge, hardened his gaze for a moment. He didn't reply. He simply lifted her by the ass and slid his cock into her wet sex with one long, slow thrust.

Jade arched her back and hissed in pleasure. He took advantage of her exposed throat, rolled his glamour over her and sunk his fangs deep. The actions were the ultimate in control.

Exquisite pleasure filled her body and mind. He took her slow, his cock gliding easily in and out of her body as he drew on her veins. He kept her riding a climax, a long, drawn-out tremor in her body that ended in a shattering that made her vision darken. He tipped his head back and roared out his release and she felt him jump inside her, his thick and hot come filling her up.

If she'd been tired before, she was exhausted now. Too worn out, too satisfied to contemplate what had just happened. How he'd marked her again, taken her so possessively, right after she'd denied him any possibility of an extension of this arrangement.

Sleep…it's all she wanted.

"You're mine, Jade," she heard him whisper into her ear as he stroked her hair. "Mine."

Chapter Seven

Niccolo watched Lex from a table across the room. He looked same as he remembered him. His dark hair hung longer now, but his build was the same, his eyes still a deep green.

Every day for the last week they'd watched Dray skate from one meeting to the next, one lunch to another. He drank, he smoked and he picked up women. It was normal modus operandi for Dray when he wasn't scheming or double-crossing someone to get ahead. Nothing much of interest. It was downright boring, in fact. They'd learned nothing concrete or even if Drayden was really working with the Dominion's manifestation.

He was growing frustrated, as were Jade and Adam. If Dray wasn't working with the Dominion, their talents could be used to greater effect elsewhere. If Dray was innocent, they were just wasting their time, and it ate at Niccolo like he knew it ate at Jade and Adam.

Niccolo had used a light glamour to disguise himself. His age afforded him some unique abilities. Jade looked as she always did to him, though to the world she appeared a blonde-haired, blue-eyed Nordic woman. Viewed through the glamour, he could've passed for her brother. He'd even managed to disguise their scents. Age definitely had its benefits.

The restaurant was an expensive, exclusive one and Jade had dressed to fit the part. She wore a dark blue corset that pushed her beautiful small breasts up to overflowing, and a short silk skirt of matching blue. The fashion was retro these days and Jade fit the part. Though she'd opted out of the huge belled skirt that was in fashion because she feared she wouldn't be able to move in one if the situation demanded it. It was odd to see her in a skirt and she didn't look at ease in it.

Far more comfortable in flat, steel-toed boots, she'd tripped three times on the way to the restaurant in her high heels. The boots she wore under the gown were—Niccolo shuddered—exquisite. Black leather, with four-inch heels, the tops hit her about mid-thigh. A nice swath of creamy flesh could be seen between the edge of the skirt and the tops of her boots. Niccolo wanted to run his tongue over it.

All Niccolo could think about was how she'd look in *just* the boots. God, he wanted to pull that sexy dress over her head, part her creamy thighs and bury himself inside her...while she wore those boots and *only* those boots.

He let his gaze trace the curve of her bare shoulders and trail over the mounds of her perfect breasts. He'd had her in his bed every single night since she'd agreed to their bargain. Every single night he'd shown her how good sex could be, and she'd done likewise for him. They were good together. She was ripe to experiment. There was a need for it within her that Niccolo felt all too ready to satisfy.

He looked up and locked with her gaze. Her smoky eyes had caught him taking her in. One hand gripped her wineglass on the table. Her breathing quickened.

Niccolo took a drink of his bourbon, barely feeling the burn of it down his throat as he held her gaze. *Dio*, he wanted her again. He wanted her all the time. She was like a drug he needed in his bloodstream constantly. The scent of her skin, her perfume, the feel of her hair brushing him, all of it was an aphrodisiac to him.

Not since Antonia had he felt this way about a woman, felt like he could make her his forever. With Jade at his side he felt like a better, stronger man. She filled a hollow part of him, a yearning inside him he never thought would be satisfied. They matched in a way he'd never thought to experience with another person. She alone made this assignment a bearable one.

He reached across the table and twined his fingers with hers. Uncertainty and fear filled her eyes for a moment, and then she relaxed and tightened her fingers with his. Yes, she was acerbic a lot of the time—not to mention touchy as hell—but, God, she could be so sweet and vulnerable the rest of the time. The dichotomy in her was heady to him.

At some point, he'd stopped *fucking* her and started *making love* to her. What they did now meant much more to him. Niccolo didn't know what Jade was feeling, but he'd already decided that they meshed well. He'd already decided he wanted to keep her.

It was just a matter of convincing Jade she wanted to keep him.

Niccolo rubbed his thumb over her knuckles. She bit her lower lip and sighed as she watched the action. Her lower lip popped from between her small white teeth all red and plumped. He wanted to kiss it.

Drayden laughed loudly across the room with his friend across the room. Knowing Drayden, he'd probably be there all evening, downing whiskey and talking. Niccolo had time to play a little.

"What are you wearing under that skirt?" Niccolo asked softly.

Jade's eyes narrowed and interest flared through their blue depths. "Something lacier than I've ever worn in my life." She looked away, toward Drayden, her other hand tightening on the stem of the wineglass. Her apprehension was apparent, yet the scent of her arousal wafted to him like a fine aphrodisiac.

Niccolo slipped his hand under the table and pulled her chair toward his easily.

She gasped in surprise, "Goddamn it, Niccolo."

"I want to feel for myself." He dropped his hand to her thigh under the tablecloth.

It clearly startled Jade, but she didn't move away. He eased the material of her skirt up higher, the faint rasp of the silk against her thigh-high stockings loud in his ears. It seemed louder than the conversation and the clank of dinnerware around him. He held her gaze and watched as her eyes grew heavy lidded. It was a sure sign of her growing excitement.

He leaned close, brushed her long hair to the side and gently kissed her earlobe. "You want me to touch you, Jade?"

He wasn't really asking for permission. She'd already given it by parting her thighs for him. He eased her skirt up a little more under the table, allowing the air to bathe her inner thighs. His fingertip skimmed the top of one of the thigh-highs and rasped over the garter attaching the corset to it.

In his pants, his cock swelled. If they'd been alone he'd spread her legs and fuck her while she was still wearing them—the corset, the garters and the boots. Just the thought of it tightened every muscle in his body.

"Hook your feet around the legs of the chair, *cara mia*, so you're nice and spread for me."

While she did that, he dragged his fingers up and found the lacy panties. She parted her thighs a bit farther for him and he ran his index finger over the swollen folds of her pussy through the fabric. Her dampness had soaked through the material. He found her clit and traced it with the pad of his index finger, then set to stroking it through the smooth material.

Jade's breathing quickened.

"What's exciting you more?" he asked as he slid his finger under the panties and sought skin-to-skin contact. Jade bit her lower lip and briefly closed her eyes. "Is it my hands on you or the fact that you're surrounded by people in this restaurant *while* my hands are on you?"

She leveled her gaze at him. "Both," she sighed out.

He caressed her with his index finger and felt her shudder. Searching out her perfect, aroused clit, he stroked it and watched the rapid rise and fall of her cleavage.

"You want me to make you come, *cara mia*?"

"Yes," she gasped.

"You want me to make you come right here? Right at the table, in front of everyone?"

"Yes, you bastard," she murmured.

He could tell she was ready…and more than a little pissed off at the same time. He loved that she felt so eager for him that she'd agree to things she normally wouldn't. Softening and slowing the strokes, he held her at the edge, letting her gather energy to make it better when he finally brought her.

"Bastard," she breathed again. Her fingers found and grasped a spoon.

He smiled. "You love it when I'm a bastard."

The waiter approached the table holding a bottle of expensive red wine and a serving bottle of bourbon in his hand. "More wine for the lady?" he asked amiably.

Jade stiffened beside him, but Niccolo never let the slow stroke of his finger on her clit falter. She seemed unable to answer to the waiter. She was too busy trying to pretend like he wasn't stroking her to a screaming climax under the table, right under the waiter's nose.

"Yes," Niccolo answered smoothly. "The lady would like…*more*."

The waiter refilled her glass, but Niccolo asked him to pour slowly. Nonplussed by the odd request, the waiter complied. At the same time, Niccolo increased the pace and pressure on her clit.

"More bourbon?" asked the waiter blandly, oblivious to the fact that his female patron was just tipping over the edge and starting to drown in a climax. Jade's body stiffened. Her breathing came faster and Niccolo felt her cunt twitch in the first throes of a climax.

"Yes," Niccolo answered the waiter. At the same time, he slid a finger down and pushed into Jade's wet heat as the waiter slowly refilled his glass. Her muscles clenched and spasmed around his fingers as he thrust deliberately in and out of her.

Jade closed her eyes and bit her bottom lip with small white teeth until a dot of blood appeared.

The waiter simply turned and walked away.

* * * * *

Jade fought the rising moan in her throat as Niccolo skillfully manipulated her body into ecstasy. The waves of pleasure darkened her vision and she fought the urge to move on Niccolo's fingers, to thrust her hips back and forth and fuck herself on them.

God, how she wished it was his cock.

The waiter went away finally and the waves of the climax ceased.

She took a moment to catch her breath as Niccolo withdrew his hand from under her skirts, then she pushed away from the table. "You fucking bastard," she shot at him in a low voice before she got up and went to the ladies' room.

She hated that he could do that to her. She hated how much control he had over her.

Goddess, how could let herself fall under this man's thrall so easily? Worse, how could she enjoy being there so much?

He caught her arm and pulled her into the women's bathroom before she'd even walked ten paces.

"What the hell are you doing?" she yelled at him once they were inside.

He checked the stalls and finding them empty, locked the door.

"Niccolo," she said in a warning tone.

He stalked toward her. "You liked it."

She stood her ground. "Of course I did."

"Then what's the problem?"

She glanced away, licking her suddenly dry lips. The problem was she felt out of control around him and she hated it. Even though he was helping her get over her psychological blocks, she begrudged him the power he seemed to have over her. Those were truths she didn't want to admit out loud.

She shook her head. "I don't know," she lied.

Niccolo drew her back to a wall and pressed her against it, his finger pulling the pins out of her hair and letting it fall around her shoulders. He plunged his hands into it. Niccolo loved her hair. His fingers were always in it, sometimes stroking it idly or fisting in it as he took her hard and fast from behind.

"You don't know how bad I want you right now," he said in a low voice. "I want you all the time, Jade." He lowered his head to hers and kissed her hungrily.

Desire swept over her immediately. When he raised her skirt to her waist and dragged her fingers over her sex she didn't stop him. When he ripped the seams of her panties and let them to fall to the floor, she didn't make a move. When he unbuttoned his pants, she didn't so much as utter one word of protest.

Making an impatient sound in the back of his throat, he cupped her ass and lifted her, then slid his cock right inside her, pressing her hips against the wall behind her. He impaled her on his cock with one smooth, deep thrust.

Jade cried out. It echoed around them in the posh, cavernous bathroom. It felt so good to have him inside her. Every time it felt like coming home, like she was regaining a part of herself that had gone missing.

Her cunt throbbed and pulsed around his length. He set her feet back down to the floor, without sliding out of her, and hiked one of her legs over his hips. Niccolo backed out and thrust back in to the hilt.

"Ah, *Dio*, that's what I wanted," Niccolo murmured raggedly near her ear. "Hot, velvet tightness around my cock, that's how you feel, Jade." He pulled out slowly and thrust back in again.

Jade thought she'd go insane at the sensation of him filling her up so completely. She opened her mouth and gasped as she hit his shoulder with her fist. Pleadings for *more* rose up in her throat, but she choked them back down. She closed her eyes as he stroked into her body again, then again.

She opened her eyes and saw the mirror opposite them. Saw her wide eyes and the needful, fevered look on her face. Saw her leg thrown over his hip and her skirt pushed up to her waist, revealing the thigh-high boot with its feminine, spiky heel.

Niccolo thrust into her again and she watched the play of his hips as he eased himself inside her, the dimples on his gorgeous ass. She let her gaze trail over his strong hand splayed flat on the wall beside her head and how his other arm embraced her hip.

He took her slow and easy and with a single-minded intensity that made her come fast. She tipped her head back against the wall and panted out her climax, not wanting to make much noise, as Niccolo kissed and licked over her burgeoning cleavage.

He increased the pace of his thrusts, pressing her back against the wall behind her in tempo with the glide of his cock in and out of her. "Niccolo," she gasped breathlessly. "Goddess, yes." The first climax seemed to make her pussy even more sensitive.

"Is it good, *cara mia*?" he asked, his words sounding slurred.

"Uh-huh."

He lifted her and carried her to the sink and sat her down, and then pulled her so her ass almost hung off the edge. The height was good and lined her sex up to his cock nearly perfectly.

Using his thumbs to spread her wide, he thrust harder and faster. She grasped the edge of the counter in a death grip against the intense pleasure of it. In this position she could watch the slide of him in and out of her between her spread thighs. Her eyes widened as she watched Niccolo thrust into her body. The sounds of her soft moans and his groans filled the air.

Her body tensed and she came again. The pleasure bloomed out from her pussy and enveloped her whole body. She wanted to scream, but she couldn't do that. Instead, she put her mouth to Niccolo's ear and whispered his name over and over as the climax took her.

"*Dio*, I'm coming," he murmured. "You're making me come." He thrust deep into her and pulled back out slowly a couple times as he tipped his head back and groaned gutturally.

Jade closed her eyes and sighed as he filled her, his body shuddering against hers.

Niccolo buried his face in her neck, keeping himself thrust up deep within her. "Jade," he breathed. "I have no control when it comes to you."

He thought *he* had no control? How laughable. From her perspective, he had it all. She was like his little plaything, her body responded to him powerfully and instantaneously to his every demand. Saying no to him, denying him, was only a dream. She couldn't do it.

She shook her head. "No. It's not me. It's that you're making up for years without sex, just as I am. We've both been in prison."

He raised his face, cupping her chin in his palm and staring down at her. "No, that's not why."

His gaze was intense and full of emotion. It made her heart skip a beat. She stared up at him, stunned by the look in his eyes. The expression on his face left her speechless. She looked away.

He forced her to look at him. "Jade, I haven't felt what I feel for you in a very, very long time. You understand what I'm saying?"

She struggled against him, pushing past him. What he was saying now scared the absolute hell out her. Did he mean he had feelings for her? How could that be? She was damaged, not ready or worthy of someone's emotion or commitment.

Jade turned away from him, and smoothed her skirt back into place. In a weird way, she felt like she had to cover herself. She felt exposed in more ways than one right now. She walked across the room, scooped her torn panties up and disposed of them. Then she just stood there, staring at the wall.

"Jade?" he asked.

She crossed her arms over her chest, suddenly chilled and confused. Jade knew how to do all kinds of things, but dealing with someone else's emotions was not one of them. "I don't know what to say," she responded, finally.

Niccolo stared at her back, and then sighed. "Come on, let's go see where our sleazy double-crossing friend is," he said.

Jade took a minute to adjust herself, easing herself out of the awkward moment she'd just shared with Niccolo. When they were both ready, Niccolo unlocked the bathroom door.

She felt the tingle of Niccolo's glamour slide over her right before they stepped out into the corridor. Three sour-faced older women stood outside, tapping expensive retro-Renaissance boots under their voluminous skirts.

Niccolo stopped for a moment and smiled dazzlingly, "My sincere apologies, ladies," he said with a slight incline of his head.

All three of the women relaxed and burst into smiles of their own. Niccolo had a way with women of all ages no matter if he appeared glamoured or not.

They continued down the hallway into the main room. Drayden still sat there, still sipping brandy and smoking a thousand-dollar cigar with his friend. Jade sat back down wearily in her chair and took a sip of her wine while Niccolo sank into his. Shakily, she smoothed the napkin into her lap and did her best not to look at Niccolo.

Getting back to the apartment would be a blessing this evening. She needed some time alone, time to think.

After about a half hour later, Drayden got up, paid the bill and left the restaurant. She and Niccolo did the same.

Niccolo had masked their scent somewhat, but there was no sense in taking chances. They stayed well behind them as they exited the restaurant and stepped out onto the bright, noisy streets.

Jade knew that Niccolo was likely telepathically communicating with Adam, telling him that Drayden was on the move. Adam was waiting in a car a distance away, their backup if they lost Drayden anywhere.

They waited until the computerized valet brought Drayden's car around before commanding their own. Niccolo's cycle would've screamed his presence. There were few vintage bikes around and Drayden knew that model had been Niccolo's favorite.

The shiny silver PTV pulled around automatically and they got in, shutting the doors against the loud voices, laughter and the sound of traffic outside.

Niccolo settled back into a chair and pushed a hand through his hair. He still wasn't completely comfortable giving up all his control to a computer and it showed. Clearly, he felt uneasy in a PTV.

Jade leaned over and programmed the vehicle to fix on Drayden's car. They'd follow his vehicle wherever it went. His vehicle's identification number had luckily been in the information uncovered by the hacker.

She fell back against the seat beside Niccolo and watched as the PTV zoomed by buildings. Hopefully Drayden was just going home. She couldn't wait for this night to be over so she could change her clothes. She couldn't remember the last time she'd put on a dress and heels, and she felt damn uncomfortable in them. Not to mention they'd hinder her fighting ability if it came down to that.

She glanced down at herself. Although she had to admit she enjoyed the reaction Niccolo had to them.

"I can't reach Adam."

Jade stiffened. "What?"

"I've been trying since we left the restaurant. I thought maybe he got caught in a conversation with someone or something, but he still hasn't answered me."

"That's not good ne—"

Something hard smashed into the side of the PTV, flinging her and Niccolo into the window opposite them. Pain and shock blossomed throughout her body, but especially in her head where she'd cracked it against the window.

The vehicle rolled over and over again and she and Niccolo went with it. The crash of glass and the crunch of metal filled her ears. She could do nothing against the terrifying force of it. Her vision darkened for a moment and she struggled to stay conscious under the intense pain of her head.

The vehicle finally came to a halt and she felt something hot and sticky running down her face. Disoriented, Jade lifted her hand to find out what it was and she drew it back coated in blood.

Her eyes struggling to focus, she flipped herself onto her side, biting back a scream at the pain in her shoulder. It was dislocated.

Niccolo lay on his back next to her. He pushed up, spit out blood and crawled toward her. He put his hands on her shoulder, her face. "Jade, you okay?"

She wasn't, but she nodded once anyway. She wasn't dead, that was a plus.

"Your weapon."

Understanding swept through her. This might not be an ordinary car crash. "My purse," she groaned.

Damn dress or boots hadn't afforded a good place to stash a weapon.

Niccolo moved to search for it in the ravaged interior of the vehicle. A short in the destroyed control panel at the front sent up sparks. The PTV now rested on its side and the feminine computerized voice kept repeating *motor vehicle collision* over and over.

As if they hadn't already figured that out.

Above her the crumpled door whined open. Jade's body tensed for whatever might come through it. She hoped for only emergency medical personnel called to the scene of a completely run-of-the-mill automobile accident, but with Adam missing...

The door clanked open and Drayden's face appeared. He leveled two guns at them. "Surprise!" he said brightly. "Man, that was fun! Can we do it again?"

Jade pushed herself up despite the screaming pain in her head and shoulder.

Niccolo growled low and dangerously and then launched himself at the door without warning. Jade watched in horror at the way Niccolo lunged straight through the opening. Drayden had a split second to look appalled before Niccolo took him flat backward, out of Jade's viewing range.

Horrible sounds—the sounds of bone cracking, blood spilling and death—reached her ears. There were more men out there, Drayden's men. Men scrambled, screamed and died.

Goddess.

Niccolo.

Was that the sound of Niccolo ripping through them...or them ripping through Niccolo?

Her heart slamming in her chest, she cast around the vehicle frantically one-handed, searching for her damn purse. Finally, she found it, pulled her gun and forced herself to her feet among the wreckage of the interior of the PTV and inched cautiously toward the doorway.

Her shoulder hurt so badly she thought she'd pass out. Her head throbbed like someone had hit her in the temple with hammer. What had happened in the crash was probably the equivalent. Sheer willpower and concern for Niccolo kept her on her feet. She had to proceed cautiously since she was working blind.

Outside someone screamed. Men scuffled. All fell silent. Jade stilled near the opening above her.

Drayden laughed.

Drayden laughing...not good.

Terror for Niccolo tightening her chest, drowning out the pain of her head and her shoulder, Jade dove out of the opening and rolled off the side of the crumbled PTV to land on her feet.

That had been a rash move, but she'd been desperate. She couldn't wait in that crumpled tin can waiting to find out if Niccolo lived or died.

Jade hovered on her feet for a moment, balanced on the razor's edge of unconsciousness. She lifted her weapon with her good arm and scanned her immediate area, though for a moment she saw two of everyone. She blinked, trying to make the world come into focus.

"Jade."

Niccolo's voice. He sounded concerned. His dark velvet voice sounded rasping and full of deep emotion.

She looked up, focused as hard as she could. He stood covered in blood and surrounded by five men, all of them held hawthorn batons on him.

At his feet, all around the area, lay bodies. Not one of them still breathed.

She looked back up at Niccolo, understanding. Slow horror filled her at the swift death he'd brought.

The blood on him wasn't his.

"I knew I'd have to sacrifice a few men to take the great Niccolo." Drayden whistled low. "But *that* was spectacular."

Jade shot Drayden. Point-blank. Straight in the heart. No preamble. No hesitation.

The men surrounding Niccolo didn't move. More men, different men, came for her.

Before they grabbed her and wrested the gun away. Before they bound her wrists, catapulting her straight into the past to make her scream and fight and tear her shoulder even more, before her whole world went utterly black... She saw Drayden fall and felt satisfied.

Chapter Eight

Drayden walked into the cell, rubbing his chest where the bitch had hit him. She'd even done it with a gun loaded with hawthorn slugs. Damn lucky he'd worn double-grade armor. He'd be standing there dead if he hadn't been.

He entered the dimly lit room where Jade—Niccolo's woman, he strongly suspected—now lay. He'd constructed the basement of his house for just such a happy occurrence—for the time when he might get his hands on Niccolo to make him suffer. He was looking forward to being able to do that now.

Mr. Jones said kill him, but that only provided fun for a short time. Drayden wanted to prolong the pleasure.

Anyway, that bastard Jones wasn't the boss of him.

Behind him one of his minions dragged Adam. He'd drugged the vamp near out of his mind. Mostly, so he couldn't shift. Adam's form was a wolf—a big one. It wasn't an animal he wanted to deal with right now.

They'd drugged Niccolo too. Didn't need to deal with any big felines, either.

Drayden's form was a large, white owl. Cool, but less deadly than a wolf or jungle cat.

Drayden pushed the door open and watched the half-blood fae priestess shift on the red and gold silk couch where he'd had his guards lay her. They'd popped her shoulder back in place while she'd been unconscious and had bound her wrists and ankles with cold iron. Cold iron negated the abilities of the Sidhe, even a half-breed like Jade.

But when she'd returned to consciousness, she'd pitched a screaming, spitting, out-of-this-reality hissy fit. She'd practically chewed her own wrists off in an effort to get out of the cuffs. She'd fought blind, like a crazy person, until she'd lost consciousness again.

Fuck. The woman really had something against being bound.

The second time she'd done it, Drayden had the cuffs taken off. Now an energy field surrounded her. He figured since she didn't have any magick to speak of, it was safe enough to leave the cold iron off her. She could only go as far as it was programmed for, which was about a ten-foot radius around the couch. Her wrists and ankles were raw and bloody now from her fight against the cuffs.

She had injuries from the crash that would've killed a human. Since she was half-Sidhe, she'd survive. Drayden was still deciding whether or not get her medical attention.

Mr. Jones had said kill them with his own bare hands. Drayden was pretty sure Jones wouldn't like that he was keeping them instead of killing them.

He directed his men to chain Adam up a few steps beyond Jade's prison.

He glanced from Adam to Jade and pushed a hand through his hand. Why hadn't he killed them yet? Hell, he wasn't sure why. Playing with Niccolo was like playing with loaded gun. He knew that.

Still, he couldn't seem to bring himself to do it. Death didn't come naturally to him the way it came to Niccolo. It never had.

Drayden left Adam, whose blond head rolled from side to side under the influence of the drugs, and knelt beside Jade. The energy bubble would let him or anyone else in, but wouldn't let her out.

Her eyes flickered open and instantly narrowed. Light blue laser beams aimed straight at him. A look of disappointment—probably that he was still alive—briefly crossed her beautiful face.

This was not a woman you wanted on your bad side. This was not a woman one wanted for an enemy.

He let his gaze travel over her body. Her corset and skirt was ripped in places from the crash, revealing nice amounts of flesh. She wore sexy thigh-highs and a garter belt. Yum. Niccolo had always had good taste in females.

He wouldn't be able to bind her though, so he'd never be able to fuck her. Not that this one had any intention of letting him touch her, anyway. Niccolo liked to bind his women, Drayden remembered, but it wasn't a requirement like it was for him.

"So, I wonder what the Order would think if they knew you were doing your assignment," he said. "You know, really *doing* it."

Blue eyes narrowed to catlike slits.

"Don't feel guilty about being weak," he continued. "The women never could resist Niccolo. They just fell right into his bed."

She swung her legs around, her hands instantly cradling her injured head. She cast him an impatient glance. "Don't you have someone to go be a toady for, Drayden?"

He smiled and propped himself against the edge of the couch like he was her girlfriend on a sleepover. "I'd rather stay here with you. We have so much to talk about."

She rolled her eyes and caught sight of Adam in the corner. Her whole body stiffened, but she quickly masked it. She had to be wondering where Niccolo was. She had to be scared, but true to her Sidhe heritage she wasn't going to let it show.

"Hey, I just wanted to let you know that you really would've fooled me, you know, in the restaurant and while you were tailing me. Really. But, you see, I planted the hacker." He smiled brightly. "It was a setup. That whole week you followed me around? I planned it all." He shrugged and smiled. "You were doomed from the start."

Ah, there it was. She slipped. For a moment she looked positively stunned. That was satisfying.

"You bastard," she said in a low voice. "Where's Niccolo?" A thread of fear laced her voice.

"Aww, you're worried about him. How sweet. I'm afraid he's unavailable at the moment. I figured you and Adam can hang out together for a while. I have unfinished business with Niccolo."

"He used to be your friend, Drayden."

"Friend?" He laughed. "I haven't had any *friends* in my life."

"He knows more about you than anyone, Lex. Yeah, he was a friend…until you betrayed him."

Drayden stiffened. It was true. Niccolo knew everything about him, every deep and horrifying secret. Maybe on some level he wanted to punish Niccolo for that knowledge.

"Sounds like you know, too," he said in a low voice full of threat.

Wisely, she didn't answer. She only glanced at him, then away. It was response enough.

"Watch it, faerie. I'm being more merciful than you can even imagine. Don't push your luck." He stood and walked toward the door.

"Drayden, you bastard! Where is Niccolo?" She stood from the couch, followed him and hit the energy barrier. It yanked her back, straight down on her ass.

Oh, that had to hurt.

He reached the door, turned and looked at her as she sat on the floor, clearly fighting another bout of unconsciousness.

"Drayden—" she started.

He closed the door on her.

* * * * *

Niccolo watched Drayden enter the room through the dark hair that had fallen over his face. They'd strung him up, arms extended out on either side and held in heavy chains, just liked how they used to do him in Harcourt. He'd no choice but to let them, since they had Jade somewhere and she was injured badly from the crash.

They'd drugged him just enough so he couldn't shift. Anyway, if he shifted now, he'd string his panther form up in the chains and be even worse off.

He put all his hatred for Drayden into his gaze. He put everything he wanted to do to him right into his eyes as he watched Drayden walk toward him. It wiped the cocky smile off Dray's face for a moment. It rocked him back on his heels for the briefest of heartbeats.

"Niccolo," Drayden said, recovering his ever-present smile. "Long time, no see."

Niccolo said nothing. He only stared at him, fighting the growl trickling up from the center of him.

Self-control was all Niccolo had right now. He had to keep it. Being back in chains made his breath come short, made his heart pound, Goddamn it, the last thing he wanted was to be someone's prisoner again, not after tasting freedom.

And there was Jade…

"Talkative as ever, I see." Drayden stopped in front of him and clasped his manicured hands at the small of his back. "Prison didn't do much for your social skills. Definitely didn't take away your knack for bestowing death, however. That was a most impressive display at the crash site."

The dried blood still covered him. The smell of death hung in his nostrils and the sickening feel of it clenched his stomach.

Niccolo's control snapped. He lunged toward Drayden like a dog on a chain that was just a little too short. Pain blossomed in his shoulders and upper arms.

Drayden took a few hasty steps backward.

One point for Niccolo.

"Come on, Nic," Drayden cajoled. "It's a gift you have. You should embrace your ability to take away life. You're very, very good at it."

Niccolo clenched his fists. "Fuck off, Drayden. I don't feel like chatting."

He shrugged. "I'm just making the rounds, seeing how all the prisoners are."

Niccolo stilled, trying to master his expression and knowing he was failing. Had he been to see Jade? She was injured and they'd cuffed her.

God...they'd *cuffed* her.

Drayden laughed. "Damn, man, it's all over your face. You got it bad for the little faerie girl, don't you?" He sobered and blinked slowly. "That's actually really good to know. She's a real little hellcat, by the way." He touched his chest where the hawthorn bullet had hit him. "Bet she's great in the sack."

Rage bloomed again from the center of his stomach and Niccolo fought to control it. "The lowest living creature is a traitor, Dray. You know that. You betrayed me once. Almost got me killed. I can let that slide. But what you're doing now, helping the Dominion...threatening Jade." Niccolo shook his head. "Drayden, you're going down for this. I'll kill you for this."

"I don't know if you've noticed this, but the only people who are going down are you, Adam and your pretty little girlfriend."

"Dray, it's not too late. Let us free and we can work together to stop whatever the Dominion has planned."

Something flickered in his eyes for the briefest of moments. Drayden looked away and when he looked back that familiar arrogant glint had returned. The split second of hope Niccolo had died.

"Now why would I want to do that?" Dray asked. "The Dominion are giving me far more of what I need than the Embraced ever have...more than anyone ever has."

"You help let them in and they'll ransack this place. You know that. All those pretty things they've promised you, Drayden? None of it will matter in the world they want to create. They'll make this place a living hell."

He only turned and walked away. "Have a good rest, Niccolo."

Chapter Nine

Jade had lost track of the days. They ran together in her windowless prison. She didn't know what time it was or even if it was day or night. It didn't matter if her eyes were open or if they were closed. It didn't matter if she slept or remained awake.

She tried to count days by the times Dray's flunkies brought food and water, or injected Adam with his drugs or a dosage of blood to keep him from going bloodhungry and insane.

It didn't work. She had no sense of how long they'd been imprisoned.

At least she wasn't bound. She had vague, hazy, terror-inducing memories of that. She'd been of no use to them trying to rip her own arms off and then passing out, so they'd encased her in this moving bubble of energy instead.

Drayden had effectively leashed her.

She'd tried everything from employing her miniscule amount of magick on the bubble to running flat out across the room to break out of it. The former had given her a migraine and the latter had only knocked her on her ass, but she still tried over and over.

Now she reclined on the couch and closed her eyes, for the thousandth time pitching her awareness out to feel the bubble that surrounded her, searching for a weakness or tear, anything that she might be able to exploit.

All she found was smooth, impermeable energy. It felt like steel encasing her.

Frustrated, she opened her eyes and glanced over at Adam. Jade felt sure they'd put him the same room with her to frustrate them both. They didn't trust Adam to an energy bubble. Drayden likely feared his other form. Instead they kept him chained.

Constant, bleeding cuts had formed on Adam's arms, where the iron rubbed his skin. They kept him drugged, too. Sometimes, when he was due for another infusion of whatever drug they were shooting him full of, he'd be lucid. It was the only time they could talk. He'd been defanged in a major way.

When they could talk, they were careful what they said. They didn't know if anyone was listening in.

She'd asked about Kara, but Adam had told her of the unique relationship between an Embraced and his or her familiar. Kara could go without food or water for a very long time, feeding from a mystical bond. Apparently, the bottom line was that Kara would live if Niccolo lived.

God, where was he? *Did he still live?*

Jade's throat choked with emotion. Their guards never spoke to them and when she asked…*screamed* at them to tell her where he was, they still remained mute. Drayden hadn't visited her since that first day and she almost wanted him to, if only so she could try to get information about Niccolo's whereabouts out of him.

In her fantasies she penetrated the bubble the moment Drayden entered the room and then tortured the information out of him.

Across the room, Adam roused from his drug-induced stupor, rolling his blond head to the side. A growth of beard concealed his face. Jade had been also trying to measure the passage of time by the length of Adam's beard. His blue eyes blinked, unclouded and focused on her.

She rose from the couch and went as close to him as she could.

"Jade," he rasped at her.

"Adam." She offered a smile.

"We have to get out of here," he gasped.

Her smile faded. Gee, that was news.

Jade figured the time hadn't worn on him as it had worn on her, since he spent most of his time drugged. To him, it likely felt they'd only been imprisoned a day or so.

"I'm working on getting us out," she responded tiredly. What a lie.

He shook his head. "Help is coming."

Jade frowned. Maybe he was still under the influence of the drugs. He was talking gibberish now.

He shook his head again at the look on her face. "No, you don't understand," he said haltingly. "Dreamwalkers. I contacted Fate. They're sending help."

Jade's eyes widened in surprise and hope. Waiting around to be rescued wasn't something she liked very much, but she'd take what she could get at this point. "But...how?"

Adam shook his head again. "They mistook the dosage...last time. It wasn't enough to keep me from..." he trailed off.

"Traveling," she finished from him.

He nodded tiredly. "Be ready."

"I've been ready to get out of here the moment we entered, Adam."

He smiled.

Just then the door to the room opened and the guards walked in, carrying a syringe full of Adam's next dose. Jade retreated to the couch and watched as they administered it to Adam.

In the next few moments Adam's head drooped as the drug took hold. Soon he was back to insensibility.

Jade leaned her head back into the cushions. Alone again. She closed her eyes and sought her prison again for any kind of a weakness or crack. Carefully, slowly, she scanned from edge to edge. One of the few abilities she had was hyper-awareness of her surroundings and, anyway, it wasn't like she had anything else to do.

* * * * *

Drayden watched Mr. Jones approach with trepidation. The nothingness in its eyes always made him feel uneasy. Right now all that evil blackness was focused right on him.

"They're here," drawled Mr. Jones.

Shit. Mr. Jones knew Drayden had Niccolo, Adam and Jade. "They're here and they're secure. They won't be bothering you any longer, Mr. Jones."

Mr. Jones' thin lips pursed. It walked toward Drayden, its boot heels clicking on the marble floor of Drayden's office. "But they're not dead."

"I didn't see fit—"

"They're not dead."

"I didn't think it would be wise—"

"They're. Not. Dead."

Drayden paused and drew a careful breath. This creature had the ability to thrust him into his worst nightmares. He needed to watch himself. "They're neutralized, sir."

Mr. Jones shook its head. "The only acceptable state for them is dead."

"I thought perhaps we could get some information from them."

"Don't lie to yourself, Drayden, and especially don't lie to me. They're still alive because you want to torment them—one of them, perhaps all of them. They're still alive because you want to disobey me, or because they're your people. In any case, they're still alive because you want them to be."

"They will not trouble you, sir."

"They're troubling me right now, Drayden."

Mr. Jones took another step toward him and Drayden willfully stifled the urge to step back away.

"This was a simple thing I asked of you," said Mr. Jones softly. "Something I shouldn't have to bother with now. These individuals are like gnats that need to be swatted. This should not have been a major operation. I should not have to take care of *your* little details."

The thing pushed past him, reaching out to take a pistol loaded with hawthorn bullets from Drayden's desk as it passed.

Damn it. Jones was going to kill them all. They wouldn't have a chance. Niccolo and Adam were helpless as babes, since they were drugged and chained up. Jade was in her little energy prison with nowhere to flee.

Emotions coursed through Drayden in a jumbled flood. He should let Jones do it. He really should. Hell, if he fought Jones over it he'd lose everything he'd been working toward.

He should've never risked this in the first place.

Drayden pressed a palm to his eye. He should've just killed them when he'd first captured them, but he could hear this other little voice way deep inside him. That voice didn't seem to be listening to logic or Drayden's desire for self-preservation.

They're my people, the voice whispered. *The Embraced. My people to torment, mine to kill.*

Not the Dominion's.

The second voice proved stronger and Drayden lunged forward, catching Mr. Jones' shoulder and whirling it around before it could leave the room. Even the civilized gray tweed of Jones' jacket felt nauseating.

Mr. Jones simply backhanded him, sending Drayden careening back through the room to land against his desk. Pain exploded across his face and blood trailed into his mouth. He shook his head, willing the world back into place. Mr. Jones was a lot stronger than he'd first surmised.

He blinked, seeing Mr. Jones walk through the door. Dray narrowed his eyes and launched himself after it.

If anyone was going to kill Niccolo, Adam and Jade, it was damn well going to be him.

He followed Mr. Jones down the hall and slipped into the room where Adam and Jade were being kept. He hit a series of buttons on the keypad by the door, releasing Jade from her bubble.

The instant he turned around, a strong hand closed around his throat, bearing him back against the wall behind him. Drayden blinked and choked at the same time, seeing Jade's icy eyes narrowed at him, a satisfied expression on her beautiful face.

Oh, shit. This just got better and better.

"God, I wish I had a camera right now," Jade growled in a low voice. "The look on your face is priceless."

Drayden ineffectually choked out a warning. It would be mere moments until Mr. Jones found this room. His eyes bugged out as she tightened her grip.

"*Shut up*," she commanded. "You don't speak unless I allow it."

Fuck! Precious moments were passing while she asserted her dominance!

Just then the door slammed open and Mr. Jones stormed in looking like a college professor with a fist full of essays he'd given Fs, only instead of a handful of papers, there was the gun.

A really big-ass gun loaded with hawthorn.

Mr. Jones raised it to Jade's temple and Drayden watched her face go from irritated to pissed off to comprehending.

And then she moved.

Moved wasn't really the right word to use for what she did, but Drayden didn't know any other. The gun fired and Jade moved to the side faster than he could follow—faster than a vamp...faster than the fucking bullet.

Drayden slumped down to the floor at the sudden rush of blood into his head. He sat choking while Jade turned and plowed straight into Mr. Jones.

They struggled with each other. Dray watched Jade land a few punches that didn't seem to faze Jones. In the melee, Jade grabbed Mr. Jones by the lapels and pulled it down to the ground with her. The gun slid from its grasp and Drayden lunged forward to grab it. His hand closed around the cold metal a split second before Jones' hand closed over his.

Dray looked up into Jones' eyes. They'd gone blacker, otherworldly and cold. Drayden glimpsed the Dominion in them...and they were *really* ticked.

Drayden rolled to the side, gripping the gun as hard as he could. Jones roared and came after him.

"Jade! Get Adam out!" Drayden yelled.

A moment later and he found himself hurtling through the air, propelled by a pissed-off Jones. He hit the wall, pain exploding through his body. When he crashed to the floor, he was still holding the gun. He raised it and fired point-blank into Jones.

Nothing. Round after round he shot into Jones' chest and still Jones didn't cease its stalk toward him. The thing didn't even slow down.

Drayden dropped the gun to his side, his eyes going wide with terror. The creature was unstoppable.

Jade grabbed a sword off the wall and used it to break the lock on Adam's chains. "You're helping us," she hissed accusingly at Drayden over her shoulder.

"Well, duh. Glad you finally figured that out," he replied. Dray struggled to his feet and inched his way along the wall, trying to get away from Jones.

Adam's chains released with a loud clanking sound and the vamp collapsed onto the floor. It was close to the time when he should've been dosed, so he was more lucid than normal.

Adam looked up at Dray with cold, burning animosity. Drayden stood mesmerized as Adam shifted. In a moment he was staring into the gray eyes of a huge timber wolf.

In the next moment, Mr. Jones backhanded him across the room again. Drayden hit the wall and ended up on the floor for the third time. Pain blossomed all over his body, and he fought to stay conscious. Damn it, he'd let himself become distracted.

His head and shoulder pounding in pain from the impact, he looked up in time to see a gun barrel aimed at his nose. He must have lost the gun as he'd traveled though space for the third time that day.

"Get up," came Mr. Jones' icy, terse command.

Drayden struggled slowly to his feet and spat out blood.

Jones pushed him toward the door. "You're coming with me."

Drayden halted, fear rushing coldly through his body. He remembered what he'd said...they'd make him relive his childhood forever.

The hard muzzle of the gun against the back of his head had him moving again. Frantically, Drayden worked out ways to escape.

Mr. Jones turned at the doorway and surveyed Jade and Adam. "I know when to pick my battles. I'll see you both later."

* * * * *

Jade stood with Adam's warm wolf body pressing against her leg. She watched the manifestation guide Drayden away.

Wow, she was confused.

But she also knew when to pick her battles, and fighting the Dominion's manifestation right now would not be a wise move. They were ill-equipped to take it on right now—despite her formidable rage—with Adam half drugged and Niccolo held captive somewhere.

Beside her, Adam shifted back to his normal form and collapsed to the ground. She went to her knees beside him and laid a hand flat on his bare chest. He let out a gut-deep groan at her touch and closed his hand over hers. Blood crusted his wrist.

"Are you all right?" she asked him, worry creasing her forehead. His normally healthily tanned skin was now sallow. Dark circles marked the skin beneath his blue eyes and his full lips were dry and cracked.

He nodded. "I will be once the drugs wear off." He tried to push to his feet, but Jade held him down.

"No," she chided. "You stay here and recover. I'll go look for Niccolo."

She stood, but Adam caught her hand before she could straighten all the way. "Be careful," he rasped.

"I will," she assured him.

He released her and she left the room, sparing one last look over her shoulder to see Adam lying there with his eyes closed, his breathing shallow.

The house was still and silent. Jade entered a marble- and gold-bedecked foyer cautiously, ready to fight anyone who might feel persuaded to battle on behalf of the now absent Drayden.

Jade didn't understand why Drayden had trapped them, tormented them and then tried to help them escape death at the hands of the manifestation. What was Drayden's purpose in all this? Had he finally found some shred of his conscience? Could it be possible the vamp had any left?

For now Jade put aside her confusion and speculation, instead concentrating on her perilous search through Drayden's home to find Niccolo.

If Niccolo was even still here.

If Niccolo was even still *alive*.

Jade gave her head a sharp shake as if to rid herself of the unpleasant notion, but it didn't work. Fear gnawed at her. If anything had happened to Niccolo, she'd kill Drayden, providing the Dominion hadn't already done that for her.

She searched room after room and came up empty, the dread in her growing by the moment. Finally she stopped in an immense corridor on the third floor and tuned in to her surroundings, reaching out with her mind and her senses to try and find him. Sensing a presence on the fifth floor, she followed it there and opened the door to the room from which it emanated.

Niccolo.

The sight of him hit her first, followed by the heavy scents in the room. *Blood and roses.* Bunches of fresh, deep red roses scattered the room. The sweet scent of them warred with the metallic, cloying scent of blood. Her gaze ate up Niccolo, ignoring the rest. They had him spread-eagle and chained like Adam, but Niccolo looked much worse off. Worse than he'd looked at Harcourt. His hair concealed his face because his head was bowed.

Emotion overriding all thought, Jade rushed toward him, his name rising from her throat with a choke.

Then he looked up.

Jade came to halt in the center of the floor, staring into the coldest eyes she'd ever seen. Nothing of Niccolo seemed to remain in them.

She took a closer look at him. He wore only the dress pants he'd worn to the restaurant the night of their capture and he looked emaciated. How long had they been here? With no way to judge night from day or mark time, she wasn't sure. Perhaps close to a month?

It looked they'd starved Niccolo for the entire time.

She glanced around and reached out to brush her fingertip across the flush of a rose. It came away stained red with fresh blood. She fisted her hand around the bloom, letting the blood run between her fingers.

Sweet Goddess.

They'd taunted him, tried to make him go insane. They'd put in this room and starved him, all the while filling his environment with blood-soaked roses. They'd starved him until he'd gone bloodhungry.

Cold fear washed through her. Had they succeeded? Bloodhungry or insane, either way Niccolo was as dangerous as he could ever be right now.

If Niccolo had been starved and turned loose, he would've been shot like a rabid dog. It was good fortune that he was chained. Maybe she could infuse him with blood and bring him back to himself.

Maybe.

"Niccolo," she queried softly.

A thin, animalistic growl trickled from between his lips. He didn't see her, Jade, now. He saw food.

Jade turned and left the room. She needed to find synth-blood and a way to administer it. She wanted more than anything to touch him, but she didn't even dare do that much.

Jade searched the now silent and near empty house for what she needed. Finally, she had packages of synth-blood to last an army for six months. She could find no way to administer the blood, and knew she'd have to do it by hand.

Cursing Drayden under her breath, she popped the top of the first package, readying it to feed to Niccolo.

"You know that might not work," said Adam in a low voice from the doorway.

She fumbled the package for a moment. She'd been so intent on what she'd been doing, she hadn't heard him approach.

"Yeah." She paused. "I know."

Adam limped into the room and came up behind her as she cautiously approached Niccolo, who looked at them both with narrowed, alert eyes. If Niccolo had been free, they'd both be dead, Jade had no doubt.

It made cold dread curl through her stomach to see Niccolo look at her that way. It made her realize how much she'd come to care for him in the time she'd known him. She hadn't formed a bond in a long time, but it appeared she had one with Niccolo. Jade could tell by the way she hurt so much now.

As she stood there staring at Niccolo, probably with a stricken expression on her face, Adam eased the package of synth-blood from her fingers. "It's okay. I'll do it," he said gently.

She looked at him and blinked. It took a moment for her to understand what he'd said. By the time she comprehended, Adam had already moved to Niccolo.

Niccolo strained against the chains, growling at Adam, tempted by the scent of food so near him.

Jade doubted it was the synth-blood he wanted.

Carefully, Adam placed the mouth of the package to Niccolo's lips. Niccolo took what was offered, drinking it down as quickly as he was able.

All the while Adam fed him, he talked to him of things of the past and people they knew. Adam spoke with caring and gentleness. It was a side of Adam that Jade had never seen. Adam was an attractive vamp, playful and seemingly carefree. She had never really stopped to wonder if there was anything deeper to him. Now she suspected that his playful and carefree nature might mask an entirely different Adam. Perhaps the Adam he'd been long ago, before he'd been Embraced.

Package after package disappeared down Niccolo's throat and, little by little, more of what made Niccolo a person with feelings and a soul returned to his eyes. Even though Niccolo still didn't yet seem capable of speech, more and more, Jade relaxed.

Finally, Niccolo consumed the last pack.

Jade had retreated by then to a chair near the door. Adam laid the empty pack with the others and turned toward her wearing an exhausted expression on his face. "Now we wait."

Her gaze traveled to Niccolo, who had bowed his head once more. His breath seemed to be quicker now that his body was metabolizing the blood he'd been given. Suddenly Jade felt filled with raw, cold gut-clenching rage. If Drayden had been anywhere in the house, he'd been dead at this moment, regardless of the help he'd given them.

She felt a light touch on her arm and flinched. Jade looked up to see Adam staring down at her, concern evident on his handsome face.

She glanced away, willed her grasp on the arms of the chair to ease and the hatred to fade from her gaze.

Adam settled on the floor near her with a groan. "Are you all right?"

She snorted. "I should be the one asking you that, Adam. You got the worst end of this deal."

"Niccolo got the worst end," he corrected her.

"Yes."

"I care for him, too, Jade. Don't worry. We'll get him back. If he'd gone any longer without help, it might have been too late." He sighed tiredly and winced. "But I think we got here in time."

She stood staring at him for a moment, then stood without a word and sought a first-aid kit. When she returned, she sat down on the floor near Adam and gently took a wrist into her fingers to clean and wrap in a bandage.

"You don't need to do that," said Adam in a soft voice. "I'll heal it up pretty fast."

"I can help prevent you from scarring by doing this. Anyway…I need to do something while we wait."

They lapsed into silence for a while until Adam said, "You're coming to truly care about him, aren't you? I mean, care more than the normal amount."

She shrugged, happy he'd left the word *love* out of his question. "Niccolo has been so tormented already in his life, it makes me angry to see more of it heaped on him. He doesn't deserve it. He's a good man."

"Torment is something you know a lot about, don't you?"

She paused in her work and looked up at him sharply. "How would you know that?"

"Easy now." He smiled. "I guessed. Not even a guess, really. It's in your eyes. They look the same as Niccolo's. You two share more than your bodies with each other, I can see that."

She turned her gaze away from him, back to bandaging his wrist. It was true that she and Niccolo reflected past hurts back at each other. They were kindred in that way. It was something most wouldn't be able to understand, wouldn't be able to relate to. In this, she and Niccolo were very well suited. They could understand each other's grief.

"It takes one to know one," she mumbled at Adam.

Adam chuckled. "Me? I'm having fun, darlin'. I'm far from tormented."

Jade looked up and held his gaze steadily. He probably didn't realize she'd read his file and knew better. She reached up and laid a hand to his bearded cheek. "Bullshit," she responded simply.

The smile faded from his sensual mouth. He glanced away. "Yeah, okay, so I've known my fair share of tragedy, but let's be honest… It's not a drop in the bucket compared to what's reflected in Niccolo's eyes." He paused. "Or your eyes."

She knew things about Adam most didn't, thanks to the information provided by the Order of the Morrigan. Adam had been married once. He'd had a family. He'd lost all of them in one tragic incident, when a drifter had come to his home while he'd been away. His wife had been raped and murdered. His children, a seven-year-old boy and a four-year-old girl, had been slain. Adam had been the one to find them.

It seemed not many got by in this life without the touch of tragedy on their shoulder.

Adam seemed lost for a moment, perhaps caught in a web of memories. His normal jocularity had completely disappeared.

Jade finished wrapping his wrists and scooted back away from him. She sighed and pushed a hand through her hair. "I didn't mean to bring back bad memories."

Adam held her gaze for a moment before speaking. "Bring them back? They never go away. Not really."

"Then…I'm sorry," she said, at a loss for words.

A smile broke over his face and his eyes lit up with their usual good-natured glint. "Hey, that's life, darlin'. It's never boring."

Behind them, Niccolo groaned. Jade turned and watched him raise his head. She pushed to her feet and walked toward him, but Adam rose and put a firm hand on her shoulder, stilling her in the center of the floor.

"Niccolo?" she asked from afar. "Are you all right?"

Niccolo moved his arms, making the chains clank. "Let me free," he grumbled.

Adam's grip on her shoulder relaxed and she moved to Niccolo. Approaching him carefully, she searched his eyes. The animal was gone, replaced once again by the man she knew.

"Niccolo," she breathed. "Thought we lost you for a minute there."

A smiled flickered over his mouth. "Never."

She laid a kiss to his lips, tasting the synth-blood on them and feeling the scrape of his beard. He growled and pressed his mouth to hers, searching out a deeper contact. He nipped at her lower lip in a barely restrained, primitive way that made her shudder with both apprehension and arousal at the same time.

Jade could taste synth-blood in his mouth, but his body's chemistry made it sweet. Anyway, what Niccolo tasted like was of no importance. Goddess, she was so happy he'd recovered that tears stung her eyes.

She broke the kiss and backed away from him, her fingers going immediately to the locks on the chains that bound him. The chains fell to the floor.

Niccolo lunged toward her so quickly that fear spiked up her spine. For a moment she thought that Niccolo had somehow tricked them, that he really had gone insane from the bloodhunger and meant to kill her now. Instead, he caught her up against him, his hand tangling in her hair and his body pressing intimately into the curve of hers.

Jade's breath left her in a rush. Relief and happiness overwhelmed her. She closed her eyes and embraced him, burying her face in the tangle of his hair. They were both unwashed, their bodies and minds ravaged from their imprisonment, but for this moment none of that mattered.

"They cuffed you," Niccolo whispered. "All I could think about until I couldn't think anymore was that they'd cuffed you."

"They uncuffed me," she murmured. "Uncuffed me and put me in a different kind of prison. I was fine."

He took her wrists in his hands and pushed her sleeves up, revealing the thin white scars that remained where she'd tried to saw her own hands off through the cuffs. He looked up from her hands with a look of cold rage, the look his enemies saw right before they never saw anything else. The hair on the back her neck stood up, even though she knew the look was not for her.

"Where's Drayden?" he asked. A world of meaning seemed to exist in those two words.

"He's the reason we're free," she answered evenly.

A quizzical look crossed his face.

"The manifestation wanted to kill Adam and I," she explained. "Drayden tried to warn us before that could happen." She shrugged. "He had a change of heart, or... I don't know. Something happened to convince Drayden he wanted us alive."

"As much as I hate to say it," said Adam behind them. "We owe our lives to Drayden Lex right now. I did manage to contact Gabriel through Fate and Penny. They were coming to break us out, but they would not have made it in time."

"Bastard," swore Niccolo. "We wouldn't be in this mess at all if it weren't for him."

"The manifestation fled and took Dray with him," continued Adam. "I think Jade's speed shocked the manifestation and it figured out killing us wasn't going to be so easy after all."

"The house is empty," Jade broke in. "Seems like all Dray's flunkies fled. Still, we need to get the hell out of here."

"Anytime," answered Niccolo.

They left Drayden's place and made it back to Niccolo's apartment. As soon as they walked in the door, Kara came scampering out of one of the bedrooms. Niccolo scooped her up and nuzzled her. She seemed none the worse for wear, perhaps a bit thinner.

While Niccolo and Adam spoke with Gabriel about what had happened, Jade took a long, hot shower. She felt like she could sleep for a week.

She wrapped herself in a thick robe and drank a cup of hot tea while Adam and Niccolo both took showers and cleaned themselves up. Her eyelids grew heavier as she sat cuddled with Kara on the sofa, clean and warm and more content than she'd been in a long time.

Before she knew what was happening, she'd dozed off and Niccolo was plucking the dangerously tilting tea-filled mug from her lax fingertips. She felt him lift her and protested a little, but she was too tired to care that he was carrying her into the bedroom. In a way, she had to admit that part of her enjoyed it—the same part of her that enjoyed the way he could make her submissive to him during sex.

Niccolo put her in bed, turned out the light and slid in beside her. He wrapped his arms around her and she snuggled into his body, rubbing her cheek against his smoothly shaven jaw and burying her nose in his still damp, clean hair.

"Sleep, *cara mia*," he murmured into her ear.

"Mmmm, hmmm."

A rumble of contentment rose up and out from his body even as she sighed in happiness. Jade felt warm and safe and almost loved. It was the most satisfied she could ever remember feeling.

The heavy hands of fatigue pulled her down until she relaxed into slumber.

She awoke to pleasure. A skillful, questing tongue laved her pussy, licking her in long, sure strokes. Jade gasped as Niccolo brought her straight from sleep and into a gentle, powerful climax. Her body stiffened as the waves of it rolled over her. Niccolo delved his tongue up into the heart of her, groaning in his throat. Her sex convulsed in pleasure under his treatment.

"I'm sorry," he said, pulling away for a moment. "I needed to taste you. I couldn't wait."

Jade's breath came fast and heavy. She stifled an insane urge to laugh. Sorry? He was sorry?

She looked down the length of her body. He'd undone her robe, leaving her bare from head to toe. She smiled. "Come here."

Niccolo crawled up, settling himself between her parted thighs. She felt the brush of the head of his cock against her opening. Suddenly, she needed him. She didn't want foreplay, no preamble beyond what he'd already given her.

She just needed to feel *him*.

Jade shifted her hips and pushed up against him. The head of his cock slipped into her body and she sighed in contentment, even as Niccolo grunted in surprise. He thrust his hips forward automatically and his hands found her waist as he sunk into her as far as he'd go.

Her back arched and she hissed out in pleasure as he began to move. He rocked his hips back and forth, rubbing the long, thick and ridged length of him in and out of her sensitive slit. His chest brushed against her swollen breasts with every stroke.

Jade whimpered in pleasure and held him close to her. She set her teeth to his shoulder and bit down just a little. He answered her with a shudder and a groan.

He thrust balls-deep within her and stayed that way, allowing them both to enjoy the sensation of being so intimately joined. In that moment, there was nowhere else in the whole world Jade wanted to be, and no one else she wanted to be with.

She tilted her head to the side, offering the smooth expanse of her throat to him. "Please," she murmured. She wanted to sustain him. Jade wanted her blood to help him heal. She wanted them to be joined even closer than they were already — at vein as well as at sex.

He brushed his lips across her skin, followed by the scrape of his fangs. The inexorable thrust of his cock within her had another climax flirting with her body even as he bit and the glamour rolled over her, plunging her into a haze of ecstasy. Niccolo grasped her hips and drew on her blood as his strokes became faster, harder and deeper.

Finally, he broke his hold on her throat and tipped his head back as he came inside her. Jade came in the same moment and together they moaned in a thick wash of pleasure.

Niccolo cradled her in his arms afterward and she found didn't have the will to pull away from him. Instead, she let his body heat comfort her as she drowsed, contented and satisfied.

He took her hand in his and traced her scars with a gentle finger. "You know you need to get over this hurt, Jade," he said softly.

She resisted the urge to take her wrist from him. "What do you mean? The wounds are healed now."

He wrapped his big hand around her slender wrist. It looked so delicate in his grasp. She knew he could crush the bones to dust if he wanted. He shook his head. "No, they're not. They're not healed inside. Because of that they'll always pose a danger to you. Do you trust me?" he asked as he tightened his grip.

Cold fear washed through her. "Yes," she pushed out with effort.

"Your fears could kill you one day, Jade. Do you realize that? What if Dray hadn't taken the cuffs off you? What would you have done?"

She shook her head. "Chewed off my own hands, perhaps, like a wolf caught in a trap."

Niccolo nodded sadly. "You see then... A fear that could kill you. We don't know Drayden's intentions now. He's a question mark, but he knows one of your weaknesses. Don't you think it would be better to eliminate it?"

He'd begun to rub her wrist, even as he held it prisoner. The gentle touch of his skin against hers calmed the beating of her heart, even though she hated the fear that burned in the back of her throat.

She nodded slowly. "But how?"

He reached over and took her opposite wrist. She jerked it away, but he held on, rubbing little circles on her flesh with his thumb. "By replacing bad memories with good ones. But to do it, you'll have to trust me. Tell me again that you trust me, Jade. Say the whole sentence to me." He wed her wrist to the first one and held them both in one of his massive, capable hands. "Say it," he said again, his voice a little harsher.

"I—I trust you, Niccolo." Her voice shook and her heart beat fast. All she wanted in the world was to rip her wrists from his grasp. She could feel perspiration break out on her brow.

"You don't sound sure." He propped himself up, holding her wrists above her head. Gently, he pressed them down onto the pillow and lowered his head toward her breast. Right before his sensual lips closed over a rosy-tipped nipple he said, "Tell me again."

She gasped in pleasure at the feel of his tongue on her nipple and arched her back. For a full heartbeat she forgot about her restrained wrists. "I trust you," she cried out.

He moved to the other breast, this time tightening his hold on her wrists until it almost hurt. "Again," he murmured, his lips brushing against her hardened nipple as he uttered the word.

"I trust you, Niccolo," she managed to say steadily and with conviction right before his hot mouth enveloped the tip of her breast.

He laved and sucked at it until her clit plumped and her sex grew heavy and aroused. He skated her to the edge of an orgasm with his tongue on her breast alone, but before she could climax he drew away and released her wrists.

Jade felt relief at the fact she was now free, and yet felt sad that the release of her wrists had meant the removal of the pleasure. She watched with wary eyes as Niccolo got up and searched out two long silk scarves and returned to the bed with them in hand.

"What are you going to do with those?" she asked suspiciously. Her arousal was fading just at the sight of them and what she thought he meant to do with them.

He said nothing as he laid them on the bed and lit the three candles around the room. The warm glow of their light felt calming, but her anxiety seemed to be growing nonetheless.

"Niccolo..." she said in a voice of warning.

He picked up the ties and drew them across his palms over and over as he stared down at her. The candlelight flickered over his body in a pleasing way, warming his already warm-toned skin and turning it coppery. "You said you trusted me. Did you lie?"

"No. I just want to know your intentions."

"My intention is to show you that sometimes when you're restrained it can be a good thing, an exciting thing...a pleasurable thing. My intention is to replace the bad memories you have of being restrained with good ones." He lifted a dark brow. "*Very* good ones. My intention is to spend the entire night doing it."

Oh Goddess.

She closed her eyes briefly as a feeling of longing welled up from deep inside her. Jade wanted to trust him, but she wasn't sure she could do it. Desire and trepidation swirled within her. Part of her wanted to offer herself up to him and tell him he could do as he willed with her, and the other part wanted to run screaming from the apartment.

"Trust yourself to me, Jade," Niccolo said in a low, soft voice. "Trust your body to me and don't be afraid. I'll only make you happy. I promise you that with all I am."

She closed her eyes for a moment and gritted her teeth. "I don't know if I can do this, Niccolo."

He stared down at her, unspeaking, unmoving. "You must, Jade. It's important that you shed this fear. When I was chained at Dray's all I could think of was you in those handcuffs and what you'd do. I couldn't stop wondering if your fears would end up killing you before Dray even had the chance."

She swallowed hard and extended her arms out on either side. "Let's try," she whispered hoarsely. He was right. She needed to be brave and defeat this fear, or one day it could be used against her. If that happened, it could mean the end of her.

A satisfied smile curved Niccolo's mouth. "There's the brave woman I know you are. I love that so much about you, Jade."

The words *love* and *you* in the same sentence jarred her. She turned her face to the side and pushed away the tumult of confusing emotions she felt at them.

"I need to tell you something," Niccolo said.

She turned back to him. "What?" He sounded so serious.

"I know what happened to you. I know about the shifters who kidnapped you. I know what they did to you."

Cold terror washed through her, followed by anger. She pushed up into a sitting position. "How?"

Niccolo pushed a hand through his hair. "I broke into the headquarters of the Priestesses of the Morrigan here in New York City and checked out your file."

"Bastard," she breathed. She tried to slide off the bed, but he was there. He pressed her back onto the mattress and covered her body with his. She struggled for a moment, but he felt like a rock on top of her and she went limp.

"Stay still and listen to me for a minute," he growled. "I only did it because of the way you acted that first time, Jade. You were so damned afraid of me. I only wanted to help you. In order to help you I had to know what was wrong, and you weren't talking."

She felt tears sting her eyes and she didn't know why. Was it because he'd gone behind her back and snooped into her past, or because she actually felt happy he knew about it and hadn't run in the other direction.

"How did you know it was something that had happened to me in my past that caused the reaction?" she whispered, on the edge of crying.

He lifted up, caught her gaze and drew a hand through his hair. "It was in your eyes. It was obvious."

She squeezed her eyes shut for a moment and felt a teardrop trail down her temple. Niccolo caught it on a fingertip.

His gaze grew hard. "If they were still alive, if you hadn't tracked them down... I would, Jade. You know that I would."

She nodded and blinked away tears.

"All I wanted when I read your file was to tear those men from limb to limb...and hold you tight." He dipped his head and kissed her. "So," he murmured against her lips. "We both discovered a secret."

"I snooped into your past, too. We're even," she murmured, feeling the tears recede. A part of her felt relieved that Niccolo knew. She felt tired, too, emotionally drained.

"If, one day, you ever want to talk about it..." he trailed off. "I want to be the one you come to, Jade."

"Why?"

He smiled and it made something in her stomach hitch. "I've grown to like you, *cara mia*, like you a lot."

"Same here."

"Mutual like. Well, that's a good start," he replied. "Not necessary where I want to end with you." He reached over and grabbed a tie off the bed. It hung between them like a promise.

The silk scarves felt cool and soft against her wrists as Niccolo tied first one and then the other to the bedposts. Fear clenched in her stomach and the familiar bile burned in the back of her throat. It made her muscles shake and ache at the same time. She drew long breaths in through her nose and blew them out through her mouth.

Niccolo hushed her, trying to calm her, and drew his hands over her body, up her legs and torso, over her arms, across her face and back down again. It was a gentling touch, a soothing massage. He did this over and over until her heartbeat slowed and the taste of metallic fear in the back of her throat had thickened and transformed to something sweeter.

Soon the trembling from her barely restrained fear gave way to a different sort of trembling. Soon her pussy grew swollen and damp and her nipples peaked red and hard on her breasts. Soon her body yearned for a different kind of touching, one less calming and more exciting. Still, Niccolo passed his hands over her, caressing.

She began to forget her wrists were bound at all. Yet in the back of her mind she knew that if Niccolo wished to harm her, rather than give her pleasure, she wouldn't be reacting this way. She knew that if anyone but Niccolo had her bound, she'd be panicking. But maybe by Niccolo doing as he did now, her terror wouldn't be as great.

Niccolo perhaps sensed her rising sexual need because instead of stroking her breasts, he palmed them, pinching and teasing the nipples until Jade squirmed on the bed beneath him. The scarves tightened around her wrists with her movement, sending her into a panic for a moment. Niccolo hushed her and she drew long, deep and even breaths once more in an effort to control her fear.

He resumed the caress of her breasts until she writhed again and moaned. Her clit pulsed between her thighs, demanding attention, but Niccolo refrained from touching her there. He clearly meant to bring her to the edge of a climax by stimulating her breasts first. Jade had to admit he was coming close. Every nerve in her body seemed to have flared to glorious life. Her breath and heart rate became faster and it had little to do with the scarves.

"You see, Jade?" Niccolo murmured. "Good things can happen when you're bound."

"Bound by the right man, you mean," she answered breathlessly.

A smile curved his lips. A moment later he dropped his head to her breast and pulled a nipple into his mouth, running it gently through his teeth. Jade cried out and arched her back. The small bit of pain after so much pleasure sent her spiraling deliciously close to an orgasm.

He nipped and licked his way down her stomach slowly, delving his tongue into her belly button and dragging it over her mound to her sex.

He didn't touch her pussy. Instead, he spread her thighs wide and kissed up from the inside of her knee to the place where her leg joined her sex. Jade squirmed and moaned and had words of begging on the tip of her tongue by the time he leaned in to lap at her needy, swollen clit.

"Niccolo," Jade breathed. "Oh Goddess, yes, Niccolo."

The fact that he'd denied her stimulation there for so long only increased the pleasure now. Her hips bucked forward and he held her forcibly in place as he sucked the small bit of aroused flesh between his lips and massaged it. Right before her body braced to climax, Niccolo shifted downward and speared his tongue into the center of her. He made a sound of pleasure deep in his throat and lapped at her there, consuming every bit of her cream like she was the best thing he'd ever tasted.

Jade tried to spread her thighs farther apart in an effort to allow Niccolo into her body even deeper than he already was. She wanted to feel his cock inside her. She wanted to feel him filling her up as much as possible, but she had no say in what he did now. Her hands were bound and, with it, her ability to maintain control.

That thought should have frightened her, but it did not. Her excitement and trust of Niccolo had drowned the fear out.

He licked her from anus to clit in long, steady, slow strokes. Jade bucked and twisted under the teasing, tortuous sensations, but Niccolo held her in place firmly, hands on her inner thighs and pressing them down onto the bed so she couldn't move.

At last, he sucked her clit into his mouth once more and teased it with his tongue. Finally, he allowed the climax to wash over her body. It slammed full force into her like a tidal wave of pleasure. For a moment she couldn't think, couldn't even remember her own name, if someone had asked her. She felt lost to pure ecstasy under Niccolo's hands and mouth.

As the waves of pleasure ebbed, he entered her. She felt him sink balls-deep into her and she arched her back in response. He pulled out and eased into her once more, pressing her hips down into the mattress, and filling her up so beautifully she wanted to weep.

In her ear, he murmured her name over and over. It was a salve for the fear that simmered in the pit of her stomach. The uneasy feeling that nagged at her, kept part of her pleasure at bay and made her constantly have to fight not to give in to it. This scenario brought back the ghost of memories she didn't want, but the gentle way he took her chased them away every time they came to the forefront of her mind.

He took her slow, deliciously slow.

He took her like she was something precious to be savored. He kept her right on the edge of orgasm, the mind-numbing, insanity-causing edge of it. Niccolo did that deliberately until she wanted to scream from the want of completion. Instead, she whimpered and moved her hips, asking without words that he increase the speed and power of his thrusts.

He took the hint and started to move. All fear of her bindings disappeared in a flood of desire and the need to have him faster and harder inside her. Jade grabbed on to the scarves, braced her feet on the mattress and thrust her hips up, meeting him stroke for stroke.

Her climax washed over her in a flood and she screamed as it stole her ability to do anything but experience it. Niccolo exploded in his own climax within her. His breathing harsh in her ear, he groaned out his pleasure. Smiling, Jade enjoyed every moment of it.

They lay tangled together, breathing heavily. Jade closed her eyes and felt the steady thump of her heart. Goddess, she'd been tied the whole time...and she'd loved it.

"Thank you," Jade heard herself whisper hoarsely.

Niccolo moved at the sound of her voice and untied her bonds. He rolled her over and pulled her against him, scattering kisses on her face and over her throat. "I just wanted to show you that sometimes being tied can mean pleasure instead of pain," he murmured.

"You did show me that."

She had no illusions. If Drayden ever cuffed her again, she'd still panic, but perhaps less so. Maybe next time she'd be able to think back on this experience and be able to calm herself and think clearly. Maybe she'd be able to think back on this one time when the man she cared about had bound her in love.

That last thought made her breath hitch, made her go still in Niccolo's arms.

Love.

What she felt for Niccolo came dangerously near to that. A caring so deep it was almost love. She remembered how she'd feared for him at Drayden's, how much she'd wanted blood when she'd seen what the bastards had done to him.

Disturbed by the direction her thoughts had turned, she pulled away from Niccolo, stood and pulled a robe on. "I need some water." She needed a little distance more. "Do you want anything?"

Niccolo shook his head slightly, his eyes nearly closed. She took a moment to allow her gaze to sweep over him lying in bed. The sheets tangled him from the waist down and he'd flung one well-muscled arm over his head.

She tore her gaze away from the lovely sight and headed to the kitchen. Jade pulled a glass from the cabinet and set on the counter, then opened the refrigerator and pulled out a jug of purified water. When she closed it, a figure stood near her, next to the counter.

Startled, Jade jumped and nearly lost her grip on the jug. Warm fingers closed over hers, steadying her grasp.

"Sorry," Adam said. "I didn't mean to scare you. I heard someone out in the kitchen and came out to see."

Jade drew a steadying breath, brushing off her scare, and turned to pour herself some water. "Can't sleep?" she asked him.

"No. I keep having nightmares about being drugged and feeling helpless."

"Want some water?" she asked, as though that would make it better. She glanced at him through the darkness of the kitchen and saw him nod.

Jade pulled down another glass, filled it and handed it to him. Then she turned and leaned against the counter, sipping her drink. It tasted sweet and felt deliciously cold as it trailed down her throat.

Adam took a long drink of water while they remained companionably silent in the night-darkened kitchen. Finally, Adam spoke. "You were the only thing that kept me sane, I think. Those times you talked to me when I was most lucid, I mean."

"We kept each other sane."

He nodded. "How's Niccolo?"

She shrugged. "He's good, nearly totally recovered."

"He's the strongest vamp I ever met. He saved my life once, before he went to prison. I'd had my throat slit by a bunch of rogue vamps, slit ear to ear so deep and so bad that I was going to die. Niccolo's blood is the only thing that saved me. It helped me heal faster than I could on my own, faster than I could lose blood. I owe him a lot."

She nodded. "A lot of people owe their lives to Niccolo," she answered softly. So did she, after a fashion. "He's a good man."

"He is," Adam agreed. "A good man and a good friend."

In silence, she finished her water and set the empty glass on the counter. Adam did the same. When she moved past Adam toward the hallway, he grabbed her arm and pulled her close.

"What the hell—" she started.

"I just need to touch someone," Adam said quickly. "I know you're Niccolo's. I just need contact with another person, simple contact and nothing more."

I know you're Niccolo's. The truth of those words made her stop gently pulling away from Adam. She hated that truth so much. Yet, she couldn't deny it. The knowledge made something hot burn in the back of her throat.

Adam drew her near, his strong arms going around her in an embrace. Jade allowed it. Maybe it was because of what he'd said, about her being Niccolo's. Maybe she had to prove to herself, that she could enjoy the feel of another man.

Adam slid a hand down her back, pressing her to him, and let out a deep, shuddering sigh. She'd noticed tension in his body at first, but now he seemed to be relaxing. She knew that Adam craved the touch of others, perhaps she was now getting a glimpse of why. Maybe in truth Adam was more lonely and afraid than anyone had ever suspected. Maybe his emotional defenses were far more sophisticated than she'd assumed. Jade put her arms around Adam, feeling the tautness leak from his muscles.

After a few heartbeats, Jade relaxed also. She liked the way she fit into the curve of his body. He was a little shorter than Niccolo, though no less broad. She inhaled the spicy, soapy scent of him at the curve where his shoulder met his neck, thinking she understood why so many women seemed attracted to him. He was a strong and striking man, and yet the bravado he displayed hid a tender heart, hid a man in need of love.

When Adam moved his head, she barely noticed it. His lips captured hers softly, yet aggressively and she jerked, startled. His arms tightened minutely stronger around her and she relaxed, giving in to the kiss. She didn't feel for Adam the way she felt for Niccolo, she realized, though the kiss was nice...even exciting.

Her mind reeled at the revelation. By kissing Adam, she felt how much she loved Niccolo. Tears pricked her eyes.

He braced her at the base of her spine, pulling her in toward him as he tasted her lips patiently. He never went any further. He never tried to part her lips for a deeper kiss or allowed his hands to stray from the small of her back. He simply held her and kissed her.

Finally, he let her go and the velvet darkness of the kitchen held them close for a heartbeat as they stared at each other across the short distance separating them. All she could hear was their breath mingling in the soft air.

"Thank you," said Adam quietly.

Jade nodded, a little confused. She turned and went down the hallway toward the bedroom and Niccolo's waiting arms.

Once there, she slid into bed beside him and curled herself around his sleeping warmth. She laid her head against his chest, snuggling against him, and listened to the steady beat of his heart. Jade sighed and closed her eyes, letting sleep tug at her with silken fingers. Although the difference she'd felt when she compared her feelings for Adam and Niccolo during Adam's kiss disturbed her.

I know you're Niccolo's.

Jade stiffened and opened her eyes, sleep suddenly distant. Uncomfortable, she turned and gave Niccolo her back. He reached out in his sleep and drew her against him, tucking her against his chest like a child with his favorite teddy bear.

She started to move away, but he just tightened his grip. Jade relented and relaxed. As she closed her eyes and she finally drifted off to sleep, she couldn't help but think, *Maybe it wouldn't be bad to be his.*

* * * * *

The holo-trans dispatch pulsed through the apartment, signaling an incoming call. Jade set down her cup of java and wandered over to receive it. It was likely Gabriel again. They'd been home two weeks since the ordeal with Dray had ended, and the trail had gone cold with his disappearance. They'd been taking their orders from Gabe, following up on other leads in this region.

She sat down at the terminal and glanced at the identity of the caller. It blinked anonymous. Frowning, she clicked the accept button.

An image of Drayden flickered to life in the center of the unit.

"Think of the devil," Jade murmured.

The transmission showed Drayden from the waist up. His face seemed a little pale, a little more drawn than usual. He appeared to be wearing an expensive gray suit and his blond hair was trimmed and slicked back fashionably from his handsome, strong-jawed face.

His full lips split in a warm smile. "Jade, darling, how have you been?"

Jade closed her blue silk robe more firmly at the top in a nearly unconscious gesture. Drayden always made her skin feel like it wanted to get up and walk away without her. "I thought your partner in crime finally ate you for breakfast, Dray," she said with feigned coolness.

His smile grew wider. "He tried. I escaped."

"What a pity." She shifted in her seat. "What do you want?"

He pretended to think for a moment. "Beside a basket full of kittens and world peace? Why, only to help you and Niccolo, my darling."

Her anger rose to the boiling point quickly. She leaned forward, wishing she could reach in and wring Dray's scrawny little holographic neck. Unfortunately, virtual reality didn't mean that much reality.

"You tried to drive Niccolo insane, you pathetic excuse for an Embraced," she said in a low, threatening voice. "You imprisoned me and Adam. You betrayed your own people. Do you really expect me to believe that you've suddenly switched sides? You really expect me to trust you when you say you want to help us?"

She felt the presence of others behind her and glanced to see Niccolo and Adam standing behind her.

"Ah," said Drayden. "You're both all right. Good."

The bastard sounded genuinely relieved.

"What do you want, Dray?" Niccolo asked. The tone of his voice sent shivers of dread up her spine.

"I have information," Drayden answered simply. No snappy comeback. No bullshit. His voice had turned all business now that Niccolo was here.

"What?" barked Niccolo. "Say it fast. I'm a heartbeat away from hitting the disconnect button."

"I know, and you have every right to do that, seeing how I treated you," answered Drayden. He seemed circumspect toward Niccolo, and almost...guilty.

Jade didn't fall for it, not for a second.

"Okay, here's the deal," Drayden continued. "I was helping Mr. Jones. You know me, I'm all about who has the power and, believe me, Mr. Jones has that. It didn't take me long to realize the error of my ways. I started to see that I'd made a deal with the devil long before Jones ordered that I execute you. When it told me to kill you all, I found that I couldn't do it. What's more, I couldn't let the Dominion murder my own."

"My own?" Adam echoed hollowly. "You turned on *your own*. You hung us out to dry."

Niccolo sighed and shifted impatiently. "Drayden, if you're looking for absolution, you're not going to find it here. We don't have to time to deal with you right now, but once this is over, you're going down."

"Well, then I don't have much to worry about then, do I?" Drayden shot back angrily. "Not when we consider the fact the Embraced are failing miserably in the face of Mr. Jones' plans. Since I've royally pissed off the Dominion and lost my favored standing, I'll be *going down* relatively soon...along with the rest of the Embraced and, eventually, humankind."

Jade really hated to admit that Drayden has a point.

Drayden drew a breath. "So, I really want to tell you what I know in order to make sure we all get through this. *Then* you can take me down, okay?" He cracked a smile. "Or, at least, you can try," he finished cockily.

The room became quiet.

"Okay," Niccolo said finally. "Say what you've got to say."

He shook his head. "In person."

Adam groaned and Jade threw up her hands.

"We don't trust you enough for that Drayden," Niccolo growled. "Do you think we're stupid?"

Drayden grinned, but said nothing. "I'll be in touch soon." The holoscreen went black.

"Asshole," Niccolo breathed.

Jade stared at the black screen for a moment, wondering if Drayden was setting them up for another trap. Her gut told her that he was sincere, that he was telling the truth. He'd gotten in too deep with the Dominion, realized the error of his ways and was now trying to set things to rights.

It didn't make her want to kill him any less, however.

She rose and followed Niccolo and Adam back to the kitchen. Kara followed them, the little bell on her collar making a tinkling sound as she walked.

As Jade warmed her coffee, she snatched an open bag of sugar cookies from the counter. Pulling one out, she leaned back against the counter and nibbled at it, her eyes unfocused as she lost herself in thought about Drayden.

"We'll take any info he's got," said Niccolo near her. "We'll take it and check it out. Use it if it appears to be good. Doesn't mean when this is over we don't hunt him down."

Jade glanced up and watched Adam splay his big hands on the counter. "I don't see that we have any choice," he said. "He was right about one thing, the Embraced and the OtherKin are failing."

Jade swallowed her last bite of cookie, brushed the crumbs from her fingers and retrieved her now warm mug. She shrugged and took a sip. "Well, there's only one single physical conduit for the Dominion and we have no way to track it. It's not easy."

Niccolo ran a hand through his hair and blew out a noisy breath. "We have to keep knocking on doors and running down leads. If Drayden gives us info on Jones, all the better. I don't have to tell either of you to handle Dray with care if you come across him."

"I really don't want to handle him *with care*," Adam grumbled.

Niccolo's eyes went darker. "I'll let you handle him a little more violently when we get through this."

"*If* we get through this," Adam answered.

Chapter Ten

Jade hung on to Niccolo as his bike ripped down the street, the stars shimmering in the night-black sky above them. He seemed like he was one with the piece of outdated machinery beneath him. He and the bike moved like one animal. Fluidly. She could barely tell where one ended and the other began.

She'd been apprehensive when Niccolo had led her down to the garage and told her to climb on, but that unease had soon given way to exhilaration when she realized how fun riding on one of these things could be.

She gripped the heavy black leather of Niccolo's jacket and tilted her head back, enjoying the feel of the wind hitting the exposed skin between the top of her coat and the bottom of the helmet. She could get used to traveling this way. The freedom of it was seductive, almost as much as the man driving the bike.

They were headed down to the wharf to check out another lead, another rumor. Their eyes and ears, the network of Embraced and OtherKin who lived within the city limits told them of suspicious activity and one by one, they checked each incident out, hoping they'd get lucky...hoping for anything they could use against the Dominion and head off the opening of the doorway.

They needed a location.

They needed a timeframe.

They needed *anything*.

Time was running out and everyone knew it. Desperation had become modus operandi.

They turned a corner and open water came into view. Behind them an off-track PTV pulled up behind them. Jade glanced back. It was strange to see a non-commercial off-track down here, so she noted it. It was a pricey black sedan, disturbingly nondescript.

Just then, another one exactly like it pulled out in front of them. The car in front had pulled out at the last possible moment before all three vehicles found themselves flanked on either side by tall steel shipping containers. There was nowhere for the bike to go, and Jade suddenly felt very fragile sandwiched between the two larger vehicles.

Well, this didn't bode well.

Niccolo gunned the bike and tried to pass the car on the right, but the vehicle moved to block him. He moved quickly to the left—blocked again.

The car in front slowed and came to a stop. Niccolo and the driver behind them also brought their vehicles to a halt. Oh, good. They were trapped.

Not liking the way the helmet constricted her view, she removed it.

Niccolo got off the bike and faced her. "They just want to talk," he said.

Jade narrowed her eyes at him. "How do you know that?"

"Because if they didn't, we'd be hurting already. Stay here."

He walked around in front of the bike. The headlight illuminated him for a moment before he walked into the shadows. Two men climbed out of the vehicle in front of them, and Jade heard the doors of the PTV behind them opening and closing.

If Niccolo thought he could command her to stay behind, he was one confused vampire. She swung her leg over, hopped off the bike and followed him. Niccolo had stopped a distance from the group of men. She came up beside him. Their breath showed white in the cold air.

"Jade," Niccolo growled low. "I told you to stay back."

"And I should've listened because…? Before you get all chivalrous on me, I'm a Priestess of the Morrigan, remember? I can handle myself."

He sighed.

Jade sent her awareness out toward the men, probing them as much as she could with her very limited psi abilities. She stiffened. "Shifters," she breathed. "These are OtherKin wolves."

Beside her, Niccolo went tense.

He had to be thinking exactly what she was thinking. What the hell did they want? There were at least ten of them—a whole goddamn pack—and they had them surrounded.

"Get back, Jade," Niccolo ordered in a low, angry voice.

She shook her head. "There are ten wolves here. You can't take them all on by yourself."

"I can injure a few before they injure me."

"Math, Niccolo?" she asked wryly. "Three from ten leaves…"

"Well, since you're refusing to stay out of danger, you can take some, can't you?"

"Yes," she answered.

"Good, because I might have been wrong about them just wanting to talk."

One of them moved forward. The tall, dark-haired shifter slipped a hand into his trench coat and produced a gun.

"Niccolo—" she started, but Niccolo was gone.

Gunfire ripped through the quiet air. She dove to the ground.

The sickening sound of crunching bone filled the air, followed by a man's pain-filled shriek.

Remembering the scene after the car crash, Jade was afraid to look, but she did anyway. She raised her head and saw three of the shifters lying at Niccolo's feet. The salty, metallic tang of blood reached her nostrils on the cold air. One of the men groaned in pain. She didn't think the shifters at Niccolo's feet were dead, but they weren't exactly healthy either.

The leader, the one who'd pulled the gun from his coat, slumped near the door of his car. Blood coursed from the man's nose, and the wolf had the look of a beaten dog. Niccolo now held the weapon.

She glanced around, taking in the six other shifters who hovered around them looking uncertain. A couple of them had shifted, but even they hung back, their ears laid flat against their heads. It appeared that they were afraid to move after seeing how fast Niccolo had taken out the first three wolves and their leader.

Carefully, Jade pushed up from the ground, feeling the grit from the pavement press into her palms. She glanced warily at the wolves near her and left her hands relaxed at her sides. Her own gun lay nestled at the small of her back, underneath her jacket. One of the wolves eyed her speculatively, probably thinking about taking her hostage.

"Touch her and you die," Niccolo growled.

The quiet engine-noise of a third vehicle filled the tense air. Jade drew a ragged breath and slowly drew the gun from the small of her back. She felt better with it in her hand. The wolves around her, cowed by Niccolo's speed and strength, didn't move.

Car doors opened and closed. Jade turned and peered into the darkness, hearing a series of noises she couldn't identify. A glint of silver caught the moonlight and a wheelchair rolled toward them in the narrow space between the car and a shipping container. Drayden sat in the chair, his face as drawn, thin and pale as it had been in the holo-transmission. He wore a dark blue suit that reeked of money.

Drayden coolly surveyed the scene as four more wolves stalked up to flank him. "Well," Dray drawled. "I can see my wolves aren't everything I thought they'd be."

"What's going on?" Niccolo asked.

"I *said* I'd be in touch," Drayden snapped. He seemed upset at the ravaging of his wolves.

"What's with all the drama, Drayden?" Jade asked.

"It wasn't meant for your *entertainment*. It was protection. I didn't know if Mr. VampAmerica here was going to take my head off first and ask questions later. Our last communication didn't go very smoothly, as you'll recall."

Jade lost the thin grasp she had on her control. "If you hadn't kidnapped us and tried to starve Niccolo, perhaps you could've expected a warmer reception."

"Enough," said Niccolo. "Drayden, what's with the wolves?"

"They're just hired muscle. Normally wolves make the best bodyguards."

Niccolo reached down and helped two of them to their feet. They limped away bloody, obviously in pain. They kept their eyes averted from Niccolo's. Niccolo had shown his dominance by kicking their asses. They now recognized Niccolo as dominant and didn't want to challenge him again.

"Well, some of your employees need medical assistance," said Niccolo. His gaze took in the wheelchair. "So do you by the looks of it."

Drayden grimaced and shuddered almost imperceptibly. "Mr. Jones did its best to break me before I got away, but I'll recover. Look, I'm leaving the city, but I needed to deliver a message to you personally. I didn't trust any other method of communication for something this important." He paused and drew a shaky breath. "The doorway will open a week from tonight, on the full moon. It's set to open at 1:13 a.m." Drayden reached into his pocket and drew out a slip of paper. "Here. The enemy of my enemy is my friend."

Jade walked to him and took it. What looked like a longitude and latitude was scrawled on it.

Drayden fell into a coughing fit. He pulled a handkerchief from his other pocket to cover his mouth. Jade saw the pristine white material come away stained red. "That's where it's opening," Drayden gasped. "Gather up the Super Friends, get there beforehand and find a way to kill the bastard. If you can't kill it, delay it. It only has so much time to open the doorway. It has something to do with the alignment of the stars making the barrier between the dimensions thinner."

Drayden waved his hand and a wolf came forward, turned his wheelchair and started rolling him back into the darkness.

"Why are you doing this, Drayden?" Jade called after him.

"I told you. I want world peace and a basketful of kittens."

"How do we know we can trust you?" asked Niccolo to Drayden's disappearing form.

"You can't," Drayden responded from the dark, then he laughed. It was a jarringly brittle, fragile sound. Jade wondered for a moment what kind of hell the Dominion had put him through before he'd escaped.

Thirty seconds later, the wolves had gathered their wounded and all three cars had disappeared, leaving Jade and Niccolo to stare at each other.

"Could be a trap," said Jade.

Niccolo rubbed a hand over his chin. "Could be."

"We don't have much choice but to walk into it anyway, do we?"

He leveled his hot gaze at her. "Nope."

He walked to the bike and climbed on. "Come on, beautiful, no sense checking out this lead. I'm sure it was planted by Drayden to get us down here."

She nodded.

He dropped his voice down to the silky octaves that usually dropped her pants. "Let's go home."

* * * * *

They walked into the apartment just about the time Adam was getting home from checking a far more legitimate lead than the one they'd been running down.

They exchanged their stories—Adam's lead had yielded no useful information— and agreed to check out the location Drayden had given them in the morning.

Adam and Niccolo called Gabriel to tell him of what had happened and discuss how they'd proceed. While they did that, Jade went into the bedroom and changed into her nightgown, a light blue silk sheath with spaghetti straps, then wandered back out into the main part of the apartment.

Jade collapsed onto the couch near a sleeping Kara and watched avidly as Niccolo peeled off his shirt while he walked through the apartment. Her gaze traced the solid lines of his body with appreciation. It never failed to make places low in her body start to get warm.

"I'm taking a shower," Niccolo said with a glance toward Jade.

Images of Niccolo wet and all lathered up with soap danced through her head. She flicked a glance at Adam, who'd sat down at the middle island in the kitchen.

"You don't have to be bashful, Jade," Adam said with a laugh.

She narrowed her eyes at him. "What do you mean?"

Adam laughed. "Come on, I know you two have been going at it pretty much every night. There's no reason not to follow Niccolo into the shower just because I'm here. You think Niccolo's hotter than hell. So does every woman I've ever met." He shrugged. "I'm a little jealous, but that's the way it goes."

Niccolo mouth twisted in a wry grin. "Don't feel bad," he teased his friend. "She's attracted to you, too."

Jade's mouth hung open. "Excuse me? How would you know that?" She snapped her mouth shut, realizing she'd confirmed that what he'd said was true. She was attracted to Adam. Niccolo chuckled. "I've seen you looking at him, appreciating him."

She shifted uncomfortably on the couch, and then stood. "Well, come on, a woman would have to be half dead not to react to having you two around." She cleared her throat uncomfortably. "My finding Adam attractive doesn't mean anything."

"Oh, now *that* hurts," Adam said with a laugh.

"You know what I mean, Adam. I find you physically attractive, but my attraction to Niccolo is…different, deeper." She was careful to not look at Niccolo. Jade couldn't believe she'd just admitted that out loud.

Adam stood and walked toward her. "You know I've always been attracted to you, too." He brushed his knuckles lightly across her collarbone. It sent a little ripple of pleasure through her.

The memory of Adam's kiss in the kitchen came back. It had been nice kissing him. His arms had felt good around her and she'd fit well into the curve of his body.

She glanced away, uncomfortable that she was actually getting turned on. "Well, gee, thanks for letting me know, Adam. Are we all done sharing now?" She took a step away from him.

He leveled a warm gaze at her. "Come on, Jade, why the shyness?" He moved toward her again, and she forced herself to stay put. He reached out and took a tendril of her hair between his fingers, then brushed her throat with the back of his hand. "You must have lots of men chasing after you. It's the way of the OtherKin, after all."

It was. The OtherKin were a sensual race, every bit as sensual as the Embraced. "Men don't chase after me, Adam," she answered. She glanced at Niccolo. Adam didn't know about her past and how much it had affected her sexuality.

"Well, they must be blind, stupid or both where you come from." Adam shrugged. "I just wanted you to know I think you're gorgeous. Niccolo is lucky as hell to be able to touch you."

Niccolo leaned against a wall and watched them with half-lidded eyes.

"You're attracted to anyone female, Adam," she responded. "That doesn't make me feel very special."

Adam grinned. "There's no denying that."

Niccolo pushed off the wall and walked across the room to join them. "I'm more than just attracted to you, Jade," he murmured as he eased her away from Adam. He pulled her against his body and kissed her until she felt breathless and couldn't think very well.

Jade curled her fingers into Niccolo's upper arms and held on for dear life as his skillful mouth worked over hers. She felt Adam's hand on her shoulder and she started. She pulled away from Niccolo, breathing heavy and her body tingling with sudden sexual awareness. Both Adam and Niccolo watched her with half-lidded, yet alert eyes. Suddenly she felt like prey, and she wasn't so sure she didn't like it.

"What's the deal?" she asked, looking between them. "It's almost like you're tag-teaming me, like you're-you're trying to…"

"Seduce you?" Niccolo asked with a raised eyebrow. He glanced at Adam. "The both of us? Well, we never talked about it. I mean, this wasn't planned, but it's not a bad idea."

"Umm," was all Jade could manage. Two men? At the same time? The last time that had happened she'd been forced.

The look on her face must have betrayed her sudden rush of memory because Niccolo reached out and drew her against his chest. He stroked her hair. "I'm sorry. That was a stupid thing to suggest. Forget it, Jade. It's just our way. You know that. It's the way of the Embraced—to find pleasure where pleasure presents itself. I just...forgot for a moment. Forgive me."

She closed her eyes, listening to the steady, comforting beat of Niccolo's heart. It *was* their way. All the long-lived races were overtly sexual by nature. It came from having such long lives. It was simply a part of their culture.

It was a part of herself that she'd yet to reclaim.

Adam turned and started to walk away, likely wanting to give them some privacy.

"Wait," she said suddenly.

Adam turned back with a speculative look on his face.

"Just wait a minute. Let me think."

Adam walked back to her and rubbed her back. "Jade, if we do this, it will only be about pleasure between you and me, nothing else. It might be about something more between you and Niccolo, but with me it's only about sex. But if you want me to get lost right now, I will. No hard feelings. I'll leave you and Niccolo alone."

She backed away from Niccolo and glanced between the two men, remembering the gentle kiss that Adam had bestowed on her in the kitchen. She was attracted to him. How would it be to have two men she trusted making love to her? Two men touching her, kissing her, intent on giving her pleasure.

It had been so long since she'd enjoyed sex that she found herself yearning suddenly for the experience of it. It was something that any other OtherKin female of her age had experienced many times over.

Adam took a step toward her, taking her wrist and drawing her close. He pressed his warm body to hers and Jade relaxed into him. "What do you think, darlin'?"

"Uh," was all she could say. "I guess, I..." she trailed off, feeling suddenly shy.

He brushed the hair off her shoulder and laid a soft kiss where her neck met her shoulder. "We'll be gentle," he murmured. "I promise you'll like it." Adam's hand slid down her back and over her hip slowly, his strong fingers caressing her as he went.

Jade drew a deep breath, feeling the beginnings of arousal start to spark and smolder deep within her. She wanted Niccolo touching her as well. She found Adam attractive, and she respected and liked him very much. Adam's touch and his kiss heated her blood, but it was Niccolo she had the deepest feelings for.

Adam reached up and slid the strap of her nightgown down over her shoulder. She felt the spaghetti strap fall down. He brushed his fingertips lightly over her skin, over her scars, and then laid a kiss. Jade shivered. She wasn't even conscious of her scars. Adam seemed to find her beautiful despite them, just as Niccolo had.

"Mmmm," Adam murmured. "Like silk. I thought so."

Behind her, Niccolo was suddenly there, warming her back. Now she was sandwiched between the two men...and she liked it. No fear threatened her pleasure. Niccolo had been successful in vanquishing all her fear. Niccolo slid his strong hands up her outer thighs, gathering the skirt of her nightgown past her hips, and revealing her bare bottom.

Adam reached down under Niccolo's arms and around, to smooth his palms over her ass. She arched up, allowing Niccolo to pull her nightgown all the way over her head. Her bared breasts crushed against Adam's chest. His shirt scraped against the distended peaks, drawing a gasp of surprised pleasure from her.

Now she stood naked between the two mostly clothed men. Why that seemed erotic, Jade couldn't say. It just was.

Niccolo's hands slipped between her and Adam and closed around her breasts. He caressed them casually as he laid a kiss to the side of her throat, tweaking and teasing her erect nipples until Jade let out a long, low moan. Pleasure bloomed out from her breasts and she bent her head to the side, letting Niccolo nibble his way down her throat.

The sound of their combined breaths and their lips on her flesh filled the quiet air. Jade fought back a rising moan at the heat between her thighs. Her shyness was quickly fading, being replaced by need.

Adam leaned in and laid a kiss to the other side of her throat. She felt the scrape of their fangs from both sides, the feel of their lips brushing her skin and the soft, butterfly kisses of their tongues along her neck. Jade closed her eyes, shuddering in pleasure.

Niccolo trailed his hand down her stomach and dragged his fingers over her mound, seeking out the source of her sweetness. At the same time, Adam lowered his head and pulled one of her nipples into his mouth with a groan. He caressed her other breast with his free hand.

Jade's thoughts suddenly left her as lust crashed into her body.

Niccolo eased his finger between her thighs, seeking and finding her clit. He stroked the pad of his finger over it as Adam pulled her rigid nipple between his lips and laved at it with the flat of his tongue. He groaned and closed his eyes as he rolled the nipple of her other breast between sure fingers.

Niccolo urged her thighs apart a little farther and worked his fingers in to slide up into her body. Jade's knees went weak for a moment at the feeling of Niccolo fucking her slowly with his fingers and Adam teasing her breasts at the same time.

It felt like somewhere beyond heaven to be sandwiched between these two strong, male bodies. She could've spent hours standing there between them, enjoying the way they explored her, but she wanted to touch them back. She wanted them out of their clothes so she could feel their bare skin slick against hers.

Reluctantly, she cupped Adam's face in her hands and pulled him up so she could kiss him. Adam came to the kiss readily, slanting his mouth over hers with a groan. He parted her lips and slipped his tongue inside her mouth. Jade eagerly returned the openmouthed kiss, sliding her tongue against his.

He kissed differently than Niccolo, less aggressively, with a slow, easy confidence that made her clit thrum between her thighs. He made a low sound in the back of his throat and dragged her up against his chest, as though he wanted more of her. She embraced him and crushed her mouth to his.

Adam had left enough space between their lower bodies to allow Niccolo to continue the slow glide of his fingers in and out of her pussy. He pulled out and used her moisture as a lubricant around her clit, sending a tremor of pleasure through her and drawing a moan from her throat. Adam caught the sound against his tongue.

Niccolo's hands left her and she heard the rustle of his clothing being removed behind her.

Thank Goddess.

Suddenly impatient to have them both naked, she reached down and yanked at the hem of Adam's shirt, wanting it off. She worked at the buttons of his pants and Adam broke the kiss and chuckled softly.

"You've gone from unsure to eager in about three minutes," Niccolo murmured, pulling her back away from Adam.

"I'm a fast learner," she replied breathlessly.

He eased her down onto the couch behind them and kissed her deeply. Her hands roved his body and she noticed with much contentment that he was gloriously nude...and incredibly hard.

When Niccolo finally broke the kiss, she felt dizzy from the possessiveness of it and the taste of him on her tongue. Niccolo moved down and took one of her nipples into his mouth and Adam knelt beside her, cupping her other breast.

Adam had doffed his clothing also. His skin was a burnished gold from the sun and light blond hair marked his powerful chest. His cock was long, wide and hard as a rock, she could tell. Her fingers twitched to touch it, but he dropped his head and took her other nipple into his warm mouth before she had a chance to reach out and close her hand around it.

Niccolo rasped his fang over her breast, sending a bolt of extreme pleasure through her sensitized nipple. Adam licked and suckled at her other breast, drawing the erect, rosy peak into his mouth from time to time.

Her pussy felt hot and needy. It throbbed, ready to be touched, more than ready to be fucked. She moved her hips restlessly, wanting them to touch her lower down. She didn't know how much of this torment she could take.

Niccolo glanced up at her and laughed low. "Patience, *cara mia*," he murmured before going back to work.

She watched their heads as they sucked her nipples, one light and one dark. The sight of that alone—those two men working together to bring her pleasure—was almost enough to make her come on the spot.

Niccolo's hand trailed down over her belly and traced slowly and sensually across her inner thigh to come a rest a breath's space from her aching pussy. Adam's hand did the same thing. Jade spread her thighs for them, wanting desperately for them to touch her. Adam flicked out a finger, minutely brushed her swollen labia, only to retreat back to rest on her inner thigh.

"Teases," she groaned. "Both of you."

She felt Adam smile against her breast, then increase the pace of his pull on her nipple. Niccolo did the same. It drew an agonized pant from her.

Finally, blessedly, Niccolo eased his hand to her aroused cunt and drew his skillful fingers over her flesh. She let out a moan of satisfaction and Adam joined in, fingering the entrance of her pussy. Adam slid a finger inside her while Niccolo stroked her clit. Jade writhed for a moment uncontrollably. Her hips canted forward, looking for something to fuck.

They gave it to her. Each of them eased a finger into her and together they thrust at the same time. Jade gasped and choked back a cry of pleasure. They worked their fingers in and out until Jade thought she'd scream.

"Is it good, Jade?" Adam asked in a heavy voice.

"Yes," she replied in a breathless whisper.

"Do you want more?"

She could only moan in response as Niccolo used her cream to slick over her aroused clit and Adam rubbed his finger through the folds of her labia. Jade stared down her body, watching them stroke her. She felt drugged with lust.

Goddess, it was so good, but she needed to touch them.

She pushed at Niccolo, urging him back onto the floor in front of the couch. She followed him down, letting her skin slid sensually across his and laying a line of kisses down his chest. Going to her knees and straddling his legs, she dragged her tongue through the tangle of hair at the juncture of his thighs, then up the length of his gorgeous, hard cock.

He shuddered in pleasure when she lowered her mouth over him, taking every inch of his cock into her mouth that she possibly could. He felt so good between her lips. The hardness of his cock against her tongue felt like pure heaven. She groaned in the back of her throat and closed her eyes for a moment, enjoying the taste of him against her tongue.

Niccolo's hands grasped her arms and she glanced up, seeing the needful look in his eyes. Giving him a coy, playful look, she wrapped her hand around the base of his and started to suck.

"Ah, *Dio*, Jade, yes," Niccolo hissed.

Jade felt Adam's warm hand on her hip and she positioned herself more steadily on her knees, presenting her ass to Adam. Adam took the not-so-subtle hint and settled himself behind her. On instinct, she spread her legs a little farther, all the better to display her pussy to him from behind.

Still, she jumped a little in surprise as she felt Adam spread her labia with his thumbs and lick the length of her. She took a moment to moan around Niccolo's cock as Adam tongued the entrance of her pussy, licking up all the cream they'd already drawn from her. He speared his tongue into her, fucking her with it, and her hips jerked involuntarily. His hands on her hips kept her steady. Jade found herself sucking Niccolo's cock in time to the tempo Adam set behind her.

A whimper of pure need escaped her when Adam's fingers found her swollen clit and rubbed it. Her pussy felt so engorged, so swollen that it almost ached for a long, hard fucking. Adam stroked the pad of his finger gently over her clit as he continued licking her.

She took Niccolo's cock down her throat even farther as the first glimmerings of climax skittered through her body. Niccolo groaned and his body tightened beneath her.

Adam never relented, knowing how fast and hard he was pushing her. He stroked her clit with just the right speed and pressure, just enough to keep her on the edge of a shattering orgasm. She moved her hips restlessly under the treatment of his fingers and tongue, moaning from time to time around Niccolo's cock, and wishing for one of them to fill her. Adam seemed to read her mind and thrust his devilishly skillful tongue inside her again.

Niccolo found her breasts and toyed with her nipples. "You're so beautiful, Jade," he murmured in a guttural voice. "*Dio*, so pretty."

And that was it.

Waves of sensation coursed through her as a hard climax took her body. Adam never let up stroking his fingers over her clit and thrusting his skillful tongue into her body as her pussy convulsed in pleasure. Her whole cunt spasmed in ecstasy, yet felt empty for the want of one of their cocks. She lost her hold on Niccolo, arched her back and cried out.

"Yes, baby, come for us," Niccolo groaned, watching her.

Jade dug her fingers into the area rug on either side of Niccolo, feeling the gentle rasp of Adam's tongue sliding in and out her cunt. After several more moments of ecstasy, the climax lost its hold on her body and she relaxed.

Niccolo eased her down onto her back and cupped her cheek in his palm. She opened her eyes to see his dark brown orbs flaring with lust. "Was it good, Jade?" he murmured. "Does he touch you the way you like?"

She bit her lower lip, smiled a little and nodded.

"Do you want more of us, baby?"

"Yes."

She felt Adam move to lie beside her. Her body flushed once more in passion with the knowledge that they were both hers for the night. She shifted over to straddle Adam and bowed her head to kiss him. Her pussy brushed his hard cock, making him shudder beneath her and made the muscles of his body tense.

"Damn, I like touching you," Adam murmured. He snaked his hand to the nape of her neck and sealed his mouth to hers, thrusting his tongue between her lips to dance against her tongue aggressively. Jade could taste herself on his tongue. He slanted his mouth over hers harder, growling like a wolf in the back of his throat. His tongue mated with hers again and again.

Jade's body quickened, ready for more. From behind, she felt Niccolo pull her hips up and push his fingers into her. He stroked her to a needful frenzy, until she could barely see straight. She moved her hips and whimpered into Adam's mouth, wanting nothing more than for Niccolo to slide his cock into her. Instead, Niccolo set to teasing her clit, making Jade moan deep in her throat. They wanted to make her insane, Jade was sure.

Needing to feel Adam between her lips, and give him the same pleasure she'd given Niccolo, Jade gently broke the kiss and slipped down, sensually rubbing her skin along his as she went. She licked the soft, slick crown of Adam's cock and then slid her mouth down over it. He groaned and swore softly under his breath. His hands found her hair and fisted in it.

Niccolo moved to her side and flipped her long hair out the way so he could watch her work Adam's cock between her lips. She glanced at Niccolo while she slid Adam's length in and out of her mouth, her hand idly stroking Adam's balls.

Niccolo watched her avidly, one of his big hands stroking his own cock. Smiling a little, understanding that this aroused Niccolo, she gripped Adam's cock at the base and licked up and down the shaft. Adam groaned low and his grip in her hair tightened almost painfully.

Lust clearly glinting in Niccolo's dark eyes, he moved behind her. She felt his skillful fingers stroke up the length of her needy pussy and she pushed her hips up at him in invitation for something more. Niccolo dragged his fingers over her, gathering her moisture, and then speared two of them into the heart of her. They glided and out and she bucked, wanting more, wanting his cock.

She endured the thrust of his wide fingers for several more moments before she gasped, "Niccolo, please."

"What do you want, Jade? Tell us," Niccolo said.

She moaned. "You know what I want, what I need."

"So say the words."

"Goddamn you, Niccolo. Fuck me. I need to feel your cock inside me."

She closed her eyes in ecstasy as he pushed the head of his cock between her swollen labia and thrust slowly inside her. He pushed in all the way to the base of him, filling her up completely.

"Ah, yes," she hissed, closing her eyes. She guided Adam's cock back into her mouth, making him groan out her name.

Niccolo grasped her hips, pulled out and stroked back in. For a moment, Jade felt overwhelmed. Overwhelmed by Niccolo who'd thrust himself balls-deep inside her. Overwhelmed by Adam, who'd fisted his fingers in her hair and had begun gently fucking her mouth by thrusting his hips up at her.

It was overwhelming, scary, and wonderful all at once.

She whimpered deep in her throat at the sensation of Niccolo filling her from behind. This position forced him deeper inside her, filled her up the most completely.

Niccolo took her slowly and masterfully and she sucked Adam's cock in time to his thrusts. The three of them moved as if in an erotic dance, each of them pleasuring the other and feeding off the ecstasy they produced in their partners.

Jade never would've believed she'd be able to take two men this way, let alone enjoy it to such a mind-numbing degree. Despite what had happened to her in the past, she felt created for this, made to take as much pleasure as she could possibly handle. Joy filled her as she realized she'd finally defeated the demons from her past.

She'd retaken her ability to completely pleasure and be pleasured. Her history did not taint this moment at all.

Niccolo's strokes became faster and more demanding. She increased her pulls on Adam's cock at the same pace, closing her eyes and giving in to the deep thrust of his cock down her throat. Soon the rhythm became heated, frantic. The air filled with the mingled groans of the two men and the erotic sound of her own suctioning flesh where Niccolo thrust in and out of her. The head of Niccolo's cock rubbed that sensitive bundle of nerves deep within her with every inward stroke.

Her climax hit her hard when it finally came. Jade never lost her hold on Adam's cock as her body tensed and her pussy began to spasm in a delicious, powerful orgasm. She felt the muscles of her cunt contract and release over and over, milking Niccolo's pistoning cock.

"*Dio*, I'm coming," panted Niccolo.

"Fuck. Me too," Adam gasped.

Niccolo grabbed her hips and thrust his cock into her as far as he could. She felt it jerk inside her as he came, his low groans of satisfaction reverberating through the air. He stroked into her slowly, enjoying his climax as much as he could. She could feel his slick ejaculate lubricating the thrust of his shaft into her body.

She sucked Adam down her throat and braced him as his hips jerked. "Ah, hell, Jade," he groaned. His body tensed and he spilled himself. He closed his eyes, his jaw going slack as he climaxed. She felt and tasted his smooth come as it spurted down her throat.

The three of them collapsed on the floor and lay tangled and panting. Her cunt throbbed slightly and her jaw hurt, but she felt incredibly content and satisfied. She wanted to savor this moment for as long as she could. Niccolo drew her near and scattered kisses along her jaw line and over her mouth. That had been a very powerful sexual experience.

She laughed a little, just for the joy of it. "Goddess, that was…good," she breathed, closing her eyes.

She felt Niccolo's warm hand close around one of her breasts. "Say that when we're finished with you," he rasped. "We're not done yet."

She smiled. "You did say something about a shower."

* * * * *

Niccolo started the water in the large shower and adjusted the level of the showerheads and the temperature of the water. Behind him, Adam let his hands hungrily roam

Jade's body. She had fallen against Adam with her eyes closed. Her cheeks were flushed and her lips parted slightly as she dragged her fingers over Adam's erection.

Niccolo stepped into the shower and let the water hit him. He pushed his hands through his hair, tipped his head back and groaned with pleasure at the feel of the hot water sluicing down his body. Niccolo lowered his head and opened his eyes to find Jade watching him.

"Come here," he demanded softly.

She came and Adam followed. After grabbing the soap, Adam sandwiched her between himself and Niccolo and lathered his hands. When he was finished, he handed the soap over to Niccolo, and he did the same. Together they ran their soapy hands over Jade's body, from head to toe.

Her eyes fluttered shut. She tipped her head back and moaned gutturally. "Oh Goddess," she murmured. "Don't ever stop doing that. It's so good."

Niccolo massaged her tight, round buttocks and slipped his fingers between her cheeks to run his finger slickly over her pussy. She parted her thighs for him instantly, and he took another lingering pass, rubbing his fingers over her aroused clit from behind. He loved to feel her when she was excited this way, and having two men touching her was definitely exciting to her.

Niccolo shifted to her front and watched as Adam soaped her breasts. Her small, aroused pink nipples stood out prominently from the white soap bubbles. It made Niccolo want to suck them. Adam stroked them until Jade shuddered with pleasure.

"Damn, you're pretty," rasped Adam as his gaze followed a bubble sliding down the plump of one breast. "You have no idea how gorgeous you are, baby."

"She does look good wet," Niccolo answered with a wry twist to his mouth at the sound of longing in Adam's voice.

"She looks good all the time," answered Adam. He laid a long kiss to an unsoaped portion of her flat stomach.

They fell into silence, each of them losing themselves to the exploration of the curve of her hip, the slope of her back where it met her gorgeous ass, her small, beautiful breasts and the pink, tempting flesh of her pussy.

Jade bit her lip, moaning and whimpering from time to time at the intense way he and Adam had fallen into worshipping her body. Finally, she snatched the soap up and lathered her hands.

"I want to touch the both of you," she said. She slid her hands down their chests slowly and closed her hands around both their cocks at the same time and pumped. Her hands slid easily over their flesh, slick with soap.

Both he and Adam tipped their heads back and groaned at the feeling of her hands stroking them. Pleasure surged through Niccolo's cock and up his body. He eased himself away after a moment, worried she'd make him come. He still had things he wanted to do to her.

Adam yanked her against him and kissed her hard, threading and fisting his fingers in the wet hair at the back of her head. Niccolo stepped in and pressed his body to the back of hers, thrusting his cock slowly between the cheeks of her rounded ass, aided by the water and soap lather. Jade thrust her backside up at him for more. Niccolo held her hips and gave it to her, while he kissed and lightly bit her shoulder.

They slid their bodies against each other in warm, silky pleasure, the sound of the pulsing water loud in their ears. Niccolo wanted to guide Jade to the wall, place her hands flat against it, spread her thighs and take her hard and fast from behind. He could almost feel the tight, hot muscles of her cunt close around his shaft. That would leave Adam out of things, however, and Niccolo wanted Jade to experience both of them together this night as much as possible.

Niccolo moved her wet hair away from her ear and whispered, "The bed?"

She broke Adam's deep and thorough kiss. "Yes," she breathed.

Niccolo led her out of the shower and he and Adam dried her. Then they allowed Jade to dry them. She took her time with it, sucking each of their cocks into her hot mouth in turn, while the other watched and envied. Finally, they made it into the bedroom.

As they stood at the end of the bed, Niccolo ran his hand up Jade's smooth, silky thigh, marveling for the fiftieth time since she'd acquiesced to him and Adam how beautiful she was.

Adam stood nearby, watching them with a very intent gaze. In one hand, Adam stroked his hard cock, his eyes fixed on Jade's gorgeous nude body.

He and Adam had often shared women before he'd gone to prison. Among the Embraced, it was a common practice. He'd shared Fate with Gabriel once. It seemed like a million years ago now.

There was nothing like hearing a woman when she had two men to pleasure her. Nothing like watching her become out of her mind with lust with four hands on her body, two cocks within her.

Niccolo enjoyed giving this gift to Jade.

He had no illusions. Niccolo cared deeply for Jade. He'd come to love her. All he wanted was her happiness, her pleasure. In addition, it excited Niccolo to share this woman he loved with his closest friend.

Niccolo dropped his hand and teased her pouting, aroused pussy, making sure Adam could see the slow glide of his fingers over her pretty flesh. Jade shuddered against him and Niccolo's cock went impossibly harder. The look in her eyes was dark and full of erotic promise.

When his little priestesses had let go of her past to embrace the future, she'd turned into a lovely, wild erotic goddess.

God, how he loved it.

Suddenly wanting nothing more than to worship her, he dropped to his knees and parted those pouting lips, letting his tongue snake in to flick over her clit. Jade moaned and grabbed his shoulders as he lapped at her. With a hungry growl emanating from his throat, he grabbed her beautiful ass in his hands as Jade parted her thighs for him, and he sucked her clit between his lips, massaging it.

"Niccolo," she breathed raggedly. "It's good," she moaned.

He kept it up, feeling the bundle of nerves plump with excitement. Niccolo wanted her crazy with need, crazy and hot for him and for Adam. He wanted her writhing with need, begging for them both. Using the tip of his tongue, he caressed her softly, bringing her to the edge of climax. Her cream pearled on the entrance of her pussy and he greedily licked it up.

"Niccolo!" she cried again, this time helplessly, urgently.

He eased away and took her hand, leading her toward the bed. He and Adam eased themselves down onto the mattress and pulled Jade in between them.

Niccolo tried not to feel jealous as Adam pulled her toward him again for a lingering kiss. Instead he pressed himself up against her back and wrapped his arm around her, fondling a breast and toying with the hardened nipple. He pressed his cock to the warm cleft between the cheeks of her ass and thrust rhythmically.

Jade turned over to face him and slid her leg slowly over Niccolo's hip in invitation. He wanted to guide his cock between her slim thighs and sink into her cunt. A look of drugged sensuality had overcome her pretty face. She leaned forward and kissed him aggressively.

Niccolo groaned at the sweet taste of her and her sexual abandon. He wrapped his arms around her and slanted his mouth over hers, taking her in a deep, penetrating kiss. Her tongue brushed against his, making his whole body go tight with pleasure.

He felt Adam's hands slip down her back and over her ass. "Your body was made for this," murmured Adam. "Damn, you make me so hot, Jade."

Niccolo agreed. He broke the kiss and pressed her back into the pillows. He dragged his lips down her jaw, throat and over her collarbone. The scent of her sweet blood coursing through her veins teased him and made his fangs lengthen. That was the main course. They were still just on the appetizers.

He closed his mouth over a nipple. On the other side, Adam did the same.

Jade arched her back and her fingers sought and found fistfuls of the comforter.

Aware of the sexual torment they wreaked on her, he exchanged a look with Adam over the sweet bounty of her breasts. Together, they timed the pull and speed on her nipples until Jade was writhing and moaning under the onslaught.

She spread her thighs in mute, but pointed, invitation and Niccolo slid his hand slowly down her stomach and stroked her. Adam took the cue and let his hand follow. Together, he and Adam slicked their fingers over her folds and teased her clit, but didn't let her come. It would be better to build the next one up, make her beg for it. It would make it more powerful for her, and Niccolo wanted to make this the best possible experience.

When Niccolo didn't think she could take any more, he broke away from her nipple and eased down the length of her body. Adam did the same. They rested between her spread legs. Jade looked down the length of her body at them in a lust-laced, slack-jawed daze. Her eyes were dark with arousal.

Niccolo circled her extended, excited clit and Jade tossed her head, breathed his name in a ragged voice.

Adam gently caressed her labia, rubbing the entrance to her pussy, which glistened wetly with her cream. Jade dug her heels into the mattress and spread her thighs as far as she could. Niccolo watched Adam stroke the pad of his finger through her swollen folds, making Jade moan. At the same time, Niccolo caressed her pouting little clit.

"Please," Jade whimpered.

Knowing what she begged for, Niccolo eased a finger in and out of her, feeling the clamp of her slick muscles. Jade cried out and arched her back at the penetration. Adam avidly watched his finger slide in and out of her sweet little cunt. "Damn, it's pretty. I want to kiss it," said Adam.

Niccolo removed his hand and glanced at Jade. "You want Adam to lick you, *cara mia*?"

"Yes," she breathed.

Oh, yeah, she was lost now.

Adam didn't hesitate. Niccolo moved to the side, allowing Adam to lean in and lick up the length of her. "Oh, hell, yes," Adam panted.

Adam speared his tongue inside her and pulled her swollen labia between his lips. Niccolo couldn't resist leaning in and flicking his tongue over her clit. Jade shuddered with pleasure and he lapped at her again.

Having two tongues on her at once nearly made Jade go through the roof. Helpless, lust-filled noises he never thought he'd hear from such a hard-as-nails woman shook the walls of the bedroom. Still, Niccolo wouldn't allow her to come. He wanted her *climbing* the walls before they were through.

"Please," she pleaded. "You're both driving me crazy and I need to feel…" she trailed off.

"Feel what, beautiful?" Adam asked.

"I need to feel your cock, Niccolo. Adam's cock. *Someone*'s cock. Please."

"Patience, *cara mia*," Niccolo answered with a light chuckle. "Patience."

Niccolo rose, afraid he'd push her over the edge, and watched Adam go down on her. His friend lapped greedily at her, holding her thighs apart as she writhed beneath him. Gazing at Jade now, with her eyes closed and her dark lashes swept down over her flushed cheeks, it hit Niccolo again that what he felt for her went past anything sane.

Damn it, he loved her so much.

He loved every aspect of her—from the way she moaned as two men pleasured her, to her badass attitude, to the vulnerable, hurt woman she tried so hard to hide from the world. God, it had been so long since he'd felt this for a woman—that welling up of caring and emotion when he looked at her, thought about her. It was jarring, frightening, but at the same time, fantastic.

He never thought he'd be capable of feeling this way for another person again.

Niccolo may have helped Jade regain her sexuality, but she'd helped him regain his humanity.

Reaching down, he smoothed her silken hair away from her face. Her eyelids fluttered open and she gave him a shy smile. Niccolo felt something in his heart catch.

He wouldn't be able to give this woman up when the day came.

Chapter Eleven

Adam's tongue teased and tormented her until she could barely think. All she could do was close her eyes and enjoy it. She felt the touch of Niccolo's hand on her cheek and looked up him.

In the same moment, pleasure welled up within her, driven by Adam's tongue, and she climaxed. Jade arched her back under the waves of it as Adam relentlessly drove her harder and higher.

Niccolo cupped her breast as she orgasmed, kissing over her throat as she moaned, then pulled her against his body.

Jade lay between Adam and Niccolo on the rumpled bed. Their bodies slid like silk against each other—Adam in back of her and Niccolo in front. Niccolo stared into her eyes as his hands roamed her body restlessly. The look in the depths of those dark eyes was breathtaking, full of emotion, full of warmth and caring. To be the sole focus of both these men, but especially Niccolo, was breathtaking beautiful.

Jade slid her hands over the hard planes of Niccolo's body and leaned in to kiss him. She treated his sensual mouth to a series of soft, teasingly short tongue kisses. Niccolo groaned raggedly in the back of his throat and slanted his mouth over hers and drove his tongue hungrily into her mouth.

Emotion welled up inside her and tears burned her eyes. She loved Niccolo. Somehow, during the last few weeks, she'd fallen head over heels for this man.

Adam blessedly distracted her from her thoughts and sudden emotion by moving along her back sinuously and pressing his hard cock between the cheeks of her ass. She gasped and arched her back at the erotic feel of his shaft against her.

Niccolo seized the opportunity of her pelvis jutting toward him, grasped her hip and softly eased his cock between her upper thighs, fitting it snugly against her clit.

They both began to move in unison, one on each side. Their strong bodies sandwiching hers, their strong cocks exerting erotic friction on her most sensitive body parts. The glimmering of another climax shot through her body, making her eyes roll back into her head. For a delirious moment she wondered how many times she could orgasm in one night.

"Do you want to come, baby?" rasped Adam near her ear in a low, aroused voice.

She nodded.

"I think we should let her come, Niccolo," he said.

Niccolo laid a kiss to her throat and his fangs raked across her tender flesh. He said nothing. He only pitched the angle of his thrusts, to rub his heavily veined shaft more thoroughly against her swollen clit.

Jade gasped and arched her back, resisting the urge to claw the pillows and Niccolo—anything with her reach.

"Come, Jade," whispered Niccolo against the flesh of her throat. "Come for us."

The climax washed over her body with the force of a tidal wave. All thought stopped as pleasure permeated every pore of her body. A scream worked its way from the depths of her throat and made it into the open air.

Suddenly, she found herself on her back, her thighs spread and Niccolo sinking into her hard and deep. Every thrust sent her ass into the bedsprings. Niccolo took her with a single-minded, possessive intensity that pushed her straight into another orgasm.

When the waves from the second one faded away, she felt a pressure on her lips. She opened her eyes as Adam kissed her softly. He groaned and deepened the kiss, parting her lips and mating his tongue with hers.

There was something so erotic about having one man easing in and out of her pussy while another man kissed her so masterfully. Feeling drunk and nearly overcome with pleasure, she snaked her hand to the back of Adam's neck and pressed his mouth more fully down on hers.

His fangs had extended down into little points and she nicked her tongue on one of them. The minor pain jarred her for a moment—playing counterpoint to the pleasure—and the metallic, sweet tang of her blood spread across her tongue.

She felt Adam's body go taut against her. He growled in the back of his throat and sucked her tongue into his mouth, consuming every bit of the blood they'd inadvertently spilled. The suction on her tongue made the slight cut ache, but it was nothing compared to the pleasurable throb Adam's action caused in her pussy. She relaxed, letting him savor the blood while Niccolo slowly fucked her.

When Adam was finished, he eased away, looking as satisfied as a cat with cream. Niccolo came down over her, kissing her deep and wrapping his strong arms around her. In one smooth, powerful motion, he rolled to the side. Suddenly, she found herself on top with his cock thrust balls-deep within her.

Niccolo slid his hand to the base of her spine and then up her back, pressing her down against him. The action lifted her rear and spread her from behind, where Adam smoothed his hand down her buttocks. Niccolo pressed his mouth to hers, consuming her small gasp of pleasure.

"Do you want to take Adam, too?" he murmured against her lips.

It took her a moment to understand what he meant. Her mind was so hazy with pleasure. She nodded, even though she felt unsure. This was another thing most OtherKin females her age had experienced, but she never had.

Niccolo spread the cheeks of her buttocks, exposing her to Adam's view and offering him a silent invitation to take her from behind. Adam moved, first to take something from a nearby drawer and slick it over his erection, then to her rear.

She felt him smooth lubricant-smeared fingers over her flesh. She jerked a little at the contact.

"Shh, baby," crooned Adam. "I'm not going to hurt you. I'm going to make you feel good."

He eased his fingers down her sensitive flesh, petting her, accustoming her to the feel of his hand on that most private of areas. When she'd gentled and had begun moaning at the sensation of all those nerves flaring to glorious life, Adam pressed a finger past the tight little ring of muscles and into her body.

Pleasure rippled out from that area, combined with ecstasy of having Niccolo's cock in her pussy. The two sensations played off each other and Jade knew that once Adam thrust inside her, it wouldn't take but a moment for her to explode in climax.

Adam played softly behind her, easing her muscles into relaxation. She could feel her body giving in to him, readying itself for more. In fact, she was becoming eager for it. Adam added another finger to his gentle thrusting, stretching her to take his cock. All the while, Niccolo kissed her, smoothed the tendrils of her hair away from her face, and murmured about how beautiful, how sexy she was.

When he deemed her ready, Adam straddled Niccolo's legs and pressed himself to her back. Strong male bodies sandwiched her as the head of Adam's cock sought the entrance he wanted...and pushed the head within.

Jade cried out as the searing pleasure enveloped her. Closing her eyes, she sank her teeth into her bottom lip. It hurt a little, but, oh, it felt so damned good at the same time. Part of her wanted to demand Adam withdraw, but the other part just wanted more.

Adam and Niccolo both stilled.

"Hush, baby," crooned Adam. "It's okay. You can take me. You just have to be calm and relaxed."

She drew a breath and then sobbed out brokenly, "Please, don't stop."

Niccolo chuckled softly.

"There's my girl," answered Adam with a smile in his voice. "Mmmm, feels good, doesn't it?"

"Yes," she gasped. "Deeper."

Niccolo's eyes flared dark and the slight smile he wore disappeared. "*Dio*, Jade, you're sexy as hell," he rasped.

Adam pressed himself within another inch, then another, until he'd seated himself the whole way in. Both men seemed afraid to move, to breathe. She closed her eyes. The two of them made her feel so full and so overwhelmed. They drove everything from her mind and replaced it with pure pleasure.

"Move," she whispered. Then louder, "Please, fuck me."

She didn't have to ask twice.

Niccolo and Adam moved like they shared the same brain, their thrusts playing off each other and matching perfectly. Jade wanted to cry it felt so exquisite. She closed her eyes and gave in to it, moaning long and loud as the two men thrust in and out of her body with deep mind-numbingly powerful strokes.

She held still, afraid to disrupt their rhythm, afraid to unravel the spell that held them all in thrall. The sounds of their breathing and mingled groans were loud in the room. Their hot breath branded her skin and their hands smoothed over her excited flesh as they fucked her.

It didn't take her long to climax, with their chests moving silkily across her skin and their powerful cocks driving into her over and over. Jade raggedly cried out both of their names as her orgasm began. The pleasurable spasm stole her ability to think and almost her ability to breathe. She let go completely and let it take her.

She tipped her head back and felt two mouths on her throat on opposite sides. Two sets of fangs, searching, scraping...then penetrating.

Their combined glamour unfurled and covered her, causing her climax to strengthen and maintain itself while they took her blood. Her cries faded to a series of moans and short, shallow pants. She called their names and spread her legs as far as she could, never wanting the slow, easy glide of their cocks in and out of her body to end.

Her vision blackened and unconsciousness threatened. Adam released his hold first, tipped his head and groaned. She felt his cock jump and his stream of hot come fill her. He groaned again and called her name. His hands grasped her hips as he thrust in and out of her as he came, his thrusts growing softer and slower. Finally, they stopped and he pulled out of her.

Niccolo broke the hold he had on her throat and rolled her onto her back. He came down between her spread thighs with a feral expression on his face and slid back inside her. He fucked her hard and fast. She could hear the gentle slap of flesh on flesh as he took her.

She stared up into his eyes and he stared down at her. He came like that, with their gazes locked. Jade couldn't remember experiencing anything more intimate. His eyes widened and he groaned as his cock convulsed erotically deep within her.

Finally, he collapsed on her and fisted her hair in his hands. He scattered kisses over her face, murmuring soft things in Italian to her that she couldn't understand, but comforted her all the same.

They fell asleep tangled together on the bed.

Jade felt warm, sated and protected. She also felt exhausted.

"I love you," Niccolo whispered in her ear just as she fell asleep.

The words made something warm and nice bloom in the center of her chest. She smiled, wondering if she'd imagined he'd said it, dreamed it perhaps. That had to be it.

Chapter Twelve

The coordinates of the doorway ended up being in a remote part of Virginia, in one of the few undeveloped parts of the United States that yet remained.

They'd had no real way to check out what Drayden had told them. They visited the site beforehand, but that really hadn't been very helpful. Jade worried that this whole thing might be a ruse, a way to send them on a wild goose chase while somewhere else in the world, the real doorway opened.

They'd gambled everything on Drayden. Everything and everyone.

Gabriel and Charlie had gathered every Embraced they could and centered them in the mid-sized town of Corningsville, about five miles from the site. The Order of the Morrigan had joined them, as well as many other OtherKin. They'd overrun one whole hotel, much to the dismay of the humans who ran it. The humans knew nothing of the threat, and the OtherKin and Embraced planned to keep it that way.

Ignorance was bliss, so they said.

Using a satellite monitoring system, they watched the field for Mr. Jones. As soon as it showed up to work its mojo, they'd rush it.

It seemed unlikely that one man, even one that was a physical manifestation of the might of the Dominion combined, would be able to defend itself against such numbers. That was if Drayden had even been telling the truth and Jones even showed up.

She stood near Niccolo, looking over Gabriel's shoulder at the brightly lit vid-screen that monitored the area Drayden had said the doorway would appear. Those of Gabriel's inner circle had gathered in his suite. The room felt tense, on edge.

Behind her, Aiden paced, while Fate and Tiya spoke in low voices in the corner of the room. Fate was a powerful dreamwalker. She fought the Dominion on their turf, in their dimension, by projecting her consciousness. She'd felt great activity in the days leading up until now.

Perhaps Drayden hadn't been lying. Time would soon tell.

The vid-screen flickered and Gabriel sat up straighter. Jade leaned in for a closer look.

"Something's happening," said Niccolo to the room.

The others came and watched the screen. A small silver aircraft flew into view and landed. Tense, they watched and waited as the door opened. Mr. Jones walked down the gangway and into the grass, looking civilized and incongruous in the middle of the field.

It looked like Drayden hadn't screwed them after all.

"Go," Gabriel commanded tersely. "As we talked about, as we planned. Be careful," he added.

Everyone moved.

Jade and Niccolo traveled in Gabriel's cruiser. They set down a distance away from the location and walked in on foot. They all had guns, but Jade didn't think they'd work. She'd seen Drayden pump round after round into Jones and it hadn't even fazed it.

By the time they reached the field, OtherKin and Embraced were laying around, bleeding, wounded and unconscious. They'd already tangled with the manifestation. It didn't bode well.

Jade scanned the area, seeing Jones standing in the middle of the field with its arms raised. Above the creature pulsed a point of light.

The doorway.

She watched it grow larger as Jones mouthed words and worked its violent, alien magick.

The Embraced went after it in a coordinated effort, but Jones merely swatted them like flies. Jones punched them, backhanded them, sent them skittering away bleeding. The thing used a strange magick that pulsed from its hands and sent men down to the ground, writhing.

Jade swore under her breath. It was a one-man bloodbath.

For the thousands of years the Embraced had fought the Dominion, they'd gathered little intelligence about them — only what the dreamwalkers could bring back when they visited their dimension. They weren't familiar with all their abilities. Now that the doorway was opening and the walls between the dimension grew thinner, it was clear that Jones was able to access much more power.

How *much* more power would it be able to tap? That was a pertinent question.

Yet Jade noticed that every time the thing had to turn its attention away from the task at hand, the pinpoint of light flickered, grew smaller. That was the objective, of course, to stall, delay. The thing looked agitated and generally really pissed off. Therefore, Jade assumed they were succeeding with their goal.

Thank the Goddess for Drayden.

She never thought she'd hold that sentiment, but if he hadn't turned on Jones and then handed over this information to them, the doorway would probably already be open.

Jade, Adam and Niccolo were meant as a last resort, and so they watched with tense agony the battle that raged in front of them. The power that Jones wielded — the power of all the Dominion combined — was awesome to behold.

One man, if you could call it that, was kicking their collective ass.

Soon even Charlie and Gabriel lay sprawled on the ground, incapacitated. The sound of injured men swelled around them. The scent of blood and vomit filled the air.

Soon they, the last resort, were needed.

"Well, that didn't take long," said Adam.

"Christ," Niccolo breathed next to her.

"Uh-huh," answered Adam.

"Bullets won't kill it. My sword won't do it." Niccolo swore low under his breath. "A grenade wouldn't even have any effect. The thing's indestructible."

Jade watched the sliver in the sky widen. Her stomach rushed up into her throat. If that thing opened they were fucked, the world was fucked. She chewed her lip, deep in thought.

Finally, she said, "Indestructible, yes, but it doesn't have all the time in the world. Jones needs to finish this while the right cosmic conditions exist. I'm fast enough." Jade said in a low voice, "I'm the only one here fast enough and who has enough training to get close to him. I'll distract him, stall him."

Niccolo grabbed her upper arm. "No. One of the priestesses who have the ability with speed—"

"Most of them are already down." She shook her head and smiled. "Anyway, I'm the only one with the speed. It was some kind of trade-off I got for being half-blood."

"I'm not letting you go," he growled.

She pulled her arm away from him. "Please, Niccolo, this is our only option."

"He...damn it, Jade, he's going to kill you."

"Better a few die than millions. All I have to do is keep him occupied until his time runs out."

Niccolo pushed a hand through his hair. "No," he said, but in his eyes she could see that he knew she was right.

Jade went on her tiptoes and pressed her lips to his. Niccolo twined his arms around her, deepening the kiss and sending her to a heaven she'd only ever known in his arms. She closed her eyes, feeling the slide of a tear down her cheek. For a moment Niccolo held her like he never planned on letting her go, but as soon as he did, in a blink of an eye, she was gone.

Mr. Jones stood in the center of the field with its arms upraised like some preacher of long ago ministering to the masses. Above it the sky glimmered and sparked as the doorway tried to birth itself. It felt her approach and lowered its head, fixing her with a gaze filled with a horrible, sickening white light. It was like looking into the dimension where the Dominion existed and it was enough to turn her stomach.

Mr. Jones raised its hand and she felt magick prickle up her side. She dodged to the left as a bolt of it came at her and just barely missed it. Mr. Jones narrowed its eyes and shot again and again, but every time she dodged it.

She reached it and treated it to a roundhouse kick, but it blocked with its forearm. It was like hitting steel. The pain shot up her leg and thought for a moment she may have broken a bone. The shock was enough to give Mr. Jones the advantage. It reached out and caught her wrist. She struggled and fought it, but the creature was so incredibly strong.

Mr. Jones grabbed her other wrist, holding her imprisoned. She felt the old panic rise up, the bile sear the back of her throat. Mr. Jones forced her to her knees in front of it. Her breath came faster as the memories rose.

"Oh, you have a lovely history to play off of," Jones murmured. "Lots to feed from here. Truly, you make it too easy."

Jade looked up at it, wondering what it meant. Then images of her past flickered through her mind's eye, as vivid as though they were happening now. She closed her eyes and shook her head, trying in vain to banish them. "I can make you live there," whispered Jones.

Something that felt like long needles stabbed into her wrists where the thing held her. Jade cried out in pain and fought her rising panic, remembering the time Niccolo bound her and how beautiful it had been. Little by little, she forced the panic away, letting the new memory cover over and replace the bad. She opened her eyes and held the thing's gaze. She had to keep her head...so she could literally keep her head.

The thing squealed, thwarted. The doorway above it flickered more softly now, since it had its attention focused on her. It tightened its hold on her and murmured a word.

And she was back there.

One of her abductors bound her wrist and another grasped her forearm. She fought, twisting and wrenching herself away from him until she felt the bone snap and pain shot up her arm, blinding her...

No.

The denial came from somewhere deep within her, only a whisper at first. It grew and grew as she decided she no longer wanted any part of this piece of her life, decided that it was history and so she would let it lie there.

The images and memories flickered, and then snapped back into place, overwhelming her once more.

The one with the red hair smiled at her and started to unbutton his pants...

No!

Little by little she gathered her power and pulled herself out of the mind trap. She screamed with the effort of it, pushing Jones back, rejecting its thrall. "Get out of my head!" she screamed at it, using all her willpower to close it off from her mind.

Its grip on her eased and the images coursing into her mind faltered.

Jade opened her eyes, gritting her teeth and pushing the worst of the experience back, and looked up into Mr. Jones' eyes. Its fathomless dark orbs widened in surprise.

"Fuck...you," she gasped tiredly at it.

Jones had a moment to look exceptionally pissed off, and then it simply wasn't there anymore. She collapsed to the grass, her wrists free.

Jade glanced up and saw Niccolo beating—actually beating—Jones back physically. Unbelievable. Niccolo unleashed was a force to be reckoned with, yet Jones was still blocking every blow. Still, the creature was on the defensive. It was first time since they'd arrived that she'd seen that.

She glanced to her left and saw Adam down, already unconscious like everyone else. They must have tried to help her when she'd been knee-deep in bad memory.

Mr. Jones landed one good shot, backhanding Niccolo ten feet. Niccolo lay still.

Very still.

Fear coursed through her. Jade stood up, shaking and weak from her battle and went toward it. Mr. Jones fixed its focus on her once more, freezing her in place.

Rage bubbled inside her. She was so damn sick of this monster.

"Come on, you freak show. I'm the one you want."

Jade turned and blinked as Drayden tottered toward the thing, propped up with a dandy-looking cane.

"What the hell?" Jade muttered.

Drayden glanced at her. "I figured you pansies would need my help. I see I was right."

Mr. Jones swung its head toward the new target, looking more like a monster scenting prey than a nattily dressed college professor. "Drayden," it said in a low, satisfied voice. It wasn't voice of a college professor anymore. Now it was infused with the otherworldly growl of the Dominion.

"That's right, your favorite Embraced has come to see you." He beckoned with one hand while he hobbled forward.

"These pathetic excuses can't take you, but I can. Come on. What are you waiting for?"

Jade goggled. Drayden was committing suicide! He had to know that.

Jones sprang. Literally, it sprang like it had springs on its feet and tackled Drayden.

Jade could see the form of the creature Jones truly was imposed over its human disguise. Skeletal and naked, the thing had huge black eyes and long, grasping fingers. Those fingers dug into Drayden's back the same way they'd dug into her moments ago. They looked like long needles piercing flesh.

Drayden let out a bellow of fear and pain and Jade knew he'd been sucked back into some hellish place in his past as the creature fed from Drayden's anguish and fear.

The memory was still fresh in Jade's mind. She wouldn't wish the experience on her worst enemy, not even on Drayden.

Opposite her, Niccolo struggled to his feet, looking dazed. He took a look at what had occurred while he'd been out and launched himself at Jones. Jade did the same.

This time, Jones threw Niccolo back easily, knocking him out. Jones caught her wrist again and pain seared up her arm. Apparently, the thing still wanted to play with her. The Dominion fed off emotion. She had enough in her past to make her really yummy, she supposed.

Gasping and going blind with pain, she collapsed to her knees as the memories folded over her once more. Only this time, they weren't only her nightmares.

Somehow, Jones was mind-melding her past with Drayden's.

The horror of Drayden's past was nearly more than she could take. She gagged on it. Images and emotions of such a dark magnitude filled her mind and she could barely function. Here was the most horrid, profane and cruel side of humanity.

Drayden had experienced it all.

It took every bit of Jade's strength to stop her slow slide into that reality. Soon it would consume her as sure it had Drayden. Sobbing, she forced her gaze to focus on Mr. Jones...at anything that was in the present. Drayden's past was a hellish place. He'd endured so much pain for so long.

Using supreme effort, she turned her head and looked at Drayden. His jaw had gone slack and his eyes were vacant. Completely lost in his past, he didn't fight Jones at all.

Jones sucked, drawing out her essence, her emotion and her humanity with a soul-twisting pain. Jade opened her mouth and screamed silently, unable to make any physical sounds. Blackness flirted with her seductively. If she lost consciousness, the pain would end.

If she lost consciousness, she would die.

She flicked a glance above it, watching the doorway struggle fitfully. Jones seemed far more intent on feeding off her and Drayden than keeping it open. She was sure, with the horror of both their pasts, she and Drayden were meals fit for a king.

Goddess, she'd meant to distract the creature...but not *this* way.

Jones' time had to have run out by now. Please, let it be so, she begged the Goddess. She didn't want to die.

Briefly, she closed her eyes as images of Niccolo filled her eyes along with tears. She didn't want to leave him. Oh, Goddess help her, she loved him. The bastard. He'd gone and made her love him. That made the prospect of dying even worse.

Above her, the slit in the sky flickered and grew smaller. Perhaps they'd delayed and foiled Jones past the available window of time. Hope surged. If she had to die, she didn't want her death to be for nothing.

From the corner of her eye, she saw Niccolo—having regained consciousness—rush Jones, but he was repelled violently backward by the swat of the thing's clawed hand.

Little by little, the creature had begun to take on more of its true form.

Her stomach dropped as she felt Jones' hold tighten to a crushing intensity, and felt herself being drawn upwards and back, toward the hole in the sky. Terror filled her. Jones was trying to drawn her and Drayden *through it*. It planned to take them with it into its dimension.

She struggled anew. If they went through there, they'd spend the rest of eternity reliving their past to create emotion for the Dominion to feed from. It would be a fate worse than death. Constant hell.

Jones squeezed tighter, making Jade gasp. The pressure grew stronger. Blackness threatened and Jade fought it until she felt weak and dizzy.

Jade felt tears run down her cheeks. She'd never told Niccolo she loved him.

Darkness closed in around her with a velvet fist. With every last bit of her will, Jade fought to stay cognizant.

* * * * *

Niccolo struggled back to his feet, his whole body throbbing with the punch to the gut the creature had given him. He watched in horror as Mr. Jones held both Drayden and Jade in its thrall. The tendrils of its other self wrapped around them both in a kind of ecstasy as it fed from their combined fear and pain.

Fear clenched in his own gut as he watched how pale Jade's face had gone, how hard she struggled against Jones' incredible power. They looked like one pale, pulsing cocoon.

Jones raised its head momentarily, looking evil and sated at the same time. "You got what you wanted, but this isn't over," it growled. "We'll be back."

"And we'll be waiting," Niccolo replied.

The thing floated backward and up, toward the shrinking hole in the sky. God, it was retreating...and taking Jade and Drayden with it.

"No! You're not taking her!" His body protesting every movement, Niccolo forced himself up. He ran toward Jones and launched himself up, grabbing on to Jade and Drayden's legs as firmly as he could. It was not taking them.

Jade made a shallow gasping sound at his touch. Niccolo pulled downward with all his might, trying to pry Jones' grasp away. Jade aided Niccolo by renewing her efforts to free herself. Her feet and arms pumped as she pummeled the creature.

Jones snarled and fought back, but when Jade landed punch after punch to the creature's face, it screamed and released her.

Niccolo was forced to let Drayden go as Jade toppled down on top of him. They landed hard on the ground in a tangle of limbs.

Niccolo looked up, seeing the thing float higher, too high for him to reach Drayden. Beside him, Jade coughed and gasped.

"You'll never be able to defeat us," Jones growled. By now all trace of the professor-like guise it'd donned had been stripped away, leaving behind the ghoulish, pale, long-fingered representation of the Dominion united. "We are your counterparts," it hissed. "Your cousins. To destroy us is to destroy yourselves."

It inhaled with a rattling sound, probably weakened since the window had closed and its time on this plane had come to an end. "We'll be back," it whispered.

The hole in the sky swallowed both the creature and Drayden. It closed up, leaving only the night behind. Silence fell. Now only the merry sound of the crickets met their ears, sounding calm, cheery and out of place.

"Drayden," Jade gasped and put a hand to her throat.

Niccolo placed a comforting hand to her back. "Don't try to speak."

She shook her head. "He...sacrificed himself to that thing...to save us."

"I know," Niccolo answered, wonderingly. "I know he did."

"Took...him."

Niccolo paused. "Yes."

Jade's eyes fluttered shut as she passed out.

Chapter Thirteen

ಐ

Jade awoke in a dimly lit room. She blinked, feeling soreness throughout her body. It took her a moment to recognize Niccolo's room. It took her another moment to realize that someone had dressed her in one of her T-shirts and a pair of the men's boxers she often wore to sleep.

"Jade?"

She turned her head toward Niccolo's voice and met a pair of soft, warm lips on hers. She inhaled, scenting Niccolo, made a soft sound in her throat and kissed him back.

Niccolo broke the kiss and sat back, running a strong hand through her hair. "You've been out for hours. It's almost dawn."

She blinked, remembering. "It took Drayden," she breathed. Drayden, who'd tried to kill them, yet had saved them all in the end.

"They did. But we defeated Jones by delaying it. We sent the Dominion back where they came from. Gabriel tells me that they won't have another opportunity like this one for another millennium."

"They're patient."

"Yes, and we'll be waiting if they ever try it again. How do you feel? The thing fed from you."

She put a hand to her head, where it throbbed slightly. "I feel okay. Much better than I did right after it had us in its grasp."

"It's over now," he soothed.

She shuddered, remembering sharing Drayden's memories. "Niccolo... Goddess, I experienced Drayden's memories like they were my own." Her voice broke. "I swear I can forgive everything after…" she trailed off, her throat choked with sudden emotion.

"I know," Niccolo replied in a low voice. "I know about Drayden's history. Remember, I told you."

She nodded, unable to speak. Experiencing it had been far more dramatic.

They both fell silent. Was Drayden even alive now? She hoped he wasn't because she couldn't imagine the hell he'd be going through right now if he still lived.

"How is everyone?" she asked, finally.

"They've recovered. Gabriel and Fate have gone home. Everyone has. Adam is still here, but he'll be leaving sometime today." Niccolo paused. "The Order has asked that you return with them as soon as you're able."

Jade struggled to sit up with Niccolo's help.

Curious sorrow filled her. She should be happy it was over, happy they'd pushed the Dominion back. But now that it was over, she'd leave. She'd go back to her apartment in London, near the Order's headquarters. Niccolo would do…well, whatever he wanted with the rest of his very long life. He was free now.

Goddess, she'd fallen in love with him. This was going to hurt.

She cleared her throat. "Okay."

"The head of the Order…Melissa…"

"Mellasandra," she corrected.

"She's waiting for you here in the apartment. She wants to accompany you home. They're very proud of you. They want to honor you."

Shock rippled through her. To have Mellasandra pay such special attention to her was already an honor beyond any she could remember a priestess ever receiving. However, right now she'd rather not have it. She'd trade just about anything for one more day with Niccolo.

She swallowed hard and looked away. "Thanks for letting me know."

"She says as soon as you're ready to travel, she'll see you home. They say you've got a promotion, and—"

"What are you planning to do now, Niccolo?" She interrupted him because she didn't want to talk about leaving anymore. "I mean, now that this is over and you're free."

Niccolo glanced away. "I'm not going back to work for the Council, that's for certain. They've asked me, I said no." He shrugged. "I'm done with that part of my life. I have some thinking to do about where I'll go next."

"Thank you," Jade said softly.

"For what?"

She looked down, studying the light blue comforter that draped her legs. "For helping me regain my life. For helping me get rid of all that junk from my past." *For helping me understand that I'm still capable of love.* She let the last part go unsaid.

Niccolo didn't answer her. He only twined a hand to the nape of her neck and kissed her. Jade placed a hand to his upper arm, feeling the bunch and movement of his biceps, and opened her mouth for him. His tongue swept in and brushed up against hers. Pleasure skittered up her spine.

Her body's reaction was immediate and ferocious. She made a small, hungry sound in the back of her throat. When the kiss broke she murmured, "Make love to me," against Niccolo's lips. "One more time."

She felt him smile. He snaked a hand between their bodies, pulling the blankets away, then slid onto the bed and covered her body with his. "It's all I ever want to do," he whispered, as his hand found the boxers and started pushing them down and off her legs.

Jade fumbled in her haste, trying to help him get her T-shirt over her head. Niccolo's clothing quickly followed. Finally, their nude bodies slid together, their skin feeling smooth and silky where it touched. Jade shuddered with pleasure at the sensation of it.

"God, Jade," Niccolo murmured in a voice full of emotion. His hand explored the curves and hollows of her body. "You feel so good. You fit so well against me."

Jade parted her thighs for him and explored the hard plane of his chest, the sinewy twist of muscles cording his arms, and the luscious, hard length of his erection. This might be the last time she touched him. The last time she ever joined with him. She'd go on, he'd go on...both richer for their association, but they'd be apart.

Tears pricked her eyes. "I want you inside me, Niccolo," she whispered. "Please. I need to feel you."

"Patience, *cara mia*. I want to take my time with you. I need to savor you."

He spread her wet labia and circled the entrance of her cunt gently, gathering moisture. Jade arched her back and bit her lip at the intimate contact. Then Niccolo dragged his finger up and drew back the hood of her engorged clit, using her cream as a lubricant. The pad of his finger slipped around and around the small bundle of nerves, driving Jade fast and hard toward climax.

She grasped his upper arms, dropping her head back to expose the arch of her throat to him. Niccolo leaned down and bit her gently, without fangs, where her throat met her neck.

"Yes," Jade hissed.

He pushed a finger just inside her, teasing her and making it slippery with her juice at the same time. Then he brought it up to gently circle her clit once more.

"Niccolo, let me come," she whispered.

"Mmmm. I like you like this," he murmured. She could feel his lips brush her throat as he spoke. "I like you on the edge of a climax, your body tense. I love the way the muscles of your perfect little cunt grasp my fingers. I love the sound of your breath, harsh in the air. If I could, I'd keep you balancing on the edge all the time."

"Please," she breathed, "don't."

He chuckled, then plunged two fingers inside her and pushed in deep. Jade bit her bottom lip and almost screamed. Then Niccolo brought them back out and circled again. Jade grasped at him desperately, her hips canting toward him.

Jade couldn't help the glide of her hips back and forth as Niccolo fucked her with his fingers deeply and firmly. She bucked beneath him, tossing her head. Wave after wave of pleasure mounted within her, and she made small, animalistic sounds as they grew stronger. Relentlessly, Niccolo stroked that small nub of swollen, aroused flesh.

She came hard against him, whispering his name.

"Yes, baby. That's it," Niccolo answered her cries.

The waves of her orgasm eased away, leaving her breathless, wet and wanting him inside her. She closed her hand around his rock-hard cock and stroked him until he shuddered.

"Now, Niccolo," she whispered. "I can't wait to have you have filling me any longer."

Niccolo kissed her long and deep, then put her legs over his shoulders and pushed his cock inside her. She cried out, grabbing the sheets as he moved powerfully in and out of her.

"Ah, Goddess, yes," she murmured, tears filling her eyes at the exquisiteness of being one with him.

He grunted and plunged steadily in and out of her, seemingly trying to get as far within her as possible. She thrust her hips to meet him, trying to deepen it even further. He responded by increasing the speed and the force.

They came together, their soft cries mingling in the air of the room. Niccolo held her gaze as their climaxes pulsed through their bodies at the same time. She felt his cock throb as he filled her, his essence mixing with hers.

"Niccolo," she breathed as they both came down from the high.

He gathered her up in his arms rolled over with her. She nearly sobbed when his cock slipped from her body. He kissed her all over, his hands roaming her. He stroked, kissed and licked her nipples, bringing fire to her cunt once more. Niccolo licked his way down her stomach, parted her thighs and sucked at her sensitive, swollen clit. It was as though he didn't want to stop touching her. Goddess, she didn't want him to stop, either. He coaxed and tempted her to yet another orgasm — this one tender and soft.

Finally, they lay tangled in the sheets, sated. Kara hopped onto the bed and lay down. Her contented purr filled the air.

"I'm going to miss you, Niccolo," she said tenderly, laying a kiss to his jaw. His stubble scraped her lips. "And not just because of the mind-blowing sex." She gave a sad little laugh.

Niccolo made a frustrated sound. "Goddamn it, Jade, don't go," he growled.

Jade stilled. "What?"

He raised his head and held her gaze. "I don't want you to leave."

Hope glimmered through her, surprising her. She sat up, pushing the sheets to her waist. "You don't? But...we're headed different directions, Niccolo. I need to keep hunting the bad guys. You're finished with that now."

He wrapped a finger around a tendril of her hair and used it to gently pull her toward him. "I know. I don't care. We'll work it out. I just don't want you to leave." He kissed her, and then pulled away, searching her eyes for a response.

Her lips parted with wonder. Their mouths were a breath's space apart. She stared into his dark eyes, unable to form words.

"I just know I want you, Jade," said Niccolo. "I want you any way I can get you." He paused. "And have for a very long time. You asked me what I wanted to do with the rest of my life. Jade, I want to spend it with you. I love you."

The expression on his face made him appear vulnerable. She knew that only a handful of people in this world had ever heard those words from him.

"Niccolo, I—"

"I never thought I'd be able to love anyone again, Jade. Then I met you. You made me fall in love with your strength and your vulnerability. I love your compassion and your sense of vengeance. You and I were made for each other."

Jade smiled. She felt speechless.

Niccolo pulled away from her, suddenly looking strangely defenseless. "I understand if you don't feel the same—"

She pounced on him. Jade forced him back into the pillows, straddling him. "Since we're making confessions and all... I didn't want to love you, Niccolo, I really didn't. I honestly didn't think I'd ever love anyone again, but you gave me my life back. You showed me that I *could* love again. I swear, I don't know what I would've done if I'd had to leave you today." She sighed. "I love you, too."

Niccolo rolled her over and covered her mouth with his. He kissed her until she felt breathless. "Well, then."

"Well, then," she panted in response.

"What about the woman waiting to accompany you home?"

Jade smiled. "I'll just tell her that I'm already home."

Why an electronic book?

We live in the Information Age—an exciting time in the history of human civilization, in which technology rules supreme and continues to progress in leaps and bounds every minute of every day. For a multitude of reasons, more and more avid literary fans are opting to purchase e-books instead of paper books. The question from those not yet initiated into the world of electronic reading is simply: *Why?*

1. **Price.** An electronic title at Ellora's Cave Publishing and Cerridwen Press runs anywhere from 40% to 75% less than the cover price of the exact same title in paperback format. Why? Basic mathematics and cost. It is less expensive to publish an e-book (no paper and printing, no warehousing and shipping) than it is to publish a paperback, so the savings are passed along to the consumer.
2. **Space.** Running out of room in your house for your books? That is one worry you will never have with electronic books. For a low one-time cost, you can purchase a handheld device specifically designed for e-reading. Many e-readers have large, convenient screens for viewing. Better yet, hundreds of titles can be stored within your new library—on a single microchip. There are a variety of e-readers from different manufacturers. You can also read e-books on your PC or laptop computer. (Please note that Ellora's Cave does not endorse any specific brands.

You can check our websites at www.ellorascave.com or www.cerridwenpress.com for information we make available to new consumers.)

3. **Mobility.** Because your new e-library consists of only a microchip within a small, easily transportable e-reader, your entire cache of books can be taken with you wherever you go.

4. **Personal Viewing Preferences.** Are the words you are currently reading too small? Too large? Too... ANNOYING? Paperback books cannot be modified according to personal preferences, but e-books can.

5. **Instant Gratification.** Is it the middle of the night and all the bookstores near you are closed? Are you tired of waiting days, sometimes weeks, for bookstores to ship the novels you bought? Ellora's Cave Publishing sells instantaneous downloads twenty-four hours a day, seven days a week, every day of the year. Our webstore is never closed. Our e-book delivery system is 100% automated, meaning your order is filled as soon as you pay for it.

Those are a few of the top reasons why electronic books are replacing paperbacks for many avid readers.

As always, Ellora's Cave and Cerridwen Press welcome your questions and comments. We invite you to email us at Comments@ellorascave.com or write to us directly at Ellora's Cave Publishing Inc., 1056 Home Avenue, Akron, OH 44310-3502.

Cerridwen, the Celtic Goddess of wisdom, was the muse who brought inspiration to storytellers and those in the creative arts. Cerridwen Press encompasses the best and most innovative stories in all genres of today's fiction. Visit our site and discover the newest titles by talented authors who still get inspired - much like the ancient storytellers did, once upon a time.

Cerridwen Press
www.cerridwenpress.com

Discover for yourself why readers can't get enough of the multiple award-winning publisher Ellora's Cave.

Whether you prefer e-books or paperbacks, be sure to visit EC on the web at www.ellorascave.com for an erotic reading experience that will leave you breathless.